I0710530

RUN FOR CHAPEL HILL

S. M. Sros Panchapor

Golden Boat Press, Inc.

Published in 2024 by Golden Boat Press, Inc.
www.goldenboatpress.com

Run for Chapel Hill
Copyright © 2024 S. M. Sros Panchapor

eBook ISBN: 979-8-218-43204-1
Paperback ISBN: 979-8-218-43172-3

Cover by S. M. Sros Panchapor
Illustration by Cotico_Art

All rights reserved. Please respect artists by purchasing copies of their labor of love. No part of this book may be reproduced or transmitted in any form or by any means without written permission of the author.

This book is a work of fiction. Names, characters, places, and incidents either are products of the author's imagination or are used fictitiously. Any resemblance to actual events or locales or persons, living or dead, is entirely coincidental.

Printed and bound in the United States of America

To a special someone…

To my niece, Seandy Sok,
and my best friend, Sharon Moy.

1

SAM, CHAPEL HILL
AUGUST 1, 2018

On a sweltering morning in August, a figure of tall and slender stature walked with measured grace past the towering bronze statue known as Silent Sam, which had become a nuisance and source of friction between community members and university students and staff. This stoic monument, with its unyielding gaze and eyes indifferent to the passersby, held its ground at the forefront of the University of North Carolina–Chapel Hill quad. The perfectly tall thirty-nine-year-old man with a chiseled jawline, his dark hair framing his broad shoulders, cast a contemptuous glance at the 105-year-old statue, his steely gaze showing disdain—or perhaps something else was occupying his mind.

He strolled through the picturesque, emerald campus, and advanced toward the brick and concrete-trimmed building bearing the inscription "Greenlaw Hall," where the American Studies Department, Comparative Literature Department, Creative Writing Program, and Folklore Program were housed. After proceeding down the quiet corridor, he stopped at the oak-framed door of the corner office, with "Samuel Wilson Angk, Professor of Comparative and World Literatures" inscribed on its frosted glass. Before he could sit down, a colleague in his mid-forties, with tousled salt-and-pepper hair like an untamed forest, poked his head in and greeted him. "Hey, Sam! Saw you come in."

"Hi, Bill." Sam glanced briefly at Bill before sitting down. He pulled his laptop and notebook out of his light brown leather messenger bag to plop on his wooden desk. He turned on his computer. While he waited for the system to finish its software and application updates, he eyed his office inbox, full of mail.

"How was your summer?" asked Bill, smiling good-naturedly.

"Good," Sam answered, with a neutral countenance, not looking at Bill while he picked up the mail and packages from his inbox, sorting them according to their importance.

"How are the kids?"

"Good," Sam replied.

"What are you doing here? Class doesn't start until August 21," said Bill.

Sam looked up at him stoically. "Right. Well, I guess I'm not the only one who has paperwork and class preparation to do. By the way, congratulations on your thirteenth anniversary at the university. Thirteen is a lucky number," Bill rambled.

"Thank you," Sam said, neither smiling nor interested in a long conversation. He glanced over to see if his computer had finished its updates while picking up and opening his pile of important mail.

Bill stood on the threshold of Sam's door, not knowing whether to come inside. He parted his lips to speak but hesitated, furrowing his brows, his right hand flipping his messy hair back. Ten seconds passed before

Sam asked, "Do you need something, Bill?" His voice was low pitched, with a steady and measured delivery.

Bill scratched his head and said, "I'm stopping by to let you know we're having the end of the summer bash and my wife wanted to know if you would like to come."

Sam remained quiet as he read his mail.

"You see, her youngest sister saw you at Wegmans a few weeks ago and asked about you. She… Debbie wants to know your situation. She wishes to get to know you," Bill said, finally pushing out his words, like the force of a mighty wave pushing a boulder from its entrenched position.

"I'm sorry; I am not interested."

"Well. There are going to be many single ladies there with whom you can mix and mingle," Bill suggested.

"I'm not looking for anyone."

"Sam, my wife and I have been thinking about you. I know it's been six years since Sara left and we can't imagine how tough it's been for you and the kids. They need a mother figure to nurture and guide them. Even after my wife and I told Debbie you have three kids, she's still interested. My sister in-law doesn't mind being with someone who has kids, especially when she can't have kids of her own." Bill said this last part in a low, almost whispered tone. "Your poor sister Vida looks exhausted running around to care for her family as well as yours. At least for her sake, huh? My sister in-law is great with kids and she can help take a load off of Vida and you," Bill said, his eyes wide and imploring.

The computer was finally updated. Sam clicked on a file on his desktop called Syllabus and proceeded to scroll to the section where he listed essays and books for his course.

"Very well. I'll leave you to it," Bill said, nodding as if he understood Sam's penchant for keeping quiet when he disliked idle talk or when he wanted to be left alone. He pulled the door closed behind him.

Before Sam finished going through his list of reading materials, a loud, old-fashioned ring tone broke the silence in his cozy office. He pulled from his pants pocket a simple looking cell phone, a basic model that served the sole purpose of making calls and checking email through Wi-Fi.

"Hello, Vida," he answered in a firm but respectful voice. His deep-set, brown eyes fixed on his white wall. Sam's square-shaped face and impeccable features exuded an air of perfection, no matter the lighting, mood, or angle.

"Sam, I've booked you and the kids a flight to Chicago," said a gentle but quavering voice from the other end of the line. She sounded like she had been crying and finally pulled herself together to make this call.

Sam's handsome face dropped. His eyes closed as he took a deep breath. "She doesn't have much time with us, does she?" Sam said, averting his eyes and focusing on an old oak tree through his window, as if looking to nature to soothe his troubled soul.

"No. I'm afraid not. I received a call from Dr. Brown who said her breast cancer is spreading and she only has a few days left, at most," Vida said, almost breaking down in tears again.

Sam sat in pensive silence for a minute before replying, "I don't want her to go," as if he had any say in the matter. "She is our only living relative. What will we do without her?"

"I know, Sam. None of us wants her to go. She has been both a mother and father to us," Vida added, sounding as though something was lodged in her throat.

"There are so many things I want to say to her. Many places I wanted to take her, to show her my gratitude for loving and raising the four of us. She's a good person. She deserves a long life," Sam said, knowing full well that's not how nature operates. "Grandaunt Betty is the last of our mother's bloodline. She hasn't shared much about our parents except that our father was killed before Mom gave birth to me. Then she died too," he said. His eyes narrowed, and his mouth grew tense, as if he was angry at himself for his complicated birth that caused his mother's death. "Time is running out just when I am ready to know more about our parents and our ancestry. She's the only bridge that connects us to them."

Vida broke down, because this was the first time she had ever heard her youngest brother speak with such raw honesty. Plus, this was the most he had ever said to her. Pulling herself together, she told him, "We'll talk about it when we are all in Chicago. The kids and I are taking a Lyft to the airport right now." Out of his sister's three children, Sam could hear Vida's two-year-old baby crying in the background. "Paolo will join us in a day or two. He has work to finish up. Listen, I couldn't get you on the same flight as ours; it's full. It'll be later today, so I went to your house and packed for you and your kids. You should be all set. I've emailed you the itinerary and tickets. Just pick up Jonny, Wallace, and Sopraffina, and the luggage, at Tomi's house. I left the kids with her since we are leaving earlier than you. Tomi volunteered to take you guys to the airport. Apparently, she's willing to blow off a trip with her husband to help you."

"Thanks, Vida."

Sam got into his 2017 Sienna and pulled out of the campus. His body appeared to be going through the motions, as his eyes gazed into nothingness. He arrived at a sprawling brick home situated on six acres of land with a lavishly fenced yard and oversized pool, overlooking B. Everett Jordan Lake. Greeting him at the door stood a thirty-eight-year-old woman with protruding eyes, a glistening dark mane, and a young, melon-seed shaped face that was small and elongated. Along with her powdery white skin, big eyes like anime, and thin lips, her face represented the ideal shape and pulchritude desired by most Asians, especially East Asians. Her slender arm reached to open the door wider for Sam.

"Daddy!" shouted six-year-old Sopraffina running from the living room, which was decorated in golden, heavy drapery, wallpaper friezes, and wall-to-ceiling bookshelves. The classy and comfortable furniture of white and gold bespoke Greek opulence. Large, glamorous portraits of Tomi hung strategically where guests could see and admire them. Sam picked up his bronze-haired little girl and kissed her on her dimpled, peaches-and-cream cheek.

"Daddy, Auntie Vida and our cousins are gone!"

Tomi stood there, hands nonchalantly resting on her back, observing the father and daughter duo with happiness in her face. She wore a neck-plunging, golden chiffon summer dress that seemed determined to showcase her east-west-shaped breasts, as though her dress had a mission to make sure everyone noticed her slim figure from all angles.

Sam flashed a warm smile at Tomi, oblivious to her fashion choices and focused on his little girl. "I know, sweetheart! So, where on earth are your silly brothers hiding this time?" he inquired of the little mischief-makers.

"Oh gosh, they're playing in the backyard. I'll get them," Tomi said in a girlish voice. She threw her hands up and pivoted toward the back, as if she had forgotten all about the boys and just realized where she had left them.

"Auntie Vida said we're going to Chicago. Why, Daddy?"

"We're going to see Grandaunt Betty," said Sam.

"Why?"

"She's not well."

"Why?"

"You'll find out. Now let's find your big brothers."

"Daddy! Daddy! Jonny hit me," Wallace cried. They burst into the high-ceilinged foyer with gold and crystal chandeliers where their father and sister stood underneath. Tomi strutted from behind them all and smiled, enjoying seeing Sam with his children.

"He took my Game Boy," nine-year-old Jonny said.

Eight-year-old Wallace retorted, "Mine ran out of battery. My adapter is at home. Auntie Vida forgot to pack it for me. Jonny won't let me borrow his."

"Boys. What did Daddy tell you about sharing and playing nice?"

"It's mine; not his!" Jonny replied.

Sam looked at Tomi as if to remind her to see the mess she created.

Tomi instinctively responded, "What? They need an outlet. Lord knows you don't have the Internet or cable at home. All they do is read and play with puzzles and board games. Those are boring." She rolled her protruding eyes.

"I see too many parents resorting to parking their kids in front of televisions, tablets, and smartphones. I don't want these electronic gadgets to become the primary babysitter for my children. I prefer they engage with nature and connect with people."

"You know you're not exactly a social butterfly yourself," said Tomi, with her arms crossing over her chest and one arched brow raised. "You know what the people at the university call you, 'the other *Silent Sam.*'"

"I just don't want my children to be spoiled by these devices," he said, ignoring her last statement. If he were annoyed or offended that anyone would associate him with the statue that represented racism and oppression, Tomi could not tell. Sam looked at her with a neutral countenance and asserted, "I would like a gadget-free zone for my children."

"Oh come on. Let them live a little. They're kids."

"My sister said something about you driving us," he said, cutting the matter short.

"Yes, I'll take you to the airport. I can keep your car here and pick you up when you return."

"You don't need to do that," said Sam. I can leave my car at the airport and drive back home from there."

"But I want to," said Tomi, in her girlish and pleading voice.

Sam put Sopraffina down. "All right, boys; let's go."

With an abundance of youthful energy, the kids dashed toward the door, jostling and nudging each other in a race to claim victory. Meanwhile, Sam gallantly took charge of the luggage that his older sister, Vida, had left behind. Tomi, on the other hand, expertly secured the little rascals into their designated seats inside the minivan. Despite Tomi's declaration to be the one behind the wheel, Sam slid into the driver's seat, taking control.

2

ETTA, CHICAGO
AUGUST 1, 2018

A long-legged woman with soft curls sat with her back against the architecture desk, looking out one of the large windows of the postmodern sixty-five-story skyscraper located at 311 South Wacker Drive. Her dark eyes, like lotus petals, with naturally thick lashes, could make time stand still. Her smooth, bronze skin and pink lip gloss on her full lips shimmered as the sun rays shafted through the two windows. She took a long, deep sigh, as if something was bothering her.

"A penny for your thoughts, Etta," a raspy voice came from behind her.

Etta swiveled her chair around to find a young, thin woman with strawberry blond curls, holding a stack of bound booklets. She looked up at the tall twenty-five-year-old woman with an athletic body figure. "Hey Kristina. Good, you got the copies ready," she said in a voice sweet, soft, and steady.

"Yep. These are copies of the presentation for your meeting this afternoon," Kristina said, leaving a stack of spiral-bound copies titled Lake Shore's Project on Etta's desk.

"So, do you want to talk about it?" Kristina coaxed.

"Talk about what?" Etta said, her eyes falling on Kristina's alabaster face.

"The way you sighed just now," Kristina responded. "Obviously, something is bothering you."

"I don't know what you're talking about," Etta retorted.

"Please, please," Kristina said, with her slender fingers curling inward in a plea, as she sat down in one of the guest chairs across from Etta. "I only have a few more months left to be your assistant before I take the bar and clerk for Judge Chang. I want us to remain good friends even after I leave here; and good friends confide in each other, right?" She moved her low-arched eyebrows up and down, showing her charm.

Etta raised her right eyebrow, natural and well groomed, at Kristina.

"I know Daron Brackenridge is your best and only friend; but sometimes, you need a female perspective. Maybe I can help; if not, I am a good listener, too."

"I can get a female perspective from Ms. Nelly."

"But she's on a leave of absence. Right now, you have me. I may not be old and wise like her, but I am young and have fresh perspectives," Kristina said, with a wide smile on her face.

"Fine," Etta said, rolling her eyes. "I trust you. You have proven yourself to be a good friend in the last year."

"Aww. I'm touched." Feeling excited, Kristina leaned forward from the guest chair with her elbows on Etta's desk and hands underneath her round chin, listening attentively.

"I'm contemplating getting out of a blind date Daron's wife has set up for me. Argh. I want to kick myself for impulsively agreeing to this. So, I ran a Google search on how to get out of a date gracefully, but there's nothing graceful about it."

"You're the only person I know who consults Google for relationship advice," Kristina said.

"Doesn't everyone?"

"No, that is something you should ask your friend or a live person."

"Not when you don't want your friend to know."

"That's why you need more friends," Kristina said, moving her brows up and down as if to charm her into confiding in her.

"Nah, I don't want the drama."

"So, what have you found out?"

"Well, an article from the Elite Daily came up. The title was something about how to cancel a date via text. There were seven scenarios, but number three was closest to my situation. Basically, it says to tell the truth. It says, and I quote, 'I've been thinking about this and don't feel comfortable meeting someone on a blind date.'"

"That's graceful. It's honest."

"But I feel bad," Etta replied.

"Why did you agree to it in the first place?" Kristina asked, as if practicing a line of questions for court.

"I don't know. Maybe because of all the pressure my family and their little community of friends have been giving me. They've been worried ever since I turned thirty-seven. More like freaking out. My parents, especially my aunt Thida, fear the community will label me as an old maid, which I am sure they already have. Aunt Thida even suggested that because I was once engaged and cohabitated with my ex-fiancé that I'm damaged goods, which no man wants to touch. I wanted to tell them, 'It's the twenty-first century. Nobody cares about that.' Anyway, I don't feel good about this date. Frankly, I am just not up for it. Argh. I should have turned the date down right then and there. I'll look like an ass if I make excuses and back out now." Etta's slender, graceful fingers made a steeple on her forehead as if to cover herself in shame for allowing others to force her out of her comfort zone.

"Or maybe you can go and see what he's like. It doesn't hurt, does it?" Kristina said. "Who knows. He may be the one. If not, you don't have to agree to a second date. At least you have given it a try. Am I right?"

Sitting with her back against her chair and hands across her chest, Etta replied, "That's just it. I don't want to go through the process of dating. I hate rejections, whether someone rejects me or I reject them."

"You don't seem to mind rejecting job applicants," Kristina interjected.

"That's not personal; it's business. I love running my successful architectural design boutique. It's my baby. My livelihood." Etta stretched her svelte arms to look proudly around her office and into the hallway through her glass door, where her human resources personnels, engineers, architect, and others were going about their work. "I only hire the best people."

"Best people, huh? You sound like Donald Trump," Kristina said, squinting her eyes.

"Except, it's true in my case," Etta replied. The two women burst into laughter.

"Factual evidence confirmed. But isn't Daron a staunch supporter of Trump?" Kristina said.

"He is."

"You know, I've often wondered how you can be friends with him. I'm totally bewildered by the stark political divergence between you and him. People I know nowadays lose friends and family members due to our politics and party affiliation. Isn't he a devout Christian and staunch conservative?"

"He is. One of his beefs with liberalism is *political correctness*, which is the bane of his existence."

"Right. The thing is: you embody compassion, love, and kindness, but Daron is an entitled, privileged asshole," Kristina said.

"Hey, only I can say that about him," Etta joked.

"Sorry."

"Well. Conservatism appeals to him because he believes in preserving a greater share of his hard-earned income. He's a Christian but hardly ever goes to church. I was raised Catholic, but I'm not bound by any religion. My parents were introduced to Catholicism by the Van Buren family. They sponsored my parents and paternal grandfather from the refugee camp of Chonburi, Thailand. Daron and I happened to be born in Weiss Hospital the same day. We grew up in the same part of our Uptown neighborhood. We have been friends since elementary school. I'm a Democrat. He's a Republican. Though I am sick of this two-party system that is going nowhere. Our bond surpasses the chasms of ideological differences because we see most Democrat and

Republican leaders as full of deceit and self-interest. They are equally tainted by corruption. A subtle distinction is only their methods. Democrats, I believe, often cloak their ambitions behind a veil of progressivism, presenting themselves as champions of organized labor, civil rights, and progressive reform. But their aspirations are often mired in the same muck of self-serving agendas that plague their Republican counterparts. Both sides hide behind the facade of righteousness, whether democracy, religion, or love of country.

"Besides these things, the Republicans, I must admit, wear their intentions more openly. Their controversial agendas are at least laid bare for all to see. Daron and I find solace in our shared understanding that both parties prioritize the interests of lobbyists for their financial gain, with little regard for the people and country they claim to represent and love. Therefore, we refuse to be pawns to their manipulation of people's primal emotions of fear and anger to protect their money and power. Empathy, compassion, understanding, and unwavering loyalty to each other as fellow citizens and human beings are our common ground. But I digress," Etta said, aware she might be revealing too much of her political views in the office.

Kristina nodded, seemingly understanding where Etta was coming from, as she herself was inclined to the liberal side.

"Now back to my problem. I would rather not go through the process of dating right now. I've had enough bad relationships to last me for a whole lifetime. I am not in a rush to go through that pain and suffering again."

"Maybe the third time's a charm," Kristina said.

"Third? How do you know this will be my third relationship?" Etta said, squinting one of her eyes at Kristina.

"Daron."

"Why, that…" Etta said, with her eyes narrowed and fists clenched.

"Actually, I overheard the conversation in the hallway when I went to the district court for an interview with Judge Chang. I think Daron had a hearing that day. He didn't say much, though. One of his clients asked why a beautiful woman like you is still single. That was when he said you have had two bad relationships and are still healing."

"See what I mean? People always want to know someone else's dating status," Etta said.

"I think his client was interested in you and Daron was trying to sway him from dating you. It sounded like Daron doesn't think he's good enough for you."

Etta smiled, appreciating Daron for looking out for her. "See?"

"Yeah, yeah. He's an asshole with a heart of gold. So tell me more about your two bad relationships. I'm sorry if it is opening old wounds," Kristina said, scrunching up her nose as if she was feeling the searing burn of Etta's stare.

"I used to have many female friends in high school. One encouraged me to date a hot football player, Thomas O'Donnell, because she heard a rumor he had a crush on me. Long story short, we dated for almost two years before he broke up without telling me. After a whole week without hearing from him, I had to call and find out if he was okay. At the same time, that friend who encouraged me to date him slept with him. She stopped talking to me the same week he broke up with me, which he failed to mention. His excuse was, he was trying to spare my feelings, and that I was bad luck. My other female friends took his side."

"What a jerk! I'm sorry. I see why you stopped having female friends."

"But that was in high school. I'm over it. I couldn't get out of there fast enough. I was glad to be far away from all of them when I studied abroad in Cambridge. Daron did keep high school bearable," Etta reminisced.

"High school. Hmph. High school relationships can be casual and fleeting. Just consider it valuable learning experiences." Kristina flashed a pearly white smile.

"Yeah, it helped me to develop important social and emotional skills for my next relationship," Etta said, sounding sarcastic.

"I heard you were engaged to Jack Edlin."

Etta narrowed her eyes on her. "You seem to know more about my relationships than you led on."

"So it is true. You were once engaged to him. What a small world. He is the best litigator in Chicago. I applied for a summer associate job with his firm. Obviously, I didn't get it. I only know of this relationship because he has a photograph of you and him in Cambridge."

"Why? Isn't he married to his associate whom I caught him sleeping with? My Christmases have been ruined since then."

"Oh, wow," said Kristina. "So that was what he meant when he said he messed things up with when I was at his office for an interview.

"Five years have passed. I've been doing fine on my own. I don't need an acquaintance whom I just met asking, 'Etta, why are you still single?' or a cousin telling me, 'Etta, forty is just around the corner. It's going to be hard having a baby at that age. You'll have all sorts of complications.' Then there is my mother: 'Etta, women are like flowers; they withered. Don't wait too long.' Lastly, here comes Rochelle, Daron's wife: 'Etta, I know the perfect guy for you!' I don't know. The whole dating scene is too much work and effort. It's exhausting."

"It won't be when you meet the right guy. Everything will fall into place," Kristina said, reminding Etta how grand love could be.

3

ETTA, CHICAGO

AUGUST 1, 2018

Suddenly, Etta's text ring tone, the Darth Vader "Imperial March" theme song from *Star Wars*, went off on her iPhone 7 Plus.

"Daron's texting me," Etta said, looking up from her phone.

"How befitting you set that music to his number. Anywho, I hope I was a bit helpful. I'll get back to my work now," Kristina said, getting up from the guest chair.

"Thanks for listening and the copies," Etta said.

"Any time," Kristina replied, leaving and closing the door behind her.

Daron: Hey Etta.

Etta: What's up, Daron?

Daron: Meet me at Monk's.

Etta: Why?

Daron: Don't you wanna eat?

Etta glanced over at her clock and it was a quarter to twelve.

Etta: I guess. I haven't got much done anyway.

Etta took a Lyft to Clark and Wells. The driver dropped her off right in front of Monk's. With its red clay, corrugated roof, the white and brown two-story German-style structure was flanked by taller buildings. She opened one of the red, castle-style double doors with wooden handles. It opened to crowds of people at the bar, booths, and tables, who were eating, talking, and laughing. There at one of the tables sat Daron, having a beer while his eight- and ten-year-old boys, Phoenix and Hudson, pushed and shoved each other, and five-year-old Rosetta played with a stack of Monk's coasters by randomly placing coins underneath them for her brothers and father to seek out. One-year-old James was strapped to Daron's chest.

"Hi Etta," said a muscular young man in black pants and a black T-shirt with the Monk's logo on it.

"Hi, Jim."

"Daron is over there."

"I see him. Thanks." She walked over with excitement.

The children looked up and said in unison, "Auntie Etta!"

"Hi kiddos," Etta said, as she hugged Phoenix, Hudson, and Rosetta. She turned to Daron, peeking at the sleeping James. She pulled the empty chair next to him. "What happened? You gave both of your nannies the day off?"

"Mommy is out of town again. Nanny Cecil and Nanny Jo have a family emergency," said the reddish-blond and blue-eyed Rosetta, as she shuffled the coasters around for her brothers to pick out while waiting for their food to arrive.

"That's what I get for hiring sisters. Rochelle thinks I should spend more time with the kids, so they don't turn out psychotic… something about nurturing them and giving them enough love and attention. I'm not really sure. I only listen to every third word that woman says." He took a swig of his beer before placing the heavy glass mug on the wooden table. "I ordered a cheeseburger with no garnish, and tater tots the way you like them. The food should be coming out soon. I know you love your job so much that you are in a hurry to get back to it," he said.

"Thanks. I do love my job. I can't imagine myself doing anything else."

"Whatever."

"Don't *whatever* me. It doesn't look good to my employees that I stay out too long for lunch. I must lead by example, although I did just chat with Kristina for a good hour or so."

"Who cares?" he rolled his eyes once again. "You're the boss. Do what you want as long as you get your work done. Besides, you're having a business lunch with me. God knows I give you enough clients to keep you busy for generations to come."

"Stop exaggerating. I'm grateful but I care about how people perceive me."

Daron shook his head in pity. "That has always been your problem. You worry too much about what people think about you. Change of subject. So, I understand Rochelle has fixed you up with some astrophysicist, astronomer loser."

"If he's an astrophysicist he can't be a loser, now, can he?"

"You know what I mean," Daron said. "Rochelle tends to have pretentious types of friends."

He picked up his beer mug again and looked at his kids to make sure they were not listening to their conversation. They were playing tic-tac-toe and cheering loudly when they beat their siblings. Jim, the waiter, arrived with a big tray, and the kids excitedly turned their attention to their food as he sat the plates in front of everyone at the table.

Etta looked at the cute, precocious children with a grin, wishing they were old enough for her to tell them how Daron and Rochelle came to name them after places where they were conceived: the ten-year-old Phoenix after a city in Arizona, the eight-year-old Hudson after a city in

Wisconsin, the five-year-old Rosetta after a port city of the Nile Delta, Egypt. Except for baby James; he was named after Daron's father, who passed away a month before James was born.

"Just say it, Daddy. You know you want to say it. We don't mind," said Hudson, egging on his father, as he stuffed a tater tot into his mouth.

"What are you talking about, Hudson?" Daron's face was red, either from embarrassment or the beer in him.

"'Asshole.' You want to say 'asshole,'" Hudson emphasized.

"Don't say that, Hudson," said Phoenix, elbowing his little brother.

"But Dad wants to say it," said Hudson, rubbing his arm.

"All right, guys. Eat your burgers and tots. Don't pay attention to adults talking," said Daron casually. They turned to their food while Phoenix pulled out a paper to continue playing a fresh set of tic-tac-toe while they munched on their food.

"Asshole, huh? Look who she married," Etta said, reaching for some tater tots.

"Jerk."

"Whatever. Anyway, were you not part of this matchmaking process?" Etta asked, picking up her glass of lemonade to sip.

"You know I love my wife, but she has poor taste in men," said Daron, taking a jab at all the other men his wife had ever dated.

"Right. Of all the good-looking and nice guys in Chicago, she chose you."

"Don't be a jerk while I am trying to help you. I told you to ask all the young people who work for you which dating site they use, but no. I must do everything for you. Give me your phone."

"What?"

"Just give me your iPhone," Daron put out his hand and gestured to her to give it up. She hesitantly handed it over. "It's locked. Need your thumbprint."

She cooperated, but craned her neck and asked, "What are you doing?"

"I've checked with the cool, hip GenZs in my office," he said, as he scrolled down the list.

Etta laughed. "Really? Do they know you call them that?"

"Shut it. This is all for your benefit." He clicked on the app icon and ran a search. It asked for thumbprint verification for payment. "I need your thumbprint one more time."

"Am I going to regret this?" She pressed her thumb on the button. He held the iPhone at a level to get a good headshot of Etta. At the sound of the snapping of the camera, Etta asked, "Are you creating a Tinder profile for me?"

"Yes, I am."

"Give it back, Daron. I'm not interested. I already have a date this evening with the guy Rochelle fixed me up with."

"It might not work out. It doesn't hurt to have more choices."

"Oh my God. I don't want to be that girl."

"What girl would that be?"

"The girl with a Tinder profile!"

"Come on, grandma. Get with the time. I told you to get out more, so you can meet someone. It could be at a church, a bar, or a café. But you insist on being a loser. Do you think *Mr. Right* can find you when you're stuck in your sixty-five-story office building and your Riverview townhome?"

"I do go out."

"Yeah, to your parents' house in Palatine."

"I go to other places."

"Your weird aunt's house in Lake Bluff doesn't count either. The people she associates with are just as weird. You gotta put yourself out there." Etta rolled her eyes, having to hear her friend refer to someone as weird or strange whenever he disagreed with them. "What will Rochelle's friend think of me?"

"I've checked. He doesn't have an account. He wouldn't know."

"How would you know this?"

"I have my ways."

"Legal?"

"Come on, now." He looked up at her. "I wouldn't jeopardize my law practice. Of course, it's legal." Baby James started to move. Etta craned her neck to look at him while Daron shifted his body to make sure the child was comfortable.

"Okay. But I don't want a Tinder profile," Etta whispered, even though the infant beside her was still sleeping in spite of the restaurant noises.

"Too bad. You're getting one."

"Why, dude?"

"Take it from a person who has been successfully and happily married for thirteen years. I know what I am doing. You're going to thank me for this. I want you to be happily married, too. You're becoming a third wheeler and it's not pretty."

"I didn't want to be a third wheeler, but you insist on taking me on your dates with Rochelle."

"You must tell the world you exist. How else would he—whoever he is—find you?"

Daron proceeded to add her professional photo from her business website, her party photo, her everyday photos from her Facebook, and the current picture of her that he had snapped earlier. Then he typed in her background information, likes, dislikes, and his assumed answers for her to the site questionnaires.

"It's not that I don't want to find someone, eventually. I do, but I don't feel right broadcasting myself like that. Tinder profile? That seems very desperate. Call me old-fashioned, but I—"

"You *are* desperate. Look, if you are so old-fashioned, then why didn't you marry that guy from Cambodia your parents arranged for you a few years back?"

"I want a man of my choice. Besides, only losers and perverts married people from Cambodia. Oh, great. Now I am a generalizing and judgmental asshole," said Etta, regretting her words and practically whispering the last word, so the kids who were busy eating their burgers and tater tots could not hear, though she knew they were smarter than the adults gave them credit for.

"It's fun, isn't it?" said Daron.

"No. I feel bad."

"You'll get used to it."

"I'll never get used to being an asshole," she said, again whispering the last word.

"There. Bam! The trick to reeling in the good ones and sifting out the crazies is to be upfront. Here, take a look."

"Don't they all lie on their profiles anyway?" He shrugged his shoulders. She took her iPhone from Daron.

"What? Twenty-five to forty? Why would I want a twenty-five-year-old? What would I do with one?"

"Come on now, Etta. You know the answer to that."

She gave him her evil side-eye.

"You look twenty-five. Just go with it. It's 2018. Cher and Madonna dated twenty-five-year-olds."

"I'm not Cher or Madonna."

"Obviously. Otherwise, you'd be with someone by now."

"There's nothing wrong with being picky. Or single! Besides, I'm not comfortable with this," she murmured softly, as if to herself. She continued to swipe her iPhone and review her information.

"So, do you want to know why I chose these particular photos?" He moved his thick brows up and down, anxiously egging her on to ask the question.

"Why these particular photos, Daron?" She feigned interest while secretly harboring a genuine curiosity about his arbitrary selection.

"It's to let your potential suitors know you're a ten with make-up and an eight or nine without it, depending on the lighting of the room." She raised one of her eyebrows, not sure if he was being biased because she was his friend. "Look. No man wants to wake up to a woman who is a ten with make-up only to find she is a blobfish without it. This way he can imagine who he is waking up to. He won't be traumatized when he wakes up to you. You're welcome."

"Thanks, I think. You rate women like your president."

"Hell yeah. Make America Great Again! Deal with it; he's your president, too."

Etta shook her head in dismay. "How did you become so good at this? Rochelle better not catch you on one of these dating sites!" Etta said, as she picked up her burger.

"Please. I don't need a date like you do. I learned it from my young associates. They know what it's like out there. Look, Etta. You're an only child. I'm an only child. Just look at it like a brother looking out for his sister. Plus, I'm a man. I know what men like and want. Trust me. You're looking at a happily married man over here. Look at what Rochelle and I produced." He eyed his four kids adoringly.

"Oh, God," said Etta sadly, rolling her eyes once again regarding his tendency to brag. "There should be more to life than just marriage and procreation, when thousands and millions of children are being starved, abused, tortured, shot at and bombed into smithereens every day."

"Don't be a Debbie Downer," said Daron, as his picked up his burger to take a bite.

"'Mr. Right must be financially independent, funny, smart, and attractive,'" said Etta, as she continued reading her dating profile. "Seriously?"

"So?" Daron responded, still chewing.

"This is embarrassing."

He swallowed and washed it down with his beer. "You must state what you want. Honesty is the best policy, Etta."

Etta sighed. "I don't feel right about this. Why can't I find a man in a natural setting?" She rested her well-defined chin on the base of her palm, absentmindedly scrolling through her phone with her other hand, contemplating the complexities of modern romance. She then snapped out of her reverie and picked up her burger to eat.

Daron, with a nonchalant shrug, interjected, "Welcome to finding love in the twenty-first century,

Etta!" He raised his glass to his lips and finished his beer, then waved to Jim for another one.

4

SAM, CHICAGO

AUGUST 1, 2018

It was eighty-four degrees—sunny with broken clouds. Vida had booked a minivan for Sam and his three kids. He drove directly from O'Hare to Northwestern Memorial Hospital, after having fed his rowdy boys and his sweet little girl. The local time was 2 p.m. when he pulled into the hospital parking lot A. His tired children groggily woke up from their nap. "Daddy, I'm thirsty," Sopraffina said. She was the apple of his eye.

"Here you go, honey." He gave her a small bottle of water.

"Thank you, Daddy."

He looked at her and smiled, lost in deep thoughts. Her delicate features reminded him of his ex-wife. He wondered where she was and if she had a kid or two with her new man.

"Dad, I want water too," Jonny said.

"Me, too, Daddy," Wallace chimed in.

"No, I asked Daddy first," Jonny said, looking at his brother with annoyance.

"No, I wanted it first," Wallace said.

"Boys. Here you go." He got out of the car and unbuckled Sopraffina's car seat. The boys unbuckled themselves and exited out of the car.

"What are we doing here, Daddy," said Jonny.

"Grandaunt Betty stays here."

"Why is she here?"

She's not well."

"Tell us the truth, Daddy. Is she dying?" Jonny said.

Wallace punched him in the arm.

"Ouch. Whatcha hit me for?" He started to hit Wallace back.

"You can't say that about Grandaunt Betty," Wallace said.

"Boys? Are you ready to go?" Sam said, unbothered by their bickering and punching.

Sam and his children exited out of the elevator and were greeted by his oldest sister, Vida. She had been waiting for him, and to lend a helping hand with his children. She knew Sopraffina would be well behaved, but the boys were more of a handful.

"Auntie Vida," Sopraffina said, excited to see a familiar face in a different city.

"Hi honey," Vida said, kissing her niece on her dimpled cheek. Vida stood at five feet seven inches tall. She seemed to have inherited her mother's Western features, but with an olive skin tone like their Khmer father. She hugged and kissed Jonny and Wallace as if she had not seen them in ages, when in fact, she just saw her niece and nephews that same morning. "Let's go and see Grandaunt Betty," she said, leading them down the hall to a secure door where they had to be buzzed in to access the patient rooms of that section of the ward. Betty's room was two doors down from the entrance, and a nurse was just walking out of the room when they reached it.

"Hey guys," Daniel and Vincent greeted his youngest brother and his kids.

"Uncle Daniel! Uncle Vincent!" The kids greeted their tall, strong, and good-looking uncles.

"Sam, I want you to meet my fiancée, Rima," Vincent said, his hand tenderly touching her lower back.

Sam's brown eyes met the beautiful emerald eyes of Rima. "Finally, we get to meet each other in person. It's nice to meet you, Sam," Rima said, extending her delicate hand to shake Sam's strong, well-proportioned hand.

"It's nice to meet you, too. Welcome to the family," Sam said, offering her and everyone a dry smile.

"Okay," Daniel said, rubbing his hands together. "Since only three adults can visit at a time, we'll be joining my wife and children in the nearby visiting lounge." Daniel walked over to kiss his aunt.

Vincent and his fiancé followed suit. "We'll be taking turns coming in and out. Don't worry, one of us will stay overnight with you," said Vincent, kissing his aunt's cheek. They lingered, wanting to make sure she was comfortable.

"Grandaunt Betty," said Sam's two boys who had often communicated with her via FaceTime with their aunt Vida.

"Hi boys," said the woman with white hair in a bob cut. Radiant and age-defying at sixty-eight, her face retained a captivating youthfulness that served as a testament to the remarkable beauty she possessed in her younger years. She kissed each of them tenderly, then reached out her arm. "And there is my sweet Sopraffina. We are finally meeting face to face. How was the flight, my dear?"

"Fine," Sopraffina said, softly, holding onto her father's leg. "Come on. Come. Come give Nana a kiss."

"Go on, honey," Sam said.

The little girl moved gingerly. Her grandaunt appeared very fragile. She seemed hesitant, as if she did not want to hurt her by giving her a big hug. Betty kissed her on the cheek and touched her face as she said, "You look just like my older sister. Your grandma. She would be so proud if she saw you, all of you." She turned to look at everyone in the room, as if she was getting a good look at them for the last time.

"Are you feeling comfortable?" Vida said, pulling Betty's blanket up. "Do you need an extra blanket?"

"Don't worry about me, child," she said. She looked at her nephews and niece, including the beautiful Rima. "Can you give me a moment with Sam?"

"Sure, Aunty," Vida said, as she looked at her other two brothers, wondering why she needed to speak with only Sam.

"Come on, guys. Let's go get some ice cream at the food court," Rima said.

"Yay," the children screamed.

"I knew I liked her," Wallace said.

"You like her because she's pretty," Jonny said.

"Watch it, boys. She's mine," Vincent said, as they laughed upon exiting the door. Meanwhile, Vida held onto Sopraffina's hand and followed the rest of them out, looking back at her aunt and youngest brother.

Sam looked at her with love and compassion. "You should rest, Aunt Betty. You have a lot of excitement today. Whatever it is, it can wait until you have enough energy."

"This is the most energy I'll ever have. Besides, I want to say my piece."

He stayed silent.

"Come here, Sam."

He moved his chair closer to her bed—close enough that she reached out to touch his face.

"You know, you look exactly like your father. You're very handsome, just like him." She looked him over for a little bit. "Oh, Sam…" She reached for his hand, those long, elegant fingers. "Life is too short. Live. Stop wallowing in sorrow."

"I'm not sure what you mean, Aunt Betty."

"I mean the void. The emptiness you feel inside, whether because of the deaths of your parents or the divorce with Sara. It's time to find love again—the love you had before you met Sara."

Sam looked at his aunt with confusion.

"Don't waste your life like I have all these years. I don't regret raising you kids, but I wish I had my heart opened. It's too late for me now; however, it's not for you. You're still very young."

His brows knitted together, as he sat in silence, still not fully grasping what his aunt was saying.

"Sam, I am very proud of you for being a great father to your children." He placed his other hand on top of hers.

"I know you don't like redundancy and idle talk, but I would like to stress how much I would like to see you happy. And your parents would want you to live your life and be happy. What happened in the past can't be changed." She cleared her throat.

Sam pulled away to grab the plastic pitcher on the nightstand next to him and pour water into a paper cup. He offered it to her with care and respect, holding it with two hands.

She took a sip and handed it back to him. "Thank you," she said. He nodded. "Do you remember when the five of us moved from Chapel Hill to live in Uptown Chicago?"

Sam hesitated before he said, "I still don't understand why you moved us to Chicago."

Her face dropped. She breathed in and out, deeply. "In due time you will know the first reason."

Sam's antenna went up. He studied her face, parting his lips to speak, but stopped himself.

"The second reason was that I wanted you and your siblings to be surrounded by Khmer speakers. I heard many Southeast Asian refugees were placed here in many numbers. I remember it like it was yesterday. 1981. Vida was eight years old, Daniel six, Vincent five, and you were two. I learned about the Cambodian refugees coming here in good numbers. I wanted to expose all of you to your father's Khmer culture, language, and religion. I bought a white and brown three-story German-styled home. I loved that house so much. I remember every nook and cranny. It was built in 1896. It sat on a quiet street, 4644 North Dover Street, where most white settlers still lived in spite of the white flight. The house had over two thousand square feet, with four bedrooms and two baths. It sat on a five thousand square foot lot with back and front yards for all of you to play in, and for me to tend to my beautiful garden."

She sighed with nostalgia for her first home in Chicago.

"I encouraged all of you to make friends. On the weekend or Friday evening, I would bring Vida, Daniel, and Vincent to the Cambodian Association of Illinois. I believe it was founded back in 1976 by Kompha Seth, Khoun Lorn, and Prak Sunnary. By the time we were there, the association was located on West Lawrence. Your siblings learned the Khmer language, culture, religion, and history. Daniel and Vincent liked it, but Vida was staunchly against it. She found the place dirty and did not feel at ease with the people. She always complained about having to go there. When you were old enough I also brought you there. In 1986 there was finally a Khmer temple for the Cambodian community to gather and perform their religious worship, ceremonies, and rituals. It was wonderful to be part of that bright and lovely community.

"Unfortunately, when you turned eight years old in 1987, you got into fights with a few Cambodian boys who bullied you. Because you were quiet and kept to yourself, they thought you were stuck up and acted better than them.

"Kids," Betty said, smiling, as if in forgiveness but also acknowledgment that the young Sam was still developing and needing adult guidance. "You had a bad cut on your forehead. Vida was fourteen years old at the time and I was having a difficult time dealing with her. She hated the Cambodian community. She thought their parents were useless and their children were gang bangers, when you got hurt. It was the last straw for her. She pleaded and yelled at me to move out of the neighborhood. She told me to stop taking all of you to the community, but it seemed all of us liked it there except for Vida.

"I loved the Khmer community. They were nice, kind, and generous, considering what they went through and how much they lost. They rebuilt their lives in what many Americans considered the ghetto. They took me in as one of their members and helped me out with whatever they could, especially introducing me to Khmer cuisine. The men would take you guys on barbeque picnics at Lake Michigan, to soccer games, and fishing trips. The men were practically helping me to raise you boys. There were many Cambodians living nearby on Beacon, Malden, Lawrence, and Wilson streets. However, there was only one Khmer family that lived across from our house on our street.

"They were a nice and kind family. I believe they have one daughter who was always playing jump rope and what they called double dutch on the sidewalk in front of her house with her friends. One of them was a chubby, ginger boy. I don't know if you remember this, but when I brought you back from the clinic that day, you saw the six-year-old girl, I believe her name is Etta, who was playing double dutch with her friends on the sidewalk.

She stopped to watch us. You stepped out of the car with a bandage on your right forehead. She cast a sympathetic gaze upon you and her eyes met yours. Her mouth and dark eyes blossomed into the most radiant smile like a beautiful pink rose. It was a tender and sweet expression, exuding warmth and kindness. As you observed the young Khmer girl's cheerful wave and smile, you smiled back just as radiantly, but your sister grabbed your hand and guided you into the house. Vida had always been like a mother hen to you. Maybe she felt bad you never got a chance to meet your parents. I did not want the girl to think we were rude people, so I waved back at her and gave her an apologetic look. But undeterred by Vida's behavior, the spirited little girl waved back with a beaming smile, seemingly oblivious to any ill-mannered conduct.

"I met Etta's parents and spoke to them briefly throughout the years. I regretted not visiting their house despite their invitation. Her father helped to shovel snow every winter during the years we lived there. Anyway, once we came inside, the day we came from the clinic, Vida continuously griped to me about her disdain for the Cambodian people and our life in Uptown.

"Meanwhile, you parked yourself on the reading nook window, peering out onto the front porch to watch little Etta as she continued to have playful interactions with her friends, full of carefree laughter. In those moments, I was not sure if you wanted to experience the same happiness and freedom she seemed to possess, or that you had a crush on her. I think it was both. Every day after school, you would position yourself at the nook pretending to read, eagerly awaiting her arrival home or watching her engage with her friends while you tackled your homework. You seemed to anticipate those encounters, even though she remained oblivious to your crush."

"I had forgotten about our life on Dover Street," said Sam, blushing, as he brushed his dark hair back.

"You were so happy, so radiant that I wished you would stay like that forever. That was what I always wanted for you, to come alive, to be happy. That little girl brought that out of you. Regrettably, it was short-lived. In 1992, when you reached the age of thirteen, your sister's desire came true. We relocated to the west side of Chicago, close to Saint Ignatius College, where you would pursue your education and met your friend Tomi. The separation meant you could no longer catch glimpses of Etta." Betty smiled at Sam's still-ruddy cheeks. "I guess over time, your memories of little Etta began to fade."

"They are but distant memories," said Sam. Staring at his aunt's hand, he seemed to be lost in deep thought.

"That's right," Betty said. "I wonder whatever happened to Etta."

"Probably married with kids by now," said Sam, dismissively.

"That's too bad, if that's the case," said Betty, eyeing him. "Although, I have a different feeling. Anyway, before I forget…" She pulled a thick, letter-bound journal from her hospital drawer and said, "Here, this is for you. You have my permission to publish it. As a professor of literature, I'm sure you will make your edits, write a foreword, and publish it for me."

"What is this, Aunt Betty?"

"It's my diary. Don't read it now. Wait until I am gone."

"Aunty Betty," said Sam, looking at her with brows furrowed.

"I know I should have done this a long time ago, when they were all still alive. To expose and bring them all down. But I was alone and scared, and I felt ashamed." Tears welled in her eyes. "I blamed myself for all the bad things that happened to me. Considering the MeToo movement and seeing these brave young women today, I now know better. I have missed out my opportunity to confront them."

Sam continued to look at his aunt with confusion and bewilderment.

"Though this story is mostly about my struggle as a victim of…," said Betty, not able to push out the word, "it is also about your loving mother and father. They were the only protectors after my beloved father, your grandfather, was killed in the line of duty. And when your parents were gone, I had no one, because my own mother, for her own self-preservation, chose to look the other way. She knew what happened to me and she let me suffer alone. She was as monstrous as the perpetrator and his protectors." Betty started to break into uncontrollable tears.

"Aunty Betty," said Sam, wrapping his arms around her. "We did not know you carry such secrets and suffering."

She tapped his arm, appreciating his consoling words and warm embrace. "This diary will shed light on what happened to your father and why your mother died a heartbroken woman."

Sam's face contorted with disbelief and anguish, upon being hit with such painful news about his aunt. He seemed to be engulfed by an avalanche of emotions. And he had not even read her written words yet.

"I'm sorry, Aunt Betty." Tearful, he nestled against her soft shoulder, his voice trembling with profound remorse and compassion. "I thought fate was unfair to me, but it has been worse for you, dearest Aunt Betty. I wish I could turn back time and make everything right for you."

Betty's delicate fingers danced through the strains of his hair, like a mother smoothing the hair of her child. "Oh, Sam," she whispered, her voice soft like a gentle breeze. "We can't turn back time. Just remember what I said. Live. Life is precious. Find your happiness. Don't mourn me too much when I'm gone. I tried to make all of you happy as best as I could, though I lived a very dark life myself. I'm sorry to burden you with this, but I figure the truth will set all of us free. You have children of your own now. I know you'll do everything to protect them from harm. I'm sorry about your marriage. But it's time for you to find happiness and someone who will care for and love you and your children."

"I'm capable of taking care of them on my own, Aunt Betty," Sam said.

"But you haven't. Vida can only do so much. And she has a two-year-old who needs her all the time. You and the kids need a woman's love and support. Go on, nephew. It has been a while. It's time to find happiness."

By the evening, the siblings and their families bid their aunt a good night and assured her they would return early the next morning while others would return to stay by her side through the night. "We'll bring back your favorite soup," Daniel said, kissing her on her forehead.

"Don't worry too much about me. It's not often you guys are together. Enjoy your time with each other. I'll get some rest," Betty said, smiling.

"I made a reservation at the Golden Bull. So, we will meet there," Vida said to her siblings and their loved ones, and they left their Aunt Betty's room one by one.

5

Like a mirage, the yellow, orange, and red glow descended upon Chicago at 8:08 p.m., a brilliant palette of the setting sun painting the city in hues of fire and warmth. Etta, having showered and put on new clothes, departed her four-story townhouse, including the basement, with a river view on East North Water Street. She maneuvered her sleek, black Acura MDX onto Michigan Avenue, famously known as The Magnificent Mile, where high-end retail stores adorned both sides to the north, while art galleries and historic buildings graced the southern stretch. Her date had arranged their dinner meeting at Athena Greek Restaurant, situated on South Halsted Street, a mere twelve-minute drive away.

As Etta's car cautiously made its way onto the DuSable Bridge, a minivan promptly pulled up behind her, closely shadowing her movements. It continued to tailgate her as she navigated the turn onto Wacker Drive, heading toward State Street. Etta flashed her right turn signal, patiently awaiting the green light. As soon as the light changed, she verified the absence of oncoming traffic or pedestrians, before she pressed down on the gas pedal to initiate her right turn onto Wacker Drive. However, her maneuver was interrupted as a car swiftly raced past her from the eastern side of Wacker, forcing her to abruptly brake and come to a screeching halt. The other vehicle had flagrantly disregarded the red light, causing a sudden and forceful impact from the car behind. Etta, feeling a jolt of violence and hearing a deafening crash, swiftly shifted her car into park, her legs trembling from the surge of nerves that overcame her. Her heart raced, and her hands trembled uncontrollably. Waves of fear engulfed her from all directions. In her efforts to avoid colliding with the individual who ran the red light, she had forgotten about the car trailing closely behind her. She hadn't anticipated the person's close pursuit and was not paying attention. The unsettling sensation of being struck brought back memories of her high school days, when a distracted businessman on a phone call had collided with her boyfriend's GT Mustang.

When she finally collected herself from all the honking as other cars tried to pass her, she put her car back in drive. Her heart continued to beat like a drum and her hands were still trembling as her shaky foot pressed weakly on the gas pedal. She drove a bit further and then pulled over to park on Wacker Drive. Tourists and passersby stood to watch for a moment and went back about their business when they saw no one was seriously hurt. Etta looked back to find the blue minivan that had followed her parked right behind her. She took a deep breath, thinking, *I hope I'm not dealing with a lunatic, or worse, a Karen or a Ken.* She grabbed her purse, phone, and insurance card from the glove compartment, and stepped out of the car.

She walked to the rear to see how much damage the other driver had caused. She then turned to see the badly damaged front of the minivan. She heard children crying, as the driver rolled down his passenger windows. Her heart dropped. She rushed to the passenger side and asked the two boys and the little girl, "Oh my God. Are you all right? Are you hurt?" They kept on crying. "Hey. I understand you're scared. I'm here to make sure you're safe. I'm calling 911 to have the ambulance check you out. Okay?"

She pressed 911. It rang. Her face remained calm and her tone casual, though her hands continued to shake as a result of the accident. The little girl seemed to calm a bit, but the boys kept wailing as loud as before, as if to defy her to calm them down.

"I think they're all right. They're just scared," said a tall, thin, good-looking man.

"911. What is your emergency?" said a female operator.

Etta's gaze locked with Sam's, as if she felt drawn into a world where time stood still, lost in the intensity of his soulful eyes. She flashed him a bright smile and said, "Whew! What a relief."

He looked at her with a dour expression, as if he had seen her somewhere before.

"Hello? What is your emergency, ma'am?" said the operator.

"Oh, I'm sorry," said Etta, lifting her iPhone to her mouth. "I would like to report an accident on the corner of Wacker and Michigan. We pulled over across from the London House on 85 East Wacker Drive."

"Are you okay?" the operator asked.

"I'm okay, but the kids might need to be checked out."

"Okay. We're sending emergency responders your way."

"Thank you," Etta said and hung up the phone. She asked Sam, "Are you okay?" when it was he who should be asking her.

He nodded. He got out of the car to make sure his children were not hurt and tried to calm them. Moments later, a police car with a loud siren turned from the other side of Wacker Drive and swirled from Michigan Avenue to park in front of Etta's car. Downtown had always been busy with policemen and policewomen in cars and bikes, so it was natural to see them responding to the scene quickly.

A female officer checked with Sam and the children while a male officer came to talk to Etta and walked with her to her SUV. She noticed the children were still crying, but Etta started to cross her arms and fidgeted with her hair when she noticed their father kept looking her way. He was talking to the female officer who was also trying to calm the children. He pulled out his insurance card and driver's license to give to the officer. Etta handed hers to the policeman who was taking her statement. She made sure to stand facing the officer whose back was turned to Sam and the female officer. Once in a while she peeked over the cop's shoulder, biting her lips, to see if Sam was still looking at her. Sam's gaze seemed to draw her in, creating a sense of connection and mutual attraction. *Hmm. Is this love at first sight that people always talk about? Or is this just an acid reflux that I'm experiencing?* "Neh. He has three kids. Obviously, he's married," she found herself saying out loud.

"Or maybe he's divorced," said the officer, smiling, as he was writing her information on a form.

"Excuse me?" Etta said, confused. The officer looked up at her and smiled. "Um. Uh. Did I say that out loud?"

"You sure did. Would you like me to ask him for you?"

"Um. Uh. No," she put up her palms to stop him from doing so. "No. Please don't," said Etta, panicking.

"All right. Suit yourself. He is a very handsome man," said the officer, laughing good-naturedly. He turned around to look back at his partner, who smiled and threw her head back laughing as if Sam had said something hilarious.

Soon an ambulance truck came. A man and woman jumped out and went to check up on the father and his children and then her. "I'm fine. I'm not hurt," Etta told them.

The police distributed reports to both of them and a tow truck was summoned to the scene. Sam looked at Etta one last time before he entered his car to see if it would need towing. Upon hearing a grinding noise when he attempted to start it, Etta stopped herself from entering her car and turned around. She walked back and thought, *It could be a sign of a faulty starter or flywheel.* Sam tried again, but it refused to start. Etta noticed that both headlights were broken. Etta's officer suggested to Sam that there might be engine and transmission damage, or an electrical system failure. Etta overheard the officer inquire about Sam's means of getting home.

Sam answered in a low, tired voice, "I'll ask my sister or my brother. They're not too far from here."

"Okay. Have a good evening, sir." The male officer turned around and saw Etta still standing there. "Or someone can give you a lift," he added, in a low voice that only Etta could hear. He winked at her. Etta's face blushed.

"Thank you," said Sam, clueless of their exchange.

"Bye, kiddos," the female officer said to the children.

"All right. Have a good evening, ma'am," said her officer.

"Thank you, sir," she said.

Etta was suddenly inundated with a surge of compassion that made it impossible for her to proceed with her scheduled date. Just as she contorted her face, grappling with this inner conflict, her phone began to ring, adding another layer of complexity to the situation.

"Hi, is this Etta?" Then she realized whose number it was. "Oh my God, Dr. Vibol. I'm sorry. I forgot to call you. I've been in an accident. The police have just left."

"Oh no. Are you okay?" said a gentle voice from the other end, as she put the phone on speaker.

"I'm fine. I'm sorry I missed our date."

"That's okay. Let me know where you are and I can come by."

"No. That's okay. I must get my car fixed. It's late. You must be up and early for your interview. I'm so sorry about this."

"It's okay. Is there anything I can do?"

"No. No. I'll be fine."

"Oh. Okay."

"Again, I'm very sorry about tonight," said Etta.

"No. You've had an accident. I'm sorry I'm not able to help you."

"No. It's not your fault. Listen, good luck with your interview. I hope you get it."

"Thank you."

"Goodbye, Dr. Vibol."

"Umm. Goodbye," he uttered with a hint of hesitation. She abruptly ended the call.

She walked up to Sam and his children with a purpose. "Hi again. Umm. I don't want to intrude, but I feel bad leaving the four of you waiting out here. Have you called your wife to let her know what happened?"

"Our Mom ran away with the milkman," said Sopraffina, innocently.

Etta let out a laugh. She thought the little girl was the cutest thing. No one else laughed. "Oh, you're serious. I'm sorry. I don't mean to laugh."

"It's all right," said Sam, with a little embarrassed smirk. "I'm divorced. Her brothers made up this story. They're teasing her."

"Oh, okay. So where are you heading? I can drop you off."

"That's generous of you. We're supposed to meet my sister and brothers at the Golden Bull."

"Golden Bull. Good choice. It's one of my favorite restaurants in Chinatown," Etta said, trying to make conversation. Sam did not respond. She fidgeted with her hair, pulling it back behind her ear. "Um. Do they know you're in an accident?"

"No."

"They must be worried. It has been over half an hour now."

"I didn't bring my power cord. My phone is dead."

"Oh. Would you like to use my phone?" She handed him her phone. Under normal circumstances, she would never allow anyone to touch her phone.

"Thank you," he responded gratefully as she extended her phone to him.

When Sam made the call, Etta overheard a male's voice at the other end. Sam replied, "Vincent, please don't react. I don't want Vida to know. She might overreact. Don't say anything but 'ah ha' and 'okay.'"

"Okay," said Vincent, playing along with his baby brother.

"I got into a little accident."

"Oh, my God!"

Sam went silent, looking disappointed.

"I mean, ah ha," Vincent corrected himself.

"Don't worry. We're okay. A nice lady offered to drive us there. We'll be there shortly."

"Okay."

"Daddy? I'm hungry," said Jonny, griping from inside the car.

"Me too," said Wallace.

"Me three," said Sopraffina.

Sam hung up the phone and handed it back to Etta. "We're on our way to the restaurant now, kids."

"Yay!" they yelled.

Sam rushed to retrieve their luggage before the tow truck driver took off with his rented minivan. He stowed it in the back of Etta's SUV, then opened a passenger door and instructed the boys to sit on either side of Sopraffina near the windows. Taking his brown leather bag, including his aunt's diary, he settled himself into the front passenger seat.

"Okay. Are our seat belts fastened?" Etta asked, playfully.

Sam looked back at his children. "Everyone is safe and secure. Are you okay back there, Sopraffina?"

"Yes, Daddy."

"Sopraffina?" Etta spontaneously replied, her gaze meeting Sam's with a curious smile. In that moment, she noticed a genuine smile grace his face. "My ex-wife and I actually had lunch at Sopraffina Marketcaffe when we visited this area. She loved the name of the restaurant. She mentioned that if we were to have a baby girl in our next pregnancy, we would name her Sopraffina."

Etta let out a laugh, knowing that Daron wasn't the only one who named his kids after a place.

"Oh. So, you're not from around here?" she asked, with laughter still in her voice.

"No."

Etta anticipated further elaboration from Sam, but he abruptly stopped, halting her from asking further questions. Choosing not to push the matter, she respected his silence. However, their conversation didn't go unnoticed by the observant boys, who seized the opportunity to tease their sister. "Haha! Daddy and Mommy named you after a restaurant," they gleefully exclaimed.

"Stop it," Sopraffina said.

Etta turned around to look at the children. When she turned back to the driving view her gaze met Sam's. She smiled and spontaneously said, "I'm Etta."

"Am Sam."

Did he just say 'Am Sam'? she thought to herself. She looked at him as if she expected him to elaborate. He just sat in silence. "Okay," she said, barely audible.

Etta pressed the start button, glanced over her shoulder to check for any oncoming cars, and then shifted into drive to proceed along Wacker Avenue. Upon reaching State Street, she smoothly executed a left turn and continued her journey southward. "Is it far, Daddy?" said Jonny.

"How do you expect Dad to know that?" asked Wallace.

"He lived in Chicago before, dummy," said Jonny.

"Don't call me that," said Wallace, reaching over Sopraffina to punch his brother in the arm.

"Hey! You're not allowed to hit me."

"Says who?"

"Says uncle Daniel. He said in Khmer culture we are to be respectful of someone who is older. I am older. You better be respectful to me."

"Not by much!" replied Wallace.

Etta's eyes widened and she gasped. "You guys are Khmer?" she said, sounding pleasantly surprised.

"Yes, we are. Daddy's father is Khmer and his mother is white," said Jonny.

Etta turned to look at Sam. He nodded and smiled. "I see," said Etta, blushing.

The boys continued hitting each other back and forth, creating a chaotic and unruly atmosphere.

Surprisingly, the girl remained composed amidst the commotion. Their father made no attempt to intervene or reprimand them, allowing them to continue their disruptive behavior unchecked. Etta glanced at Sam, wondering why he didn't tell his kids to behave. She saw Sam through her peripheral vision. He seemed to be lost in a forlorn world. As Etta caught a glimpse of the girl's reflection in the rearview mirror, a warm smile graced her face. The girl, with her charming smile, reciprocated. Etta smiled at her adoringly.

The behavior of the boys continued to escalate on both sides of Sopraffina. They persisted in hitting and kicking each other, with one of them even targeting Etta's seat, causing her annoyance as they struck her headrest.

Etta jokingly asked, "Hey, guys. Did your uncle tell you about being respectful to an adult by not disturbing anything within the proximity of her sacred head?"

"Boys, please don't hit the nice lady's headrest," said Sam, as if waking up from his reverie. Everyone became quiet.

With narrowed eyes, furrowed brows and a tight mouth, Etta felt a little peeved at Sam's liberal style of parenting. He only said something because she had said something.

Etta made a turn west onto Cermak Road and continued driving to their destination, marked with a green sign. "Here we are," she said at last, excited for them to have their dinner. She double-parked right in front of the Golden Bull Restaurant.

Before he opened the door, Sam turned to Etta and said, "Thank you for dropping us off. It's very kind of you."

"It's my pleasure," said Etta, smiling.

He went to retrieve their luggage and opened the door for the kids. Hungry and eager to be free from the confines of the car, the boys couldn't contain their excitement.

The little girl stayed by her father's side, looking shy and adorable. She expressed her farewell by waving at Etta. "Thank you for driving us," Sopraffina said, her innocent words touching Etta's heart.

Etta couldn't help but feel a deep affection for the sweet little girl with her dimpled face. She appeared to be the calm and well-behaved one among her boisterous brothers and her father, who seemed so reserved in his communication. Etta waved back at her, appreciating her polite gesture. Then something caught Etta's attention in her peripheral vision—a leather-bound journal wedged between her and the passenger seat. She picked it up. "Oh, I think this is yours."

Sam, already seeing his boys making their way inside the restaurant, turned around and walked over, extending his hand to receive the diary. "Thank you. I greatly appreciate it."

Etta responded with a casual, "No problem," as Sam lingered, eyeing her. She flashed him a genuine smile that radiated like a ray of sunshine as she waved back at him.

Sopraffina remained close to her father's side, and as soon as the boys entered the restaurant, Vida emerged to greet her brother and niece. Etta pondered if she was Sam's sister, as she seemed to fuss over him and the little girl with maternal care. For reasons unknown to Etta, she remained in her car until both father and daughter had entered the restaurant, with Vida being the last to go inside. Vida turned her gaze toward the darkened car. Etta was unsure if she was noticed by Vida.

Recognizing the lateness of the hour, Etta sent a text to her mechanic friend, who worked at her Acura dealership, arranging to leave the car in the lot and drop the key off in the designated box. She drove there and took a Lyft back home, where she prepared a quick meal of instant noodle soup before attending to her bedtime routine—brushing her teeth, taking a shower, and finally settling into bed for the night. She drifted off to sleep smiling, thinking of the handsome Sam and her fateful accident.

6

SAM, CHICAGO
AUGUST 2, 2018

At 6:30 a.m. the following morning, the phone pierced the silence of his cozy bedroom with its insistent ring. Sam had just stepped out of the shower, with a white towel draped over his well-defined abs. He rushed to reach his ringing phone from the nightstand with one hand, drying his hair with a small towel in the other.

"Hi, Vincent," he answered. His face turned pale, and he found himself needing to sit down for this news. "Have you told Daniel and Vida? Okay. I'll get dressed. We should be there shortly," Sam said in a steady voice, his countenance crestfallen.

After getting dressed and checking on his children, who were still sleeping peacefully with their cousins, Sam descended the majestic, double-side staircase of Daniel's Tudor-style home in Skokie where Vida and Sam's families, who lived in Chapel Hill, stayed whenever they came to Chicago. Once he reached the landing leading down a single staircase, he was greeted by Daniel, who stood by the foyer lit by the morning sun through the arched window above his glass and iron entry doors.

"Vida and Paolo left earlier," Daniel said.

Sam's left brow went up, showing surprise that their brother-in-law had made it to Chicago from Chapel Hill without him knowing.

"Yeah, he came last night when you went to bed. You can ride with Sopheap and me. Oh, my mother in-law brought over her famous chicken *babar*. Why don't you have some before we go?"

"I'm not hungry," Sam said, brooding.

"You shouldn't go on an empty stomach." The soft voice came from the direction of the kitchen, down the hall and around the staircase, followed by the shuffle of indoor slippers against the hardwood floor.

"Good morning, *bang srey*," Sam greeted his sister in-law. The thin, round-faced woman stood five feet six inches tall, with straight, silky, jet black hair. Walking over toward him, she put her wallet inside her purse, zipped it up, and wore it on her shoulder. Sam turned to look at his big brother and said, "I'd rather we go now."

"As you wish," Daniel said.

Sopheap opened her hallway closet to exchange the slippers for her dress shoes.

Sam turned around to look up the stairs as if he thought of something. Sopheap noticed and assured him, "Don't worry about the kids. My parents are both here. My mother is looking after baby Lily right now. My younger sister will be around to help out."

Driving down Lake Shore Drive, the husband and wife continued to discuss their assigned tasks. They had been prepared for this moment since the doctor told them their Aunt Betty did not have much time left. Sam stared outside the window of his brother's black Mercedes at the passing scenes, the trees and the blue water of Lake Michigan. They pulled into the parking lot of

Northwestern Hospital, amidst the concrete jungle of downtown Chicago.

With heavy hearts, they gathered around the bed of their beloved aunt, Betty Wilson. Intense emotions erupted as her time was getting nearer. Vida cried out loudly while her three brothers silently wept, each lost in their own grief as they observed their aunt's final moments. Betty summoned every ounce of strength with her last breaths to share parting words with each of them. Then, she reached out to Sam, grasping his hand as a gentle reminder to continue living a life brimming happiness.

"I have no regrets raising all of you," Betty whispered, her voice overflowed with sincerity. "But I do regret living in fear and worry. Please, my dear ones, do not mourn me too much. I have given you all a good life, and it brings me joy to see you with families of your own. Sam, you have my diary. It holds the legacy of our family, including information about your father and how he left us all." His siblings turned to look at him with knitted brows. Betty continued, "I look forward to meeting him, your mother, and my father—your grandfather. Take care of one another, always. I love you all very much. Say bye to the little ones. Tell them Nana Betty loves them all so much."

As Betty's final words drifted away, she took her last breath, leaving a profound void in the room.

"Aunt Betty! Aunt Betty!" Vida cried out, her plea echoing through the space. "Please don't go. Please don't go. We need you." The room teeming with the collective sorrow of everyone present, as tears flowed freely. Betty was their matriarch, and now they only had each other.

In the days that followed, Vida and her brothers focused on arranging their aunt's funeral, making the necessary preparations to bid her a proper farewell. Meanwhile, Sam held onto the diary his aunt had left specifically for him, keeping it safely tucked away in his leather messenger bag. The death of his aunt weighed heavily on him, and he couldn't bring himself to read the contents of the diary just yet. He chose not to share it with his siblings either, feeling the timing wasn't right. He knew one day he would have to face the words written within its pages, but for now, he needed time to process his grief.

As the funeral arrangements were made and the service was scheduled for Saturday, the siblings and their partners gathered at the dining table with paperwork and family photo albums spread out over the dining table. They openly expressed their sorrow late into the evening when their children had already gone to bed. They found solace in sharing their emotions with one another and reminisced about their individual and collective memories of their wonderful Aunt Betty. However, Sam's thoughts and feelings remained hidden from the rest, leaving them unaware of the turmoil he was experiencing. He sat at the end of the table staring at old photos from when they lived on North Dover Street, flipping through the album as if he was looking for something or someone. Suddenly, the doorbell rang.

"Who could be ringing at this time of night?" Rima, Vincent's fiancé, said as she helped Daniel's wife, Sopheap, put away the food they had prepared for the upcoming funeral lunch. Sopheap viewed her kitchen video screen to find a melon-faced woman looking straight into the ring camera.

"It's Tomi," Sopheap said, looking surprised. They all exchanged confused looks and then cast their eyes on Sam.

Sam got up to walk to the front and opened the glass and iron door. As soon as she saw him, Tomi dropped her luggage and lunged at him with a full embrace, which he did not expect.

"Oh, Sam. I took the first flight here as soon as I heard about Aunt Betty. She's like an aunt to me," she said, weeping but without tears. Sam hesitantly put his arms around her and patted her back to console her. She told him, "I'm here for you and the children, whatever you need, Sam."

"Is your husband here, too?" Vida asked, interrupting their embrace. Paolo, Daniel, Sopheap, Vincent, and Rima all came out of the kitchen to greet the unexpected guest.

"Hi," Tomi said, waving to everyone. "Kevin is out of the country on a business trip. He won't be able to make it in time to attend the funeral." Looking at Vida, Daniel, Vincent, and then Sam with sad eyes, she said, "I'm sorry for your loss. I hope I didn't interrupt anything. I'm here to help you, so if you need anything from me…"

"Are you planning on staying here?" Vida asked.

"If you don't mind. I just want to be near Sam… I mean near the family to help out during this tough time," Tomi said, sheepishly.

"Well, we have just finished renovating and decorating the attic. There is a bathroom up there, too. You'll have plenty of privacy," said Sopheap, trying to be a good host. "Come with me. I'll show you to your room."

"Oh. Thank you," Tomi replied. "I greatly appreciate your hospitality."

"I'll help you with your luggage," Daniel said, following his wife and Tomi up the stairs.

"Who is she?" Rima said, looking confused and intrigued.

"Sam's best friend," Vincent said, sounding sarcastic, looking in the direction of his younger brother.

"She's a good friend, always there for Sam day or night," Paolo said, sounding equally sarcastic. Vida gently smacked him in the arm.

"Don't get it twisted," Sam scolded. "She's been my friend since childhood. Plus, she's a married woman. I'm tired. I'm turning in now." He got up to check on his children before he went to bed.

Upon learning about Sam's aunt passing, Tomi had wasted no time in flying over to be of assistance, especially offering her support to Sam. Understanding his reluctance to openly express his emotions, she respected his need for space and allowed him to process his grief in his own way, so long as she got to be in the same space. In fact, Tomi became a constant presence by his side. Like a shadow, she remained close to him, offering her silent companionship and understanding. Tomi cherished the moments she spent with Sam, finding joy in simply observing him and being in his presence.

After the wake and funeral service that took place Saturday morning, friends and guests gathered once again at Daniel's home for a heartfelt "thank you" lunch fest. As Sam's older siblings and significant others attended to the guests, he stood at the back of the room, gazing out the window into the meticulously maintained backyard. It was at that moment he realized something. Approaching his brother Vincent, Sam was interrupted by Tomi, who appeared with refreshments. Expressing his gratitude, he glanced at her, meeting her sympathetic gaze. "Do you mind checking on my kids?" he said to her. She happily nodded. When she was out of the room, Sam reached

Vincent, who was talking to one of the guests. "Vincent, can I see your phone for a moment?"

Although curious about the reason, Vincent, preoccupied with speaking to the guests, handed over his phone. Sam swiftly scrolled down until he found the number he was looking for, listed on August 1 at 9:10 p.m. Feeling thankful that his brother hadn't cleared the call log, he memorized the number, returned the phone to his brother and abruptly left the house.

Sam found himself walking eastward along Golf Road and McCormick Boulevard, with no destination in mind, simply allowing himself to be consumed by his thoughts and emotions.

7

ETTA, CHICAGO
AUGUST 4, 2018

To kickstart her Saturday, Etta began her morning routine of running, a practice that both energized and helped her think. Her routine also involved meeting either Daron or Rochelle's best friend, Randall Smith, for a leisurely lunch or brunch. However, this particular Saturday veered from the usual course. Etta had made a commitment to step in for a former colleague by teaching an architecture class the following Friday on his behalf.

Consequently, she decided to stay in and dedicate her day to prepare for the class.

Nevertheless, she had made arrangements to have dinner with Daron and the gang later that evening. She knew he and Rochelle would be brimming with anticipation, eager to hear every detail of her date with Dr. Vibol. Etta had purposefully withheld any updates of her evening to Daron since their last conversation at Monk's, as well as refraining from divulging any information in their text exchanges.

Seated in her home office, facing the serene Chicago River, Etta diligently worked on her class outline. As she focused on her tasks, her iPhone chimed with an incoming text message. Surprised, she picked up her phone and saw it came from Dr. Javin Vibol.

Hi, Etta. I hope you're doing well. I'm just checking to see how you're doing. If everything is okay with you. Since I last heard, you were in an accident.

Before she had a chance to respond to Dr. Vibol's text, a call from a phone number with a 919 area code appeared on Etta's screen. Intrigued by the unfamiliar number, she paused for a moment and then decided to enter it into the Google search engine to gather more information. It wasn't listed. However, it said the area code belonged to Chapel Hill, North Carolina. Her brows knitted. *I don't know anyone from Chapel Hill. There is only one way to find out.* She pressed the speaker icon and set the iPhone on her desk.

"Hello," a gentle voice said from the other end.

"Hello?" she said.

"Is this Etta?"

"Speaking."

"Hi, Etta. This is Sam."

"Sam?"

"The guy who rear-ended your car."

"Yes, I know... I... I just didn't expect a call from you."

"Well, I never got a chance to apologize."

"Oh. You're calling to apologize."

"Um. Yes. I would like to apologize in person. Do you have time for a cup of coffee today?"

"Um. Yeah. Sure. What time?" She placed her hand over her mouth and her eyes widened, as if she could not believe how quick she agreed to have coffee with a guy she hardly knew.

"How about now?"

"Oh. Okay. Sure." She slapped her forehead, surprised at herself for agreeing to him with such ease.

"I can take a Lyft and meet you."

"I live downtown."

"Is there a coffee shop near there that you prefer?"

"There's a Le Cafe on Michigan Avenue across from the Tribune Tower. Would you like to meet there?"

"Sounds like a plan. I'll see you in forty-five minutes."

"Okay. See you then."

"See you," he said. They both hung up. Etta felt a tingling blend of curiosity, excitement, and trepidation ripple through her. Clutching her phone tightly, she fixated on the enigmatic set of digits—919—emblazoned on her call list. A smile began to form on her lips, like a ray of sunshine.

Etta stood up from her desk and touched her cheeks with both hands, as if she could feel herself blushing. "What am I doing? Did I just agree to go out for coffee with a total stranger who rear-ended my car?"

True to her nature, Etta surrendered to her impulses, and without regret. She stepped into her expansive white walk-in closet, searching for the perfect outfit with a blend of comfort and cuteness.

Knowing she had a leisurely ten-minute stroll to the coffee shop, while he would require a forty-five minute drive, Etta enjoyed trying on various outfits. She finally chose slim blue capri jeans and a salmon colored button-up blouse with flats of nude color.

Gazing upon her reflection in the full-length closet mirror, she twirled and swayed gracefully to capture every angle. Her soft, wavy tresses flowed down her back as she tucked the sides behind her delicate ears. Drawn to the perfect details that composed her face, she leaned for a closer look. For that final touch she reached for her cherished pink lip gloss and applied it. A smile of contentment graced her kissable lips. Completely satisfied by her own beauty and realizing the time, she hastily grabbed her iPhone on the counter, slipping it into her pocket, while her identification and bank card found a snug spot in the back pocket of her jeans. Feeling nervous and excited, she took a brisk stroll from her beautiful Riverview townhome, traversing the lively streets until she blended with the bustling crowds of shoppers and tourists on Michigan Avenue.

Etta crossed over to the other side. She pushed open the glass door and stepped into the busy and flourishing world of Le Cafe. A vibrant group of workers, tourists and local patrons made for an eclectic atmosphere. Indistinct voices mingled harmoniously, blending with the symphony of coffee grinders, clinking glasses, and hissing espresso machines. The robust aroma of the coffee beans and baked goods wafted through the air.

She looked around the room. Her heart skipped a beat as her gaze fell upon Sam, seated by the window at a cozy table for two. There he sat, in perfect posture, engrossed in the pages of the *Readers* newspaper, exuding a quiet confidence.

With a deep breath, she gracefully approached the table, her heart pounding with anticipation. "That's funny. Who reads newspapers anymore?" Etta said aloud to herself—a habit when she was anxious or nervous. She looked around, finding numerous patrons engrossed in their smartphones, their attention consumed by the digital world at their fingertips. Yet amidst this sea of distraction, her gaze quickly turned back and settled upon Sam. There he sat, without any electronic device, his focus solely on the *Readers*.

His countenance remained as brooding as when she first met him, the evening of the fateful accident. He seemed to be enshrouded by melancholy. Yet there was something undeniably magnetic about him, an enigma that enticed her to uncover the layers hidden within his soul. And so, with her heart beating fast, she walked over to him.

"Hi," she said, softly.

He looked up and stood up immediately. He offered her that gloomy smile. Etta's hand instinctively found its way to her stomach, a gentle gesture as if to soothe the fluttering butterflies that seemed to have taken residence within her since he first called her out of the blue.

"I'm sorry; I'm not normally late. Did you wait long?"

He looked at his wristwatch. "No. Not too long," he answered nonchalantly.

"You chose a high table," she said, though in her mind, she meant they would sit close and intimate.

"Yes. You don't like it? Do you want to switch?" Sam said, sounding serious, as he looked around to find a table that would please her. They both looked around and there were no other available tables.

"Oh, no. It's fine. I was just making an observation." Etta felt awkward but a warm smile graced her lips. Their eyes remained locked.

Sensing a shift in the atmosphere, an awkwardness that settled between them, Etta took the initiative to change the subject, to make a brief escape to collect herself. "Well. I'm going to grab myself a hot drink," she declared, her voice soft, carrying a touch of lightheartedness. She noticed he did not have anything to eat.

"Okay," he said.

"Would you like me to get you something to go with that coffee?"

He looked at his cup of coffee. "No. Am fine."

"Are you sure?" She noticed he had said "am" again instead of "I'm."

"Yes," he said, smiling his gentle smile.

As Etta patiently waited for her order, her gaze naturally gravitated toward Sam, who remained immersed in the pages of the newspaper. There he sat, a portrait of concentration, his attention captured by whatever story he was reading. With her chai latte in hand and a freshly baked croissant on a small plate, Etta made her way back to the cozy high table by the window, where Sam sat engrossed in his reading. Settling into her seat, she placed her cup and plate gently on the table, their presence adding a touch of warmth to the space they shared.

"Have you eaten?" she asked, breaking the silence between them.

"No."

"Would you like to share my croissant?"

"Sure," Sam replied, casually. Her face flushed red, as she realized the intimacy in her gesture of offering food. She took her seat across from him and the world around them faded into a blur, leaving only their shared presence in focus. Etta placed her iPhone face down on the table before Sam, giving him her undivided attention.

As the croissant's aroma wafted through the air, Etta couldn't resist taking the first piece off and putting it in her mouth, savoring the buttery pastry before she gently pushed the plate toward Sam. Her action spoke of a comfortable familiarity, as if sharing food with Sam was an effortless extension of their connection. Sam, feeling at ease, broke off a piece.

"So, how are you?" His voice carried a genuine curiosity. He put the flaky pastry in his mouth. Without thinking, he broke off another piece, suddenly feeling hungry because he had skipped breakfast and lunch. He seemed to have regained his appetite.

"I'm fine. Thank you for asking. How about you?" Etta said.

"I'm okay."

Savoring the frothy warmth of her latte, Etta's thoughts momentarily drifted before she swiftly recalled and posed her next question. A gentle smile graced her lips, reflecting her genuine interest as she inquired, "Mm. So, how are Sopraffina and the boys?" Her words carried a tender affection, an acknowledgment of his precious family.

"They're fine," he said, after swallowing and then taking a sip from his cup.

A soft, contented smile graced Etta's lips. "Good. Good," she echoed. Her cup found its place on the table, momentarily forgotten as her attention was wholly captured by Sam's gaze.

It was in this moment, as their gazes locked, that the potential for something deeper, something beyond the surface-level conversation, bloomed.

Etta's heart quickened, anticipating where this meeting would lead them.

"First of all, I just wanted to say, I'm sorry."

"Sorry for what?" said Etta, teasing him.

"For not paying attention and rear-ending you."

"You must have been preoccupied with your children. Apologies accepted."

"Thank you."

"You're welcome," she said. He let out a gentle laugh, as if finding what she said utterly adorable.

"Also, I want to thank you for taking us to meet my siblings at the restaurant. You're a very nice person."

"I couldn't let those munchkins be stranded like that," Etta said, shyly. He never took his eyes off her.

"I looked at the police report and finally know your full name: Etta Kem."

"Finally?"

"Well. You told me your name was Etta, but you never said anything about your last name until I saw the police report."

"I see," she said, believing him wholeheartedly.

"I didn't make a good impression that Thursday, but I'm glad to have *bumped* into you, so to speak."

Etta let out a gentle laugh.

"Can we have a fresh start?" he said.

"Yes. Definitely."

Sam gently extended his hand, offering a congenial smile. "Allow me to introduce myself properly. My name is Samuel Angk, although I prefer to be called 'Sam.'"

Etta reciprocated the gesture with a warm handshake, her eyes reflecting genuine delight. "Pleasure to make your acquaintance, Sam. And as you know, I am Etta Kem."

Sam showed his pearly whites, accompanied by an affectionate glimmer in his eyes.

"If I'm not mistaken," Etta ventured, "Angk is not only a Khmer last name but a royal one."

"Really? I did not know that."

"So, are you a prince?" Etta meant the question seriously, but it came off as a joke.

Sam laughed. "I don't believe so. I understand Kem is one of those popular Khmer surnames," Sam said, quick to change the subject.

"Yes, like Meas, Chhim, Chay, and Chorm," she stated, a touch of pride resonating in her words.

Sam's laughter reverberated through the air, a joyful melody that reached Etta's ears. In that moment, a sense of ease washed over her, knowing that Sam possessed a lightness of spirit, capable of genuine mirth and engaging in a meaningful conversation.

"So," he said, "how long have your parents been in America?"

"Hmm. Let's see…" Etta tapped her index and middle fingers against her subtle, dimpled chin. "You probably know the story of every Khmer family that migrated here in the 1970s and 1980s. It's the same, but not the same, if you know what I mean."

"Sure."

"You see, my parents and grandfather were displaced in the refugee camp in Thailand for a few years before the Van Buren family sponsored them. They arrived in Uptown Chicago in 1979, two years before I was born."

"Interesting. They arrived the year I was born." Sam said.

"Oh."

"So you're an American-born Khmer."

"Yes, I am. I get the best of both worlds," Etta said, smiling.

Sam's eyes shimmered with affection as he gazed at Etta. "I can only imagine," he responded, his voice full of longing for what Etta had. "To have a deeper understanding of my own roots, to explore and connect with that other side of me, would undoubtedly be wonderful."

Etta's gaze softened as she beheld Sam's adoring smile. It captivated her. A gentle warmth filled her heart, and an unspoken desire stirred within her, wishing to witness his radiant smile more often.

With a composed posture, Etta sat upright, her arms gracefully folded on the table. "So, you have a 919 area code. Is that Chapel Hill, North Caroline? Her words held an air of gentle probing, as she sought to unravel the layers of Sam's life, eager to delve deeper into his personal story.

"Yes, my siblings and I were born in Chapel Hill. My mother and her side of the family were all born in Chapel Hill."

"Really? You don't have a Southern accent."

"No. In academia, we have a neutral tone. Plus, the people in Chapel Hill have a very slight Southern accent, to begin with anyway. But that is not to say there aren't any who don't have a deep Southern accent."

"Right. So, you work at a university?"

"Yes. I'm a professor of comparative and world literatures at the University of North Carolina in Chapel Hill."

Etta smiled at him for saying his full title and the university name. "Oh, nice. So have you published anything?"

"Yes, I have published a few books on how to write. Just textbook stuff for the students."

"I see. So, your last name is Angk. Are you by any chance related to King Angk Duong who ruled Cambodia from 1841 to 1860?" Etta said, hoping to get to the bottom of Sam's ancestry. She couldn't understand why a regular person would have a royal last name.

"No," he chuckled, his voice bursting with genuine amusement, "I don't believe so, at least not to my knowledge. But you seem quite knowledgeable about Khmer history."

"Yes, thanks to my parents and grandfather."

"It sounds like you have an educated family."

"Yes, for peasants, they're very educated. You said you're from out of town. Are you visiting your father?"

"No. He passed away before I was born."

"Oh, I'm sorry. Was he ill?"

Sam's gaze deepened as he locked eyes with Etta, a flicker of hesitation shadowing his features.

"No." Sam dropped his gaze.

Etta recognized there were depths to Sam's past that he was not yet ready to reveal, and she respected his unspoken boundaries. She let it go, for now, and pivoted the conversation to something else. Admiring Sam's broad shoulders in his white shirt and black jacket, she said, "So, what brought you to the City of Broad Shoulders?"

"My Aunt Betty has just passed away."

"Oh. I'm sorry for your loss. My deepest and most sincere condolences to you and your family." Etta's heart sank, as she found herself unable to find any comforting words to say besides these usual sentiments.

"Yeah. She took great care of my siblings and me. She's the only family we had and knew. We held a funeral for her today. It's fine. We knew it was coming. There were too many people at my brother's house. I needed some fresh air. I hope you don't mind me dragging you out here."

"Oh no, of course not. Not at all."

"So, how about you? Have you always lived in Chicago?" Sam asked, shifting the questions as if he wanted to know more about her.

"Yes, my parents and grandfather love Chicago and never wanted to move or live anywhere else. They told me most Cambodian refugees who were placed in Uptown Chicago had since moved to warmer states like California, Florida, Texas, and Louisiana, while others just moved to other states for work or better income. But our destination has always been Chicago."

"I don't know much about Cambodia and the Khmer people. Do you speak and write Khmer well?"

"Yes. What about you?" asked Etta.

"I speak conversational Khmer but can't write well yet. I learned it from Franklin E. Huffman's *Cambodian System of Writing and Beginning Reader*."

"He's not a good source. You know, they have many Khmer learning apps now."

"I'm sure they do. I only get to practice it when I visit Daniel and his family. Because his in-laws only speak

Khmer and broken English, he is forced to learn it to communicate with them. I don't think my sister Vida and Vincent speak it anymore."

Etta's countenance fell at the disheartening news of his two siblings' lack of interest in their native tongue. She couldn't understand the apathy displayed by numerous Khmer children of the diaspora, who appeared indifferent, if not disdainful, toward their ancestral language. Some seemed to go out of their way to express their contempt for it, reducing it to a dying relic while elevating other Asian languages as more lucrative and influential. With a sigh, Etta reluctantly acknowledged their prerogative, the freedom to choose their own linguistic path.

"I do listen to Khmer oldies and watch classic movies to get a feel for the culture and the proper pronunciation of the language," Sam said, unknowingly bringing Etta's spirits back up.

"That's good," said Etta, enthusiastic and happy that he wanted to learn Khmer.

"So you're fluent in both reading and writing?" Sam asked.

"Yes, my grandfather and parents taught me."

"Maybe you can teach me," he said and smiled at her.

Oh my God. Is he flirting with me? She felt butterflies fluttering in her stomach again. "Sure, if you're interested," she said, trying to appear calm, cool, and collected.

"I'm very much interested," he said, reassuring her.

As with any café conversation between a man and woman who were interested in one another, Etta and Sam were in the stage of discovering one another. Sam offered Etta fragments of information he was willing to share about how he met his ex-wife, Sara Berg, at Loyola University. "After our graduation in 2000, Sara had a job offer in Chapel Hill. So I followed her there. It worked out because I got a chance to move back to my birthplace and the birthplace of my mother's side of the family. I earned a master's degree in literature from the University of North Carolina in 2002, followed by a PhD in 2004, and eventually Sara and I married in 2005. Unfortunately, after Sopraffina's birth she suffered postpartum depression."

After Sam finished telling Etta about his failed marriage, Etta opened up about her humble origins, sharing the tale of her severed engagement and the struggles she had weathered. "I'm glad it didn't work out for you," Sam remarked, a mischievous smile playing upon his lips, his words conveying a subtle hint of his feelings for her.

Oh, my God! He's totally flirting with me. Her eyes lit up, but at the same time she felt shy and embarrassed. On cue, she pushed her hair behind her right ear. As she looked down, her eyes widened as she noticed the empty plate. She had taken only one bite of her croissant; he had finished it all. She smiled. She didn't mind at all, because she was not hungry and only bought a pastry out of habit whenever she went to a coffee shop. She also realized with a shock that they had been talking, sipping, smiling, and laughing for hours, when she saw the time on the Tribune Building. She picked up her iPhone that was flipped face down on the table to make sure the time was correct. "Oh, my God, look at the time. It's already eight o'clock," she said, sounding panicky.

"What is it? Do you have somewhere to go?"

"Actually, I do," Etta said, sounding regretful. " I have dinner reservations with my friends in an hour," she said.

"Can't you cancel it? Do you have to go?"

"I do." Etta laughed, but Sam was serious.

"Do you think they mind if I come along?" Sam asked.

Oh, my God!, she thought. *Is he joking with me right now?* "Do you think that's a good idea?" she asked him with an arched eyebrow.

"I know. I know. I'm just kidding." He tossed his hands up in the air as if to surrender. "It's just that I don't have enough of you. I want to spend more time with you," he said, almost in a childish way. "Would you like to have lunch or dinner tomorrow?"

Her heart fluttered. Wow. Did I hear that correctly? Or did I just fantasize about it? Did he actually say he can't get enough of me? I wish I could ask him to repeat himself. "Um. Sure. Lunch would be wonderful."

"How about dinner?"

"Um. How about lunch?" Etta insisted.

"All right. Lunch it is. We should do this properly. It shall be in that order: we just had coffee; the next thing would be lunch; and then dinner. I'll call or text you the details."

Oh. He's already thinking about dinner—a third date, for sure. I can't believe it. It's possible that he's into me like I am into him. "Great," Etta said with glee. They both got up to leave.

Sam opened the door for Etta. "Thank you," she said. He nodded in acknowledgment. "Wow. It's dark now." Etta looked up at the sky. However, the city lights illuminated the atmosphere. They traipsed along Michigan Avenue. People still assembled on The Magnificent Mile with their shopping bags. Tourists with their cameras and iPhones snapped themselves in front of the Tribune building. Sam and Etta walked shoulder to shoulder. "So how are you going to get home?" Etta said, suddenly feeling concerned about his well-being and safety. It crossed her mind that if he asked her to, she would drive him home. She would just tell her friends she would be a bit late.

"I'll grab a taxi," he said. "Since I can't walk you home, how about I walk with you across the street? I am going there anyway to flag a taxi," Sam said. Etta felt sure he did not want to let her go just yet.

"Sure. That would be nice." They strolled, taking their sweet time, over to the Tribune Tower. To break the silence, Etta said, "Fun fact. Did you know that this neo-

Gothic building has pieces of history taken from around the world and plastered on its outside walls?"

"I heard about that."

"Yes, and two of them came from Cambodia."

"Really?" He seemed fascinated. "Where are they located?"

"We will be walking past them soon. I'll show you." They reached the end of the building on Michigan. Two small stones from centuries ago—in the great Kambuja Empire, currently known as Cambodia, now diminished to the size of Oklahoma—were plastered on the end wall in view of all the tourists and events happening at that part of the city's busy intersection. One piece of gray stone was taken from Ta Prohm and another piece of red stone was taken from Banteay Srei. Every time she passed by them, she felt a spiritual connection to the motherland of her parents. She hoped to visit one day. "Can you imagine our ancestors building these great monuments," said Etta, as her hand instinctively found its way to one of the weathered stones, and, in a serendipitous moment, their hands touched, as Sam also placed his hand on the same stone. Startled, she glanced over at him, only to find his gaze locked with hers. Time seemed to stand still as their eyes held each other in a silent exchange.

Etta's heart quickened its pace, its rhythm matching the beat of a drum. A sudden shyness painted her cheeks a delicate shade of red, her face reflecting the profound impact of the connection they had forged. Yet, before the moment could fully enclosed them, the enchantment was interrupted by the sound of the Darth Vader ringtone, punctuating the air.

Reality seeped back into their consciousness, and Etta's eyes dropped to her phone, seeing the text message from Daron. She looked at Sam and said, "Uh oh, my friend is asking where I am."

"Very well. I suppose I better let you go and meet your friends," Sam said, but not too quick to move his feet.

They stopped by one of the yellow taxis parked on the side of the street.

"Okay," said Etta, acknowledging their time to part.

"Well. I have something to look forward to. I'll see you tomorrow," said Sam, in a voice of longing.

"For sure." Etta stood watching him as he opened the cab's door. He got in, closed the door, and waved bye to her. She waved back with her hand suspended in the air as the taxi took off. She had a great time with him and wondered if he felt the same way about her as she felt about him. *He must be interested in me, as he said he couldn't get enough of me and wanted to see me again.* She practically beamed from ear to ear.

In the age of over-sharing and too much information, Etta expected to know more about him right away. As of that moment, she knew he was a divorced man with three children. He had a beloved aunt who had just passed away. His father passed away before he was born, and his mother passed away shortly after his birth. He had three loving older siblings. She did not know all their names yet. As she walked back to her home, she did a Google search on him. Nothing came up. She checked variations of his name to see if he was on Facebook. Nothing there either. No Instagram. No TikTok. No Twitter. It appeared he had no social media presence at all. So she got excited when she found him on LinkedIn. Unfortunately, it was empty, just a blank silhouette of a man and his name.

The next thing she did was to search for his school. She typed in "University of North Carolina." She went to the UNC Directory Search. She punched in "Samuel

Angk" and lo and behold, Samuel Wilson Angk appeared in orange, bolded font. She could see his Email, Phone Number, Position, Title, Department, and Primary Work Location. It had his downloadable VCard at the end. Her heart skipped a beat. Butterflies fluttered her stomach. She placed her right hand over her heart and thought to herself, *he does exist. He is real.*

A honk made her look up. "Hey, beautiful girl. Put that phone away and watch where you're going before you get run over," said a golden age man driving a Range Rover. She looked through the rolled down window and waved happily at the two familiar faces.

"Hi, Mr. and Mrs. Rodgers." They were owners of one of the townhomes to her left. At home they could see each other through their windows and terraces. "Thank you. I shall do that. Have a great evening." She waved them off and ran, skipped, and smiled while crossing North Water Street to her home to change. For a thirty-seven-year-old woman, she acted like a giggling teenager. She did not realize she had made it to her complex without paying attention to the traffic lights. Her face had been glued to her phone screen.

"That girl looks like she's in love," Mr. Rodgers said, looking adoringly at his wife of forty-seven years.

"Yes. She is like me after I met you for the first time," his wife said. They drove off smiling.

8

ETTA, CHICAGO

AUGUST 4, 2018

Etta's friends Daron, his wife Rochelle, and Randall Smith sat at a table with four seats at the London House Rooftop Bar with glass protection, overlooking the Chicago River where they could see the iconic Marina Towers—the two corncob-shaped condominium buildings. She walked up to find a man in his forties ranting and flailing his arms at Daron. "You suck as Doogie Howser! Go fuck yourself. And leave my wife alone."

Rochelle and Randall watched with their lips tightened, trying very hard to contain their laughter. Patrons and staff were watching to make sure he did not get violent. Fortunately, he walked away. Daron seemed speechless, which Etta seldom saw. He normally had a snappy comeback or told the guy to go do something anatomically impossible like that guy just said to him.

"I see someone has mistaken you for Neil Patrick Harris again, huh?" said Etta, smirking.

"The story of my life," said Daron grumpily.

"What would NPH be doing with his wife?"

"The hell if I know. Where have you been? We're starving." Etta leaned in to kiss everyone on the cheek.

"I'm sorry I am late. I…"

"Save your story. Let's order first." He flagged one of the waitresses over.

"Don't mind him, Etta. He's hangry," Rochelle said.

"Sorry," said Etta with a sad pout.

"Can I get you started with a drink, hon?" the waitress asked Etta.

"The Chicago, please."

"Sure thing. I'll bring your drink out and then take your food orders, unless you're ready to order now."

"I should be ready when you come back. Thank you," Etta said, glancing quickly through the menu. As everyone studied their menus, text alert came from Randall's phone.

"Oh shit!" Randall exclaimed. He and Rochelle had been best friends since high school, and Daron and Etta had gotten to know him through Rochelle after she and Daron had dated. It was evident he was visibly upset.

"What is it, Randy?" said Rochelle.

"A guy I've dated a few times just texted."

"What? How come we don't know about this?"

"I didn't want to say anything because I wasn't sure of our status yet."

"Oh, the status changes? Do tell us."

"Yeah, a guy who I barely knew said he used to have a crush on me in high school. He said he was shy and didn't know how to approach me back then. Plus, he had not come out yet. He was not sure of himself like now, so a few weeks ago he asked me out. Since he was nice and not a bad-looking guy, I went out on a date with him. I've been out with him three times. I guess I was not what he had imagined or built me up to be, so he just gave me the silent treatment. So, I was watching an episode of *How I*

Met Your Mother about a 'settler' versus a 'reacher.' An epiphany erupted. He thinks he is the *settler* and I am the *reacher* in our relationship because he thinks he has to settle for a less attractive person like me while I was more into him and always anxious to hear from him. Okay, so the fool is not into me; but just to be sure, I asked him where our relationship was going and if he still had feelings for me, because, you know, I don't play games."

"What? You guys use the 'I have a crush on you in high school' line, too?"

"Whatever, Daron!" He raised his hand in a dismissive gesture, as if to say, "Talk to the hand." It was clear he was not amused by Daron's joke about his sexual orientation.

"Randy. You know better than that. You let a dude use that line on you?" said Rochelle. Randy shrugged his shoulders.

"What's wrong with him having a crush on you in high school? I think it's romantic," said Etta, seeing everything as romantic after having met up for coffee with Sam.

"See, Etta, that's why you always pick the wrong guy. Let me warn you. If a guy says he has a crush on you in high school, run. It's just a slimy pickup line. It's the oldest trick in the book."

"Jeez, I didn't know that's a pickup line," said Etta.

"Men and women both fall for it. Did you not watch *Groundhog Day*?" he said as he browsed the menu.

"Actually, no."

Daron closed his menu after having decided what he wanted. "You should watch it and don't fall for that trap."

"Sure, I'll get right on it," Etta said, rolling her eyes.

"So, this is his last text to me." Randy passed his phone around for his three friends to read:

> I have been busy. It's not that I don't have
> feelings for you. I feel like I don't know
> how to be in a relationship. I hope your
> day goes well.

"Good. He doesn't deserve to be in a relationship. What a chickenshit," said Rochelle, fuming that someone mistreated her friend.

"Wow," said Daron with a blank look.

Etta appeared perplexed. "Is that a problem? It seems like he's simply asking for your understanding and patience," she remarked, trying to make sense of the situation.

"Yes, it's a problem, Etta!" said everyone.

"That's abundantly clear. He's created an out for himself. It's just another way of saying 'It's not you—it's me.' That's crap—he's not telling the truth. He's probably seeing someone else or found someone better. No offense," Rochelle said, fuming at the thought of someone mistreating her best friend.

"None taken," said Randy.

"Oh," Etta said. "I'm so sorry to hear that, Randy. If it is true, that's terrible. I know how it feels. It hurts more when someone keeps the truth from you. I would rather he be honest with me than spare my feelings. I want to know why someone breaks up with me—no matter how hurtful or shocking the truth may be. Oh, it'll hurt; but at least I know the truth," said Etta, still feeling a little bit of the sting of her past relationships.

"Yeah, like Thomas O'Donnell," said Daron.

"Oh, that coward. Don't remind me. Calling me *bad luck* and sleeping with my friends. The nerve of that fool." The Chicago came in time for Etta to take a sip of it while others drank theirs.

"Are you ready to order?" the waitress asked. The four friends quickly gave the nice woman their orders.

They thanked her and she collected their menus before she walked away.

"Um," said Rochelle as she put her Manhattan down. "I remember Daron telling me that story. High school boys are crazy and hormonal. Nothing has changed. This guy is immature. He is being a coward. He's not a real man at all."

Daron raised one of his eyebrows and said, "Was he ever a man to begin with?"

Etta, Rochelle, and Randy all turned to him and said, "Shut it, Daron!"

"He should have straight up told you the truth—that he is not into you anymore. That would've been more honest. He would have been a jerk for taking you for a ride, but at least he would be an honest jerk. We would have more respect for him that way," said Rochelle.

"Oh look. He unfollowed me on Twitter. Great. Real mature, buddy. Let me check my Instagram. Oh, dog shit, he unfollowed me there, too. Okay now, let me check my Facebook. Yep. He unfriended me there, too. Oh, I don't see him anymore. Oh, hell no. That fool just blocked me from seeing him. If he blocked me from social media, I am sure he has blocked me from his phone. What a loser."

"Seriously. What a chickenshit. He's not right. Not right at all. You're worth much more than that. He's not worthy of you, Randy. Screw him!" Rochelle said, appearing as agitated as Randy.

"Thank God I didn't," said Randy. "He would have left a bad taste in my mouth." Rochelle and Etta laughed while Daron ignored the pun. "What a drama queen. I don't need him to suck up all my energy. I have had enough of that fool. Besides, there is a yoga instructor I've been eyeing. But I need to find out if he's on my team."

"Yoga instructor? Aren't they all on your team?" said Daron. Rochelle slapped his arm and Randy gave him a sneering look.

"Interestingly, no. Straight guys become yoga instructors for many reasons," said Etta, innocently.

"And how would you know that, Etta?" said Daron.

"My assistant is dating a yoga instructor."

"Ooh. Is it true that yoga instructors are good at sex because they can bend and move certain ways?" said Rochelle, looking intrigued.

"No. She was complaining about how it was a hit or miss with him."

"Oh. Like Jack Edlin?" Rochelle said, smiling.

"Yeah, he was a manly man, but had no sense of direction. The audacity of him telling me I have a penguin mating habit that sustains me for a year! I told him, 'At least a penguin is monogamous,'" said Etta, laughing.

"What he did to you was unforgivable," Daron said, sounding serious, as if he had not forgiven him yet for what he did to Etta.

"For centuries, men have struggled to find things. That's why we have to lead them there," said Rochelle. She and Etta giggled like schoolgirls.

"I'm not listening to this," said Daron, shaking his head of red hair.

"Yeah, I'm not really into this heterosexual sex talk," said Randy.

Their food arrived and Daron and Rochelle steered the conversation back to what happened with Etta and Dr. Javin Vibol.

"No. I didn't get a chance to go out with him. I was rear-ended before I made my way to see him," Etta said, smiling, as if she was happy for that fateful accident to happen. She smiled more than usual, because she had been thinking about Sam since she left him at the taxi line.

"What? Oh my God. Are you okay?" said Rochelle.

"She's sitting here and having dinner with us, isn't she," Daron said to his wife. She rolled her eyes at him.

"So, you didn't meet him at all?" said Rochelle.

"No."

"Are you going to keep in contact with him? He might get a job and move here. That reminds me. I need to find out if he's got the job."

"What does it matter?" said Daron. "She blew him off. He'll never want to talk to her again."

"Hey, I had a good reason. Oh, crap. He texted me this morning and I never responded," Etta said, conveniently leaving out how she got so distracted by Sam's call that she ignored Dr. Vibol's text.

"Good going, Etta," said Daron.

"What? How could you forget about something like that?" said Rochelle.

"Well. I got distracted."

"By what?" said Daron.

"Well," Etta said, hesitating, as she was not sure if she should tell them this yet. Like Randy, she wanted to see where the relationship was going before she told her friends all about him. But she could not tell her friend about missing her date with Dr. Javin Vibol without mentioning Samuel Angk. After a long pause, she said, "I met a guy."

"What? I set you up on a date with a guy and you saw another guy?" said Rochelle. "Unbelievable." Everyone stopped eating and looked at Etta with interest.

"Okay. Who is this guy?" said Daron.

"This is a funny story if you think about it," said Etta, smiling her sunshine smile.

"Spill it," said Daron, looking at her, dead serious. She recounted everything that had happened on her way to meet Dr. Vibol, including her coffee meeting with Samuel Wilson Angk who rear-ended her. "Now he wants to have lunch with me tomorrow."

"Nope. You should cancel it," said Daron. He cut into his steak, forked the piece into his mouth and chewed slowly as he continued to look over something on his phone.

"What? Why do I need to do that?" Etta said, flabbergasted.

"He's not right for you," Daron said, still focusing on his phone.

"We're at the stage of getting to know each other. How would I know if he's right for me or not, if I don't meet him again and see what happens?"

"You're wasting your time. He has too many red flags already."

"Like what?"

"I can't believe you don't see this. Number one, he's divorced; two, he has small children, and three, he's a psychopath."

"What?" Etta felt offended at how her friend dismissed the man whom she could potentially be dating. "First of all, people get divorced. No one foresees how their marriage turns out. Secondly, it might not be that bad with the children. They need a loving home with a mother and father. Lastly, where do you get off calling him a psychopath?"

"Seriously, Etta. You're doing yourself a great disservice by being with a divorced man. You don't deserve it. He has too much baggage. His ex-wife is loony if what he says is true. She can create problems for you. Are you ready for that? Also, do you want to waste your life taking care of other people's children when you can have your own? Having your own kids is not the same as taking care of other people's kids."

"One doesn't have to be biologically related to love and care for a child, like one's own," said Etta, annoyed.

"Says who? Facebook? That's a load of crap. Listen, Etta, they're not your kids. The feelings are not the same. Believe us. We know," Daron said, looking at Rochelle. "We love our children very much. If we were to adopt, we wouldn't see ourselves loving other people's children as much as we love ours."

"That could just be you," Etta said, feeling so peeved that she took more of her drink instead of eating her food.

"To top it off, he's not normal," Daron said, as he scrolled up and down his iPhone. "I have been running searches on him since you mentioned his name. I don't see anything on him but his school's contact information. He has no social media footprint. What kind of person doesn't have a social media footprint in this day and age? What does he have to hide? That can only mean one thing: a psychopath."

"Are you serious? People with social media presence do crazy things and commit murders. Their images don't necessarily reflect who they are behind closed doors.

Maybe Sam is just a private person," said Etta, feeling protective of Sam.

"Private. What is that, code for a psycho? He told you he saw a therapist. Any guy who sees a therapist is crazy," Daron said, cutting his steak a little heavy-handedly.

"Come off it with your macho self. His wife suffered from postpartum depression. It took a toll on their marriage. He needed to see one for the sake of his wife, his children, and to salvage their marriage. I say that is a very caring and commendable thing to do," Etta replied, forking her mashed potatoes into a hill.

"A real man doesn't see a therapist," Daron said, smacking his lips with each bite of the succulent, perfectly grilled piece of steak. His jabs at Sam caused a look of contentment to spread across his face.

"Are you joking?" Etta said, finally taking a bite of her tender pot roast to offset the alcohol that was going to her head.

Daron rested his fork and wiped the corners of his mouth with his napkin. "Did you say she married someone else? If he's such a great guy, she wouldn't be marrying someone else."

"Hello? Were you not listening?" Etta said. "She abandoned him and their kids. He said she fell out of love with him. The marriage didn't work out."

"Gee, I wonder why. You don't know the truth, do you, Etta? You're going based on what he told you," Daron emphasized.

"You're ridiculous. Help me out here, guys," said Etta, turning to look at Rochelle and Randy.

"I don't know what to tell you, Etta. What thirty-something-year-old guy you know doesn't have a social media presence? We don't know anything about him. At the same time, based on what you've been telling us, I don't think you should waste your time with him," Rochelle said, agreeing with Daron.

"See?" said Daron, gesturing toward his wife.

"Great, you're taking your husband's side," Etta said to her, disappointed. She picked up her glass of water to quench her thirst from the dryness of the alcohol and the saltiness of the pot roast.

"What kind of guy rear-ended you, invited you for coffee, didn't even pay for your coffee, and ended up finishing your croissant?" Randy said, twirling his fettuccine with his fork and spoon.

Rochelle and Daron laughed.

"What did I tell you, Etta? Even Randy sees him as a loser," said Daron, seemingly content.

9

ETTA, CHICAGO

AUGUST 5, 2018

A mass of darkness hovered over the bright concrete landscape of Chicago. In the master bedroom of one of the Riverview townhomes on the right half of the complex, Etta could be found tossing and turning in excitement. She turned to her right side and saw the digital clock flashing 4:07 a.m. She lay on her back staring into the darkness. Whenever she thought about Sam a ray of sunshine illuminated her heart. Then anxiety hit when she realized what her friends thought about him. She did not appreciate her best friend being too harsh on her love interest by calling him a loser and a psychopath. Her mind echoed with the resounding chorus of judgmental voices. She wondered if she should forget what they said, as her spirits soared at the idea of being in a relationship with Sam.

Just then her *Sherlock* ringtone alerted her to a text message from Sam, waking her from her deep thoughts. She had set his number to the sound of the *Sherlock* theme music, because Sam was a mysterious figure she did not mind unraveling.

Sam: Good morning, Etta.

Etta: Good morning, Sam.

Sam: Did you sleep well?

Etta: Yes. You?

Sam: Am excited about our date. I couldn't sleep.

Oh, Lord. I had not been mishearing him. He actually does say "am" and not "I'm." But whatever. He has been thinking about me like I have been thinking about him. No wonder I am constantly feeling butterflies in my stomach. Etta smiled and typed, "Me too. Actually, I couldn't sleep either," before she changed it, because she didn't want to sound too needy.

Etta: I'm excited about our date, too.

Sam: Since you live downtown, what do you think about going to a restaurant in your area?

Etta: We do have lots of good restaurants around here. What kind of food do you have in mind?

Sam: Have you ever had Indian food before?

Etta: No, I can't say that I have.

Sam: Really? You're missing out. You should try it.

Etta: Okay. I'll give it a try. :)

Etta's morning was a whirlwind of multitasking as she tackled a colossal project for Monday while simultaneously getting herself ready for a nerve-racking first date with the enigmatic Sam. She carefully selected a navy blue polyester dress with a sassy, knee-length pleated design, which fit her perfectly and beautifully. Etta was no fan of lugging around clunky purses, thus she often bought dresses and skirts with pockets. With a satisfied grin over how she looked, she slipped her ATM card and ID inside her cozy dress pocket.

As if on cue, the doorbell chimed, interrupting Etta's thoughts of making sure she had everything she needed. She did not have to worry about carrying a key because her door was padlocked with a code. With a glance at the decorative wall clock, which read 11 a.m. precisely, she knew her date had arrived. *Impressive. He's prompt.* Etta grabbed her iPhone and approached the door, eager to greet her date with excitement and nervous anticipation. As she swung open the white door adorned with frosted opaque privacy glass on each side, she was met with a sight that made her heart skip a beat.

There, standing tall and slender on her doorstep, was a man who could give Greek gods a run for their money. Sporting a light blue, long-sleeved shirt that hugged his frame just right, paired with dark khaki pants, he exuded an effortless charm that was hard to resist. Etta couldn't help but notice the subtle flex of his muscular arms, the glimpse of his sculpted chest, and the hint of his toned abs peeking through the fabric of his shirt. Talk about a visual feast! *How can a literary professor look this hot?*, Etta thought to herself.

But beneath his striking visual, there was a touch of sadness in his eyes. Etta knew he was still mourning the loss of his aunt, but somehow, being in her presence seemed to be a good distraction. It lifted his spirits, if only momentarily. As he flashed her a warm, yet slightly melancholic smile, she couldn't help but feel a connection forming. She did not know what it was, but she felt completely safe and comfortable with him.

Their gazes met. She responded to his greeting with a radiant smile. Time seemed to stand still, as her heart quickened, and butterflies fluttered within her stomach. She closed the door behind her. Their exchange of pleasantries, though mere words, carried an unspoken language of how much they liked each other.

"The restaurant is seven minutes from here. Do you mind if we walk?" Etta said, feeling a pleasant soreness in her cheeks from all the smiling she had been doing at the thought of Sam.

"I prefer it," Sam said, feeling in sync with Etta.

"Great. We agree," she said. He smiled at her and she at him.

Together, they gracefully descended her doorstep, their strides harmoniously synchronized. As they strolled side by side along the bustling streets, a gentle breeze swept through them. The city, adorned with random trees and architectural wonders, carried a vibrant pulse. It seemed to embrace their presence with open arms.

"Chicago is a beautiful city," he remarked to initiate conversation. His voice carried an air of admiration, an appreciation for the unique skyline of the city.

The towering skyscrapers and the sights and sounds of city life made her appreciate and feel grateful for where she lived, especially when she was sharing it with a handsome man for whom she had developed feelings so quickly.

"Indeed. I don't see myself living anywhere else but here," she said proudly.

"Oh? Despite the high crime rate?" he quipped, maintaining a poker-faced neutrality. Etta couldn't help but raise an eyebrow, wondering if he was one of those people who believed in the exaggeration of Chicago crimes in conservative news outlets as the words "Ch-iraq, corruption city," and "gangster town" got tossed around. Even during her time studying abroad, she encountered the same tired stereotypes where people would inquire if she knew Al Capone simply because she came from Chicago, inadvertently reducing the city to a bygone era of crime and violence. And just because they heard about the shootings in the South Side and other areas of Chicago, they thought it happened all over.

"Millions of people live here. You said you used to live here. Surely, it's not that bad, right?" Etta asked, her voice abounding with curiosity.

Sam took a long pause. "Well, I wouldn't venture to a certain part of Chicago. I heard Uptown is pretty bad," he said, as if he tried to fish for her earliest memories of that part of Chicago.

"It may be a little dilapidated in some parts of town, but I don't believe it was that bad. I have fond memories even though my family heard about crimes here and there, but that is pretty much anywhere. Anyway, everything is changing. The skyline in Chicago has changed and will continue to change," Etta said, admiring her city. "What I love about Chicago is, it is clean. We have great hotels and restaurants, not to mention art and culture that the city abundantly offers. It even rivals New York, London, and Paris. The vibrant theater scene, the renowned museums, the thriving music festivals—these are my playgrounds."

Sam turned his gaze toward her, his lips parting into a gentle smile that mirrored the radiance of her own. "You're a true architect and Chicago girl."

En route to East Ontario, a palpable warmth surrounded her. She sensed the admiring gazes of passersby, their eyes alight seeing the harmonious union she and Sam embodied.

There was an intangible quality about Sam that rendered her weightless and buoyant, which brought her joy and warmth. But their stolen glances reassured her of how real and tangible they were to each other.

"We need to turn east here," said Etta once they arrived at the intersection of Ontario and Fairbank. He nodded. Their footsteps echoed against the concrete, resonating with purpose as they approached the doorway nestled at the terminus of the very same building, where they walked past Chipotle and Potbelly's chains. A cozy restaurant awaited them within—the Indian Garden Restaurant, with its door frames adorned with sleek, black metal, encircling the glass panels at the top, middle, and left side. Sam, ever the gentleman, grasped the right side of the double glass doors.

Etta voiced her gratitude for his chivalry and attentiveness with a soft-spoken expression of "Thank you."

"You're welcome," Sam said, smiling.

Ascending the regal marble stairs, their footsteps resonated with a quiet elegance as they approached the landing that led to the restaurant entrance. A glass box, meticulously placed, captured their attention, showcasing a captivating sculpture of a bare-breasted woman bedecked in ornate jewelry from head to toe.

Her delicate fingers gracefully plucked the strings of a tanpura, also known as tambura. Sam, captivated by the artistry before him, paused in admiration, his gaze fixed upon the intricate details. Etta, sensing his fascination, stood by his side, taking in the same sight.

"Do you know the difference between Khmer and Indian breasts?" he abruptly asked. Etta's cheeks flushed with warmth as Sam broached a rather unexpected topic of conversation. Her mind raced, grappling with surprise and apprehension.

"I haven't given it much thought," Etta responded, her voice carefully measured, as she tried to navigate the unexpected territory. Memories of Khmer and Indian female sculptures or intricately carved depictions on ancient temples in Cambodia and India flooded her mind. She never thought about their differences in that area. And she wondered why Sam chose to fixate on such a specific aspect—breasts—when there was a wealth of other topics to explore. *Is he being a pervert? Has he noticed mine?* Her eyes widened with her growing discomfort. *Could my friend Daron be right about him?*

Sam's demeanor remained focused and contemplative, his left arm tucked beneath his right arm, which cradled his chin. Etta couldn't help but notice his unwavering gaze fixed upon the subject of their conversation—the breasts depicted in the sculptures. His brows furrowed, indicating a genuine analysis. Sam motioned his finger to circle the area around both breasts. "You see. Indian breasts are round while Khmer's breasts are more arched." Etta pondered his words, reflecting on the influence of societal preferences and cultural norms that could have shaped these artistic depictions. The sculptures of both cultures, she realized, were likely influenced by the ideals of beauty and desires of men in those two places during that era.

"Interesting," Etta responded. "Is there a reason why you notice this particular difference?"

"I was reading about the stolen Khmer and Indian artifacts currently housed in Western museums. I had read about Khmer and Indian histories and artistries. It happened that the magazine I was reading had side by side images of Khmer female sculpture and Indian female sculpture. I noticed the differences, but they are based on the same ideas and concepts."

"Oh?" said Etta, curious.

"Round breasts represent ideal beauty, fertility, and the celebration of the female form within Indian artistic styles. Similarly, Khmer female sculptures, found in Angkor Wat and other temples built by Khmer throughout Southeast Asia, depict the 'apsara'—or celestial nymph, if you will—in arched form, to convey a sense of elegance and divine beauty, also often portrayed in dance form. Hence the arched breasts. Both represented their own understanding and appreciation for aestheticism in female forms within their artistic traditions. But this is just my interpretation." He turned to face her, to let her know he did not mean anything perverted by it. "You see, I'm teaching the art of writing about art, specifically about sculptures and abstract expressionist paintings around the world. This sculpture just gave me an assignment idea."

"Aaaah," Etta replied, suddenly realizing Sam's knowledge and appreciation for Khmer and Indian arts, as well as getting a little peek into his teaching topics. *Look who's the pervert now*, she thought to herself, walking away feeling embarrassed in more ways than one.

Once inside, the host graciously guided them to their designated table, where they settled into their seats. Moments later, their waiter approached, ready to take their orders. Sam took the lead, assuming the role of a culinary guide.

"My favorite is the lamb stew. Would you like to try it?" Sam's enthusiasm was evident in his voice.

The waiter added, "Fine choice, sir. We make the best lamb stew."

"I bet all the restaurant owners say that," Etta said, teasing the man.

"I'm telling you the truth, ma'am."

"Okay. I believe you," Etta said, smiling.

Sam put in the orders of masala dosa, lamb stew with basmati rice, and cauliflower masala.

"Would you like anything else besides water?" The waiter looked at each of them.

They both said, "Water is fine."

Sam took a sip and turned his attention to Etta. "So, what do you like to do when you're not working?"

"Do you mean besides going out to eat and hanging out with friends?"

"Sure."

"I like to jog, read, and go to the theaters. You?"

"Me too."

"That's awesome," Etta said, wondering if he really did those things or was just trying to sound compatible with her.

"What type of show do you like?"

"I like the opera…"

"Really?"

"Yes. Why?"

"I like the opera, too. I don't like any of those English operas. They're not authentic. I prefer the real deal—opera in its original format, Italian."

"Me too," said Etta, feeling shocked to discover how much they had in common.

"So, what else?"

"I like a good murder mystery, ballet, musical, orchestra, and pretty much anything good creatively."

"Why do you go to the theater?" Sam said, taking another sip of his water.

"I like it."

"What do you like about it?"

Great. I'm in an interview. Welcome to dating. Etta put down her glass of water after also taking a sip, looked at him, and said, "Well. It's a magical experience. It's escapism, just like movies and books, but it feels more real because the audience and actors share the same time and space. Also I admire and appreciate the hard work and dedication of the actors, directors, set designers, production, and all the people involved who create this escapism where we, as an audience, can identify and relate to the characters in whatever situations they are going through. We laugh. We feel sad, happy, and angry depending on how well the actors can incite these emotions from us. I love going to the theater for many reasons, but generally, it's the craft, and being with the people who enjoy these human expressions like me. More importantly, unlike movie theaters, the audience respects each other and the performers. They have etiquette. They're punctual and become completely silent from the beginning to the end. They spent a lot of money, so they expect to get their money's worth."

"That's interesting," he said, sipping his water, grinning, and admiring Etta.

"Why?"

"I think many people go to the theater to show off. I don't think they understand anything about it. You're the first person I know who likes and enjoys it for what it is. That's wonderful."

"Oh. I don't know anyone who goes and doesn't enjoy the theater for its craft and extraordinary experience."

The food came. "Wow," Etta said, impressed by the vibrant colors of the dishes and their aromatic spices wafting through the air. "Everything looks and smells so good."

The waiter placed a bowl of water with pink flower petals for them to wash their hands. Sam gestured to her to go first and then he followed suit. He waited for her to try each dish and waited for her to tell him what she thought.

"It's very good. Thank goodness you ordered, because I would have ordered the wrong thing and not liked it," she said.

Sam scooped the lamb stew onto his plate. It came with flatbread as well as basmati rice. Sam took the flatbread from the basket and tore off a manageable piece to scoop up a portion of the stew from his plate. He looked like a pro doing it—and not to mention, hot. *He might look even hotter if I invite him to have Khmer-style lunch, where he can eat rice by hand, and dip or scoop* prahok teuk kroeung *with raw vegetables.* She decided to stick with utensils by eating the stew with the rice, not ready for Sam to see her making a mess of herself.

Though she generally despised the dating scene, Etta found herself surprisingly engaged and enjoyed her time with Sam, even if he devoted most of the conversation to his children. Etta remembered her aunt Thida telling her daughters, "If one parent has to go, it should be the father, because the mother is more nurturing and would never abandon her children. Whereas men, as soon as they take on a new wife, they neglect and abandon their children in a heartbeat." Etta knew it was a generalization but felt elated to know Sam loved and cared about his children very much. He was not part of her aunt's generalization. She did not mind talking about his children at all. If they had more dates together, it could be a precursor to an actual relationship, and an opportunity for her to get to know his children better and to love and care about them as much as he did.

"You know, I've never dated a Khmer girl before," said Sam, breaking her happy thoughts.

Etta's defense shield went up. Excuse me? What am I, chopped liver—something at the bottom of the barrel that you must scrape up? Is a Khmer woman that bad that you never considered dating one? Am I supposed to feel good about myself for being the exception to other Khmer women?

His statement made her feel especially defensive because, not too long ago, a Cambodian friend of her family stated he owned a professional photography studio, and when she said she would like to take her family there for a family portrait, he proudly and arrogantly responded, "My studio is frequented by whites only." She did not understand what he was trying to prove and why he felt the need to say that when the neighborhood in which he lived and worked consisted mostly of whites. She thought, *Isn't it obvious that mostly white people would give him their business because he is their local shop?* She found it rude and ignorant for him to say that. The worst kind of Cambodian happens to be the one who thinks so highly of himself or herself that other Cambodians seem beneath them. It's internalized racism at its finest. She couldn't believe that Sam, who happened to be half Khmer, felt the need to say something along that line also. *I mean, my jerky exes never said this to me, and they had never known or seen a Khmer person in their lives before they met me. Calm down, Etta.*

She smiled at Sam, thinking she should give him the benefit of the doubt that he was just being honest. He probably did not mean anything by it. She could hear Daron telling her now, "All you libtards are so hypersensitive about everything. Give it a break, snowflakes." Quite possibly, Sam probably never had met a Khmer girl before, let alone going out on a date with one. However, as a liberal academic, he should have been more aware and more sensitive to stuff like this. *Why should he even bring that up, though?* Outwardly, she kept on smiling and brushing it off by telling herself, *He is a nice guy and pleasing to the eyes. He doesn't mean anything by it.*

"Oh, so we are dating?" Etta responded. Like most women, she was looking for assurance and confirmation. He didn't say anything further but smiled.

Their lunch and conversation lasted for nearly three hours. By the time they left the restaurant it was 2:30 p.m.

The sun cast a gentle glow upon their part of the world. Etta and Sam sauntered along the trail that traced the shoreline, where they could gaze to the majestic expanse of Lake Michigan on the east and Chicago's iconic skyline on the west. They found themselves in the company of random couples holding hands. Bikers whizzed by with exhilarating speed, joggers carved paths of determination, while rollerbladers, skaters, and scooter riders added to the urban life scene. Grateful for her choice of flats, Etta walked effortlessly. She was glad they took the long way home, because she needed to burn all the calories she had just consumed. Besides, being with Sam infused her with an invigorating energy that she could walk around the Chicago metropolis area and back.

When she switched her iPhone to her right hand, Sam's right hand brushed against her left hand. Suddenly, his strong but gentle fingers moved to find her soft fingers. A grasp reflex happened. In a beautiful synchrony, their fingers intertwined. A sensation of warmth and comfort surged when their skin met. Etta's knees turned to jelly, weakened by the sheer potency of Sam's touch. Yet, in Sam's firm grasp, she found affection and stability. Leaning into his strong arm, Etta basked in this overwhelming emotional and physical closeness. In this tender moment, she felt a profound ease with Sam, a sense of connection that transcended words. In her peripheral vision she glimpsed his stolen gaze at her, as her eyes fixated on the vast horizon.

Breaking the tranquil silence, Etta asked, "Did you ever venture here during your time in Chicago?" Her voice conveyed curiosity and nostalgia. Sam shook his head. "I remember back in the '80s and '90s, mostly Asians, African-Americans, Latin Americans, Natives, and Eastern Europeans dominated the parks and beaches from West Bryn Mawr Avenue to West Irving Park Road. We would wake up early in the morning to grab a perfect spot for our BBQs on weekends."

"The aroma of food and the sound of music of various ethnic groups floated along these areas. Despite our differences, we generally got along and tolerated one another, and lived in harmony. Gentrification in the late 1990s and early 2000s brought white Americans back. They're the majority again. Like anywhere else, Chicago changes and evolves. Everyone brought something different to this wonderful city." Etta halted her words, feeling cautious she was talking too much while coming to recognize Sam's penchant for silence. His words were like rare gems, precious and sparingly bestowed. "I'm sorry. I'm talking too much. After all, you were a resident here once," Etta acknowledged.

"That's perfectly fine. I like to listen," Sam said, a dry smile gracing his face. Their leisurely walk brought them back to the doorsteps of Etta's townhome. "Well. I guess this is it." They never let go of each other's hands.

I'm surprised our hands are not sweaty. Geez, it feels nice to hold his hand. He's so dreamy. Ugh. I'm so lame.

"Thank you for a perfect Sunday," he said.

"No. Thank *you* for a perfect Sunday," said Etta, smiling.

Etta glanced at the time on her iPhone. "Oh, my God. Isn't your flight at 8 p.m.?"

"Yes. No worries. My sister has everything packed and she'll get my children ready. I just need to get home by five."

"Well, it's three forty now. Do you need me to drive you to your brother's house?"

"No, I don't want to inconvenience you. I'll just take one of the taxis around the corner," he said.

"Are you sure?"

"Yes, I'm sure." In the stillness of the moment, Sam and Etta stood face to face with both of their hands intertwined. The world around them faded into insignificance as their gaze locked, their eyes becoming windows to each other's soul. With every movement Sam made, Etta felt the rhythm of her heart quicken. She breathed in the delicate blend of his Safari cologne. *Thank God, he doesn't marinate in it. He applies just a light touch to go with his body chemistry.* In a gentle and deliberate motion, Sam leaned in, enclosed Etta in a tender embrace. Time seemed to stand still as their bodies met. The feeling of his body touching hers made Etta's heart swell with a blend of emotions—joy, vulnerability, and an overwhelming sense of belonging.

As Sam gradually pulled away, his eyes lingered on Etta's exquisite countenance, his admiration evident in the softness of his gaze. He beheld her as if she were a masterpiece, a work of art crafted by destiny itself. And in a gesture that spoke volumes, he pressed his lips lightly against her forehead, a delicate kiss that spoke of tenderness and reverence.

If that chaste kiss sends me over the edge like this, I can't imagine what his kiss on the lips would be like. Etta found herself melting in front of Sam.

In a soothing voice he said, "Have a good evening. I'll text you." His words floated in the air, carrying a promise of continued connection and the sweet anticipation of their next encounter.

"Okay," Etta responded, as if she too was floating on air. A whirlwind of emotions, a giddy euphoria tugged at every corner of her being.

She stood on the landing of her steps, her eyes fixed upon Sam as he gradually receded into the distance. With each step he took, her heart yearned to hold onto his presence, before he slowly faded away from her sight.

10

ETTA, CHICAGO

AUGUST 6, 2018

As if summoned by a serenade of nature, a pair of sparrows graced Etta's terrace, their melodious chirps filling the air like the sweet exchanges of two lovers. The sun, a familiar presence in the sky, seemed to take on a new radiance, infusing her with joy and illumination. The noises of the city had turned into a symphony.

Clad in her work clothes, while still wearing her slippers, Etta stood in a state of bliss, her coffee cradled in her hands, and a perpetual smile adorning her face.

Perched atop her townhome, overlooking the Chicago River and Riverwalk, she was gifted with a breathtaking view of the city and the vast expanse of the lake. With each sip of her coffee, the flavor tasted much sweeter and the fragrance smelled much more aromatic.

The gentle breeze caressed her skin, showering her with a vision of a bright future. Her eyes sparkled as she observed the boats and yachts gracefully gliding along the water's surface. The sight, sound, and the smell of the city immersed her in a state of heightened awareness.

Buoyed by this newfound energy and driven by her vibrant spirit, she decided to walk to work. If Sam knew she was walking he would appreciate it very much, as he too, loved to walk.

A vase of ornately arranged, radiant red roses with baby's breath and eucalyptus greeted her from her desk. It was not unusual to find a bouquet on her desk, as she had, in the past, received flowers from friends and clients. However, she had never received red roses before. And there was no occasion to celebrate anything, as the building she designed was still being constructed. The developers would not be sending her red roses.

"Yeah, we don't know who sent the bouquet; but obviously, it came from Kelly's Flower Shop," said an excitable voice from behind. She turned around to find her assistant, Kristina, smiling at her. "I don't think one of your clients would send you an arranged romantic bouquet of red roses unless there's something I don't know about." Kristina raised one of her eyebrows at Etta, teasing her as well as trying to coax information out of her.

"Nope. You need not worry about that," Etta said. Walking over to her desk, she took in the fragrance and counted the roses.

"So, is it from the guy Daron's wife set you up with?" Kristina persisted.

"No. By the way, I'll be substituting for a friend this Friday. I'll return to the office in the afternoon. Can you print everything out from a folder called Architect 101 for me with inserted number tabs and wire binding? Please make twenty-one sets," Etta said, as she pulled out a thumb drive from the pocket of her black tote bag.

"You got it," Kristina said, taking the thumb drive from Etta. "So you're not going to tell me?"

"Thank you," Etta said, changing the subject. "I have everything organized; it should be self-explanatory."

"All right. Fine. I'll get you your copies," Kristina said. She walked away sulking, closing the door behind her.

Etta scanned from left to right and top to bottom, recounting all of the roses with her eyes. *Interesting. Two dozen long-stemmed red roses. Why twenty-four? What does that mean?* She started her Mac desktop and while it went through updates and security checks, she reached for her iPhone to run a search on Google: "What do twenty-four red roses mean?" Sure enough, according to www.proflowers.com, the first answer of her search results, it signified the sender was thinking of the recipient twenty-four hours a day. It also called into mind the purity of twenty-four-carat gold. "Oftentimes," it read, "two dozen roses are simply chosen to have twice the impact of a traditional bouquet of one dozen roses. In this way, an arrangement of two dozen roses can be used to convey practically any sentiment, with even more emphasis on the message, especially of love."

She stopped there. *Love* was all she needed to know from her sender. She gently put her iPhone on the polished surface of her desk while feeling the physical sensation of fluttering in her stomach. Her fingers, tingling with excitement, reached out and plucked a small card from the holder pick. She gingerly unfolded the card, as if it held the secrets of the universe. And there, inscribed upon its pristine surface, were words that brought her brightness and joy. "To a special someone. I hope this brightens your day. Sam A." Her giddy grin stretched across her face. Overwhelmed by a wave of tender emotions, she sank into her chair. It was the kind of weakness that invigorated the spirit. With bated breath, she allowed herself to bask in the beauty of the resplendent bouquet of twenty-four scarlet roses. She reverently gazed upon the card, appreciating its affectionate message, before delicately leaning in to inhale the musky fragrance emanating from the velvety petals of the roses. In that very moment, the haunting Sherlock ringtone filled the air. *Right on cue*, she thought, so intrigued by the enigma Sam represented in her life.

Sam: Hi there.

Etta: Good morning, Sam.

Sam: How are you this morning?

Etta: Ecstatic.

Sam: I hope that means you have received

my roses.

Etta: I sure did.

She floated through her workday, seemingly carried by an ethereal bliss. From Monday to Friday of that eventful week, Etta and Sam exchanged text messages during their lunch breaks and stole moments of connection whenever they could find them. In the evenings, after Sam had tended to his children's needs and tucked them into bed, they would engage in heartfelt conversations over the phone. Occasionally, when his children stayed overnight at their Auntie Vida's house, Sam and Etta were granted uninterrupted time together. Etta hadn't yet thought about the logistics of their long-distance romance, but such concerns didn't matter to her. She cherished every precious moment she shared with Sam, relishing in their romantic conversations and the profound happiness he brought into her life. No man had ever made her feel this elated and alive.

Her newfound joy radiated from within, evidenced by the spring in her step and the infectious laughter that graced her voice as she carried out her work. Those around her couldn't help but notice the transformation. Even the students she taught as a substitute felt joy through her genuine happiness and infectious spirit. And so, on that glorious Friday, instead of confining them to the classroom, she seized the opportunity to take them on a memorable field trip, strolling along the picturesque Chicago River.

Despite the city's nickname as the "windy city," a term open to various interpretations, the atmosphere that day was tranquil. Only a gentle breeze caressed their bodies while the warm glow of the sun tenderly kissed their faces. Standing on the Riverwalk site between the State and Wabash bridges, with her back against the "Chicago Remembers" wall and her students' backs against the rail of the Chicago River, Etta declared with glee, "Ladies and gentlemen, I present to you Chicago's magnificent architecture. I'm proud to say Chicago is the birthplace of skyscrapers and home to 1,315 high-rises. Look at its unique architectural styles. You can appreciate its monumental scale and composition from any vantage point, whether by foot, boat, vehicle, or air. Aren't they beautiful?"

Her students turned to admire the buildings on both sides of the river. From the east, their gaze could reach as far as the Tribune Building, and to the west, they could see Merchandise Mart.

"As you can see, we have a few new buildings being added along the river. In total, our current construction boom will soon bring us forty-nine additional high-rises along the Lakefront. The new towers will reshape our beautiful skyline and take us to a new era. Just to name a few, especially those in my hometown, they'll include Eight Eleven Uptown, the glassy tower that will include 373 rental units and nearly thirty thousand square feet of retail space; Sheridan and Wilson, the twelve-story glassy tower that will deliver 149 rental units and retail space; Vista Tower, the 1,186-foot tall luxury hotel and condo tower, designed by the superstar architect Jeanne Gang of Studio Gang. Vista will become the third tallest Chicago building. Then there's NU Biomedical Research Center; the fourteen-story tower will replace the Brutalist-era Prentice Women's Hospital and will be dedicated to the research of heart disease, cancer, and genetics. NEMA Chicago, a seventy-six-story, 893-foot tower, will offer eight hundred rental apartments and will be seen south of the Sears, I mean Willis Tower. To Chicagoans, Willis Tower will be forever known as the Sears Tower. I'm not going to bore you by running down all forty-nine of them. To be honest with you, I haven't got the chance to memorize them all. However, I did list them and their descriptions in your copies of the binder I prepared for you. You can read all about them at your leisure. Also, even this Riverwalk itself will get an expansion and upgrade by the summer of 2019. It will provide more space, restaurants, and vendors for everyone to enjoy. I can't wait," she added, thinking about strolling along the Riverwalk with Sam.

"Now, after having studied the early designs of Louis Sullivan, Burham and Root, and Holabird and Roche, and the contemporary designs of Bruce Graham, Skidmore, Owings and Merrill (SOM), and Studio Gang Architects, and by looking at these buildings along the Chicago River, what's your takeaway?"

A handful of enthusiastic students raised their hands. Her eyes scanned back and forth, noticing a young auburn-haired woman who eagerly waved her hand.

"Suzan?" said Etta.

"The early designs such as the iconic Wrigley Building, Tribune Tower, and Merchandise Mart used steel-framed structure, terracotta, and stone; while contemporary designs such as the Aqua Tower, the Trump Tower, and 333 West Wacker Drive used stainless steel and glass," Suzan said with confidence.

"Very good. Let's head west of the river. Shall we?"

In a charming procession, the students trailed behind her with an enchanting sense of wonder, akin to tiny chicks faithfully following their nurturing mother hen. "There's so much to talk about. I don't know if we have enough time in a day. I can go on and on, but I'm going to do my best to give you the most important details to pass your class with Professor Bryant. Before we analyze the buildings, let's examine this area and the Chicago River itself. It's amazing how the Chicago River has dramatically changed from the 'smoky hollow' it once was known as—due to its dirty water issuing from the sewage and rubbish dumps from residential buildings, factories, and railroads in the 1800s—to this 'second shoreline' with brilliant high-rises of various styles and structures built in the years since then."

As Etta gracefully meandered alongside her eager students, regaling them with tales of the captivating history of the mighty Chicago River, her thoughts remained steadfastly anchored to Sam. Each step she took, every word she uttered, seemed to mingle with her memories of him.

Upon her return to the office, still thinking of Sam, Etta found herself pouring salt into her coffee and laughed at herself for being so absent minded. Looking left and right, to make sure no one was watching, she swiftly discarded the salty concoction and prepared another cup.

Seated once again at her desk, Etta took a sip of her freshly brewed elixir, her gaze tenderly adoring her withering roses. Since Monday, she had been dutifully tending to them by changing the water to preserve their ephemeral splendor.

"What the hell is this, Etta?" A bombastic voice echoed through the room.

"Jesus, Daron. You scared the heck out of me. What are you doing here?" Etta said, waking up from her reverie.

"I'm free of work and children; I thought I'd catch up with you. Why are you sitting there and smiling at the dead bouquet like a high school girl? Who sent you these red roses?"

"It's not dead; just a little withered," Etta responded.

"Same difference. So who sent them to you?" Daron asked.

"Guess who?" Etta said with glee, pulling out dead leaves and petals.

"The nerd," he responded.

"No. Guess again."

"That loser who rear-ended you?" he said as he sat down on the couch facing her desk.

"Shut up. That's so rude."

"Why is he sending you flowers? To properly apologize for rear-ending you?"

"Stop it. Actually…" Her face turned warm in her vulnerability and red like blooming roses. She couldn't help but emit a soft, girlish giggle. "I…" Etta straightened up in her chair, her fingertips forming an elegant steeple as her mischievous eyes watched her friend. "I went out to lunch with Sam," she confessed, well aware of Daron's disapproval of him.

"What?" Daron said, as if he did not hear her correctly.

"We have been communicating. I think we're dating."

"You think? You don't know? Either you're dating or you're not! What the fuck, Etta?"

"What?" Etta said, confused at his tone.

"What do you mean? Did you not listen to any of the things we said at the London House Rooftop Bar?"

"You don't know him," Etta said, with her arms crossed and eyes narrowed.

"You don't either," Daron replied, frustrated with his friend.

"Isn't that the whole point of dating, that we are trying to get to know each other?"

"All right. What have you found out differently than what you had when you met him for coffee?"

"Well..."

"You can't even say it."

"He has three siblings."

"You knew that when you dropped him off in Chinatown."

"I know all their names now."

"Whoop-de-doo," said Daron, sarcastically twirling his finger and rolling his eyes to the back of his head.

"I'm getting to know him better," Etta said, looking at her friend with disappointment. Besides, you suggested I date someone from a Tinder App. How's that any different?"

"You can't get to know him better. You live in Chicago; he lives in Chapel Hill. I suggested that you date someone within the Chicago metropolitan area, where we could easily track him down and check out his place of work, basically making sure he's not an ax murderer. Why do you think I was not too thrilled about that astronomy professor either, granted he was looking for a job here. Anyway, you don't know what kind of life this Sam is leading over there. You don't know what he's up to. For all you know, he could still be married, and he goes to other cities to philander with gullible women like you."

"Who does that?" said Etta, her brows furrowed. "Besides, he came here with his children to attend his aunt's funeral."

"Don't be naïve. That could be a cover story. Are you sure they're even his kids?"

"Oh please," Etta said, rolling her eyes. "Why would anyone go to such lengths to just have casual affairs with women?"

"Plenty of sleazy men do that, Etta. Worse. This Sam guy could be a psycho killer."

"Pfft," Etta let out a dismissive sound.

"Look," Daron said, his tone softened, as he got up from the couch to sit on the guest chair across from Etta. I just don't want you to do anything stupid, and get hurt in the process."

"I appreciate your concern, but—"

"Okay. Look. Take things slowly. Let's find out who this guy is before you form an intimate relationship with him."

"What other way is there besides me going out with him and talking with him?"

"So far it doesn't sound like you've got much out of him."

"What do you propose I do?"

"We're going to run a background check on him."

"What?"

"You heard me."

"You better not. I think that's stalking."

"What? Are you afraid we might find something on him?"

"Can you run a background check on anyone?"

"Yes, but with consent."

"That's what I thought."

"Etta, I don't feel right about him. Rochelle agrees with me."

"You're making him out to be a monster. He's a very nice guy. I'd like to think I am a good judge of character."

"No. You're not," Daron said, his arms were now crossed as well.

"Whatever."

"Things seem to be escalating fast with you and him: he rear-ended you, he asks you for coffee the next day, and then lunch before he returns to Chapel Hill. Why don't you be like most girls and play hard to get? Don't agree to everything he asks you to do. Did you…"

"What? No! I'm not that easy. I want to see where our relationship is taking us."

"I'm just checking. All right. Fine. I'll tell you what. What do you say about taking things slowly?"

"Fine," Etta said, hesitantly, knowing that her heart begged to differ..

"Good. I'm starving. Let's go to Piece Brewery," Daron said, jumping up from the guest chair.

11

ETTA, PALATINE
AUGUST 11, 2018

During one of their phone calls, Etta contemplated sharing with Sam the conversation she had with her best friend Daron about him. She swiftly dismissed the idea as soon as it crossed her mind. Her decision to refrain from sharing stemmed from a sense of embarrassment caused by Daron's strong opposition to their relationship. Plus, she did not want to throw any negativity his way. Somehow, she felt protective of his feelings.

On Saturday, Etta visited her parents and paternal grandfather; he alternated between living with her parents in the summer and living with her aunt Thida in the winter. The tightknit families made a decision since their moves to different areas of Illinois from Uptown Chicago to get together on weekends for a cookout where food and fun activities bonded them and kept their tradition alive.

While her male and female cousins were outside with the older males of the families, where the men were starting the grill and women were either helping or watching their youngest kids, Etta remained in the kitchen with her mother and her father's older sister. The conversation about her single status and living alone came up again.

"I don't understand why you need to waste money living alone downtown when you have a perfectly nice, big home here in Palatine with your parents, and the train commute is only thirty to forty minutes long," her aunt Thida said, as she cut up the chicken into chunks.

"We keep having the same conversation, *oum srey*," Etta said. She was trying to be as respectful as she could, as in Khmer culture, the younger ones must maintain decorum and hold their elders to a high esteem like one's parents. "I need my privacy. It's my personal haven. Plus, I love my beautiful luxury townhome. It's close to my job and I can have guests over when I want. I'm an adult. I need my own space." Etta continued washing the many vegetables after her mother had removed from the vines to cut up or grate: green papaya, pea eggplant, long eggplant, butternut squash, long beans, and moringa leaves. Her mother remained quiet as she moved on to her next task of roasting rice in a dry pan.

"Kids these days, always wanting their freedom. No Khmer man from a respectable family would marry a girl who lives on her own, if she is not under the umbrella of her parents. She might be seen as loose," Thida said, chopping the meat opposite her niece of the white marble kitchen.

"It's the twenty-first century now, *oum*. If they're that judgmental then they're not worthy of being with me anyway."

Just then her father walked in to pick up the chicken and beef that had been marinated in green and yellow *kreoung* or spice paste since the night before, for grilling on skewers. "So Daron tells me you're seeing someone."

Her mother looked up from the pan; her aunt paused from cutting chicken.

"Daron? When did he talk to you, Dad?" Etta asked.

"He called the other day to throw some business my way. A relative of one of his clients was looking to order custom-made violins and violas. Apparently, he's a shopper for symphony orchestras. Daron put in some good words for me by telling him I create beautiful instruments, inside and out, with exceptionally high-quality sound. That friend of yours is a good salesman. That was nice of him."

"He can be nice when he wants to. Also, he is not wrong. You're one of the best luthiers in town," Etta replied, smiling at her father.

He returned the smile and asked, "So who is this someone you're seeing?"

"I wasn't going to tell you until it's official, but I am seeing a man named Samuel Angk."

"Angk?" Her parents and aunt said simultaneously.

"Angk is an old, old Khmer royal name," said her father.

"He said he's not sure. His father passed away before he was born."

"Hmm. That name and that story sound familiar."

"Really, Dad?"

"Royals? There are thousands of them, but they're just like any one of us now," her aunt chimed in.

"Yeah, he is part Khmer, Dad, but he doesn't know much about his Khmer or white side," Etta said, looking sympathetic. She dried her hands on a towel and pulled out her iPhone from the pocket of her apron. Scrolling through the picture gallery, she chose a headshot of Sam and said, "This is him, Dad."

"Very nice. He's a good-looking young man," her father said, smiling. "Daron said he doesn't approve of it, but as long as you're happy, that's all that matters."

"Aww. Thank you, Dad. That means a lot coming from you," Etta said, smiling ear to ear upon hearing her father's approval. She affectionately and gently slapped her dad in the back. Her father nodded with a proud smile, lifted the stacked trays of meat and exited the back glass door. One of her cousin's husbands offered to help carry the trays to the stainless grill in the blossoming yard, full of all kinds of flowers and vegetation, the results of her parents' green thumbs. Her mother liked growing flowers while her father liked growing vegetables and fruits.

"So why doesn't your rude friend approve of him?" Thida asked, putting the finished meat in a silver bowl. "What is wrong with him? Let me see that photo." She walked around the kitchen island to the sink and scrubbed her hands with soap, dried them with her apron, and then walked over to receive the phone.

Etta's mother poured the roasted rice into a bowl to cool off. She too wiped her hands and asked to see this good-looking young man her father approved of.

"Wait a minute. I know him," Thida said, staring at the digital headshot.

"Really?" Etta said, excited, as she put the washed vegetables by the stove range.

"Yeah. He's married, with three kids," Thida said. "No wonder your jerky friend doesn't approve of him."

"He was married but has been divorced five or six years now," Etta corrected her aunt.

"So he's divorced and has three children. I'm not sure he's the right man for you. That's a lot of responsibilities, and you're still—"

"I'm no spring chicken, Mom," Etta interrupted her mother.

"To me, my daughter is single, pure and innocent," her mother said, no longer looking at the photo and moving to the stove range to remove the pea eggplants to roast in a dry pan.

"Oh, Mom. Please be real. I was engaged and cohabitated with someone before. Remember?" Etta stood next to her mother, watching her use the back of the wooden spatula to press on the pea eggplants once they turned brown, to release some of their bitterness.

"I wouldn't brag about it or say it too loudly. My friends are still talking about it," Thida said while still examining Sam's photo.

"You need new friends. They gossip too much and are always creating problems and misunderstanding for the Cambodian community," Etta replied, as she turned to her aunt. Thida frowned at her niece.

"Still. I don't want to see you taking care of other people's children," Etta's mother continued. Etta felt offended by Daron and now her mother speaking negatively about caring for children who are the innocent victims of divorce. She parted her lips, wanting to tell her she sounded like Daron, but she decided against it.

Etta gently reached for her iPhone from her aunt. She slipped it back into her apron pocket and returned to her kitchen tasks. Using a handheld blender to pulsate the roasted rice, she felt disappointed in the conversation and tried to drown out the negative voices with the noise of the blender.

Aunt Thida attended to her own tasks. She scooped out a spoonful of *prahok*, placed it on the chopping board, and removed the bones. She then took out a cleaver to chop and mince the salty and pungent fermented fish. She paused and said, "I know his family."

"Really? How?" Etta asked, curious.

"Back in 2005, he and his older sister came to my store to choose an engagement ring. It turns out his older brother had also bought an engagement ring from my shop, and he must have recommended my store because of the beautiful selection that his wife would appreciate. Both the sister and brother seemed quite pretentious, but at least she knew how to put on a fake friendly demeanor. I can't say the same about him, though. He has a gloomy expression in that photo just like when he visited my store. Yeah. I knew they're half Khmer, but it seems like they don't really embrace that part of their background.

And did I mention, his facial expression appears to be in a perpetual state of mourning?"

"That's a mean thing to say," Etta replied, her voice imbued with annoyance and offense, as her aunt knew nothing more than his outer appearance. "Actually, he has a very nice smile when he wants to." She paused, a wistful smile gracing her own lips as she allowed her thoughts to reflect on the times they smiled and gazed into each other's eyes.

"I'm telling you, Etta, this is the plain truth. That man, he is no ray of sunshine. No, he's more like a dark cloud, bringing nothing but misery wherever he goes. Like my grandson would say to his friend, 'Boy, you suck up all the light and energy like a black hole.' Can you believe it? Even my Queen of the Night plant went limp the minute he stepped foot into my jewelry shop. That's how bad his energy is. Trust me, honey, you don't want someone like that in your life."

Thida poured two spoonfuls of cooking oil into the pot and threw in the pieces of chicken she had cut up. Measuring with her eyes, she poured in fish sauce and added a spoonful of Aji-No-Moto, a little bit of sugar, and a pinch of salt. She stirred the chicken until the color changed, then poured in the *kroeung* or spice paste, the pulsated roasted rice, and the minced *prahok*, and continued to give it a good mixing and stirring.

"We're a family busting with rays of sunshine, full of positive energy, and he's just gonna mess with all of that. And don't even get me started on his family. They're all uppity and high and mighty, like they're better than the rest of us. No, no, no," Thida ranted, "he's just not right for you. And you know, it's rare for me to agree with your mother, or even your jerk of a friend; but this time, we are all on the same page. If he has the audacity to ask you to marry him, my dear, don't you dare say yes. Let him go and make other poor souls miserable. But he's not gonna do it to our family, no way."

Etta's face crumpled with offense and hurt as she responded, "That's really harsh. I mean, come on, you don't really know him, do you? You only see him in passing, and you can't judge him based on that one time." Etta's tone softened as she explained, "We're just dating and getting to know each other right now. It's a process, and we're still figuring things out."

Thida turned her head away from the pot but her hand continued to stir it constantly, like the way she was stirring up problems in Etta's life. She lowered and drew together her eyebrows, her lips raised high with the corners turned down, and said with utter disgust, "Dating?!"

Etta's voice was sweet, masking her exasperation as she countered, "What's wrong with dating, *oum*? It's a completely normal and healthy way to connect and discover each other."

She assisted in the cooking by adding the washed vegetables, leaving the faster-cooking grated papaya and moringa leaves to the last, as her aunt stirred the pot. Etta's mother, who had not been saying much, because her sister in-law had been dominating the conversation, poured five cups of water into a pitcher and handed it to Etta, as Thida continued to give it a good mix. Etta then poured in the pitcher of water while her aunt continued to stir.

Thida resumed her rant. "I can't understand this dating thing with today's youth. In our times, when a gentleman took a liking to a young lady, he would conduct himself with utmost honor and approach his elders. They, in turn, would pay a visit to the young lady's parents' house, bearing gifts of all kinds, to respectfully negotiate a suitable dowry and propose a sacred union. However, this young man, Sam, fails to grasp your true worth. Instead of cherishing you, he engages in this casual dating practice."

Etta, taken aback by the contradictory advice, responded, "Wait a minute, Aunty. First, you suggested that Sam lacks the sincerity to be considered as a suitable husband. And now, you're implying that he ought to do the honorable thing by marrying me? I'm confused."

"What I'm trying to say is that he doesn't appreciate your worth as a woman. Dating, to me, is solely about men seeking personal gratification without considering the consequences it may have on your reputation and the reputation of your family. I encounter such individuals frequently when they visit my store, boasting about the women they *dite* and the exploits they engage in." Thida, with her old-fashioned upbringing, saw the word *date* as negative as the French-influenced word *dite*, which means to call—almost like a catcall—or to flirt. "I often overhear them making derogatory remarks such as, 'That girl has been involved with numerous men. She's certainly not suitable for marriage. If you're looking for a life partner, consider going to Cambodia and finding yourself a virtuous and untouched wife. You'll have better luck there. These American-born Cambodian women are so promiscuous and lacking in morals. I *dited* her myself. You can give it a try, but don't even think about marrying her.'"

"Oh, my God! Seriously, Aunt Thida, I can't even comprehend why dating has to be twisted into this sick, slut-shaming game. It's infuriating! Why is it always the girl who gets blamed when she's harassed or catcalled? It's not fair, and it's certainly not her fault for trying to find love. Relationships can be complicated, and it's not her fault if things don't work out. She deserves someone who can genuinely love and commit to her. And those guys she dated who turned out to be total dogs? Ugh, don't even get me started! She trusted them, opened up her heart, and they betrayed her. It's their fault for being dishonest and disrespectful, not hers. She deserves so much better than that!"

"As the kids say these days, let me drop some wisdom, my dear. You see, it has always been this way. A woman should always prioritize her reputation and avoid compromising situations. Respectable Khmer gentlemen—you know, the ones worth marrying—prefer women who uphold traditional values and refrain from dating multiple men. Moreover, a woman's body is a sacred temple, a sanctuary of purity. It is a privilege reserved for one exceptional person to enter and adore her with utmost reverence."

Etta shot back, jokingly, her voice full of defiance with a touch of sass, "A good temple has many worshippers."

"Oh, Lord Buddha! Can you believe what your daughter just said?" Aunt Thida said to Etta's mother, her eyes widening with surprise. Meanwhile she kept her hands busy, with one hand in an oven mitt holding onto the handle of the pot while she used a wooden spatula to stir the *samlor kakor* Khmer soup. "How could she even entertain such thoughts? It's incredibly inappropriate and simply not befitting for a young lady from the Kem family."

Etta quickly interjected, a mischievous grin spreading across her face. "I was just joking," she said, her tone light and playful.

"I'm being serious here. Listen to me, as your elder. Your mother and I are married to honorable men who cherish and value us. We only wish the same for you. Let me share a personal experience. Before I met your uncle, there was a man who approached me and asked me out for dinner. In response, I confidently replied, 'What's the matter? Do you think I am incapable of buying my own dinner? I do not need you to treat me.'"

Etta's mother continued to focus on her tasks, seemingly bothered but kept her feelings to herself for the time being, as if she did not want to gain up on her daughter while her sister in-law babbled on.

Etta lost interest in listening to her aunt and her gaze drifted toward the kitchen window. Amidst the soft rays of sunlight filtering through the glass, her eyes were drawn to her thin, silver-haired grandfather sitting in her parents' manicured yard. His weathered countenance adorned with the wisdom of years gone by, he still looked fit and healthy for a man of his age, because he tended to look at the lighter or beautiful side of things. She smiled seeing him laugh and enjoy the company of his great-grandchildren. Their laughter echoed through the air like a symphony of youthful joy, amid the beautiful profusion of pink and white climbing roses and strawberry and vanilla hydrangeas.

She was thankful neither he nor her father were as judgmental and hard on her as her aunt. She let out a smirk, finding it amusing that her aunt was always judging and lecturing her when her own children did not listen to her nor showed her any respect.

Etta changed her tack, asking in a soft tone of reflection, "How can you truly get to know someone if you never go out on a date? What if there's no physical compatibility between you two?"

Her aunt responded in kind. "We have an intuition when the right man enters our lives, my dear. Sex, you see, is primarily intended for the purpose of reproduction. It is not about indulging in perverse pleasures that the younger generation seems to seek, engaging in casual encounters from one person to another, without any regard for commitment or loyalty."

Etta pondered but found herself saying aloud, "If you don't give it a chance, how would you ever know if that person could bring you immense pleasure? I wonder if you've ever experienced the incredible sensation of an orgasm."

"What did you say?" her aunt said with alarm.

"Oh, nothing," said Etta, nonchalantly.

"I don't want to bring this up, but let's consider the outcome of your eight-year relationship with Jack Edlin. It was clear from the beginning that it wouldn't work out, dear, because, as the Americans say, he was "getting the milk for free." Did you truly get to know each other better after all those years of dating? Only after eight years, he put a ring on your finger and then he cheated on you."

Etta's face fell with disappointment and sadness. Her aunt's words pierced her heart like a knife. To cope with her emotions, she focused on carefully scrubbing the sink clean from their mess. She felt helpless, realizing that her aunt's mindset was deeply rooted in old-fashioned beliefs and unfairly placing blame on women.

Recognizing the impact of her words and sensing Etta's sorrow, her aunt decided to drop the subject. Regrettably, pride prevented her from offering an apology she knew was needed.

"She doesn't mean to bring that up," her mother murmured, her delicate fingers tenderly touching her daughter's hunched shoulder.

The weekend had come and gone. Before Etta knew it, Sunday afternoon had melted into evening. She had been anticipating her call with Sam. His voice and his presence, albeit through virtual means, had become a catalyst for her boost of serotonin. His text messages became the soundtrack of her existence, each melodious tone lighting up her face with a radiant glow.

Unfortunately, lurking underneath Etta's newfound happiness lay a disappointment—her friends, mother, and aunt were not being receptive to Sam. She possessed great compassion for him, though he remained oblivious to the criticisms and doubts cast upon him. However, steadfast in her way, Etta continued to live her blissful life in her own world and wished to shield Sam from the unwelcome opinions of those close to her. After all, only what was in their hearts truly mattered.

Etta sat in her home office, where her large windows overlooked the Chicago River, shimmering with the glowing red and orange sky. While using computer-aided design software to create 3D models of her building designs to communicate her ideas to one of her clients, her eyes kept glancing at her iPhone sitting on a stand next to her computer. Sam seemed to be taking longer than usual to call. She picked up her phone, clicked on Sam's profile, and sat staring at his handsome face. As she was about to press on his phone number she quickly put the device back down, realizing she preferred him to call her when he had time, because he might be busy parenting.

After dinner, she looked at her iPhone one last time before she changed into her pajamas and then brushed her teeth. No calls from Sam. By 10 p.m., she slipped under her cozy comforter to turn in for the night. As she reached for her iPhone to set her alarm clock, the mysterious ringtone sounded. She smiled a radiant smile upon seeing Sam's 919 area code. She tried to play it cool by not answering right away. Finally she clicked on the green phone icon to answer by the fourth ring.

"Hello," Etta said with a smile in her voice.

"Hi Etta. How was your weekend?"

"It was great. How was yours?" she said with happiness in her voice.

"It was all right. I was busy with the kids and getting ready for teaching."

"I see. When does class start in Chapel Hill?" she asked.

"August 21st, but my class starts on the 28th."

"Ah. It's just around the corner."

"Yes. Um. Listen, Etta. Before we both go to sleep, I would like to ask you something." Sam's voice carried a weight of seriousness.

"Yes?" Etta's heart skipped a beat, her mind racing to decipher the gravity underlying Sam's tone.

"My brother, Vincent, is getting married to Rima on August 18 at the Drake Hotel."

"Oh, wow. Congratulations to both of them! How exciting!"

"Yeah. Thank you. Um. I was wondering if you would do me the honor of accompanying me as my plus-one?"

Etta's eyes widened in disbelief and her jaw dropped in awe. "The Drake Hotel? It's a truly exquisite venue," she responded. "Did you know Princess Diana herself stayed there for three days back in June 1996? It's a beautiful place, Sam."

"Yes, I heard about that."

"Did you know Edward VIII, the Prince of Wales, was the first British royal family to stay there?"

"No. I did not know that."

"Yes. The empress of Japan and Queen Elizabeth II also stayed there. Of course at different times."

"Of course. Yeah, I didn't know all these historical figures stayed there."

"Well. They did. Did you also know it's one of Chicago's landmark hotels?"

"No. Interesting."

"Yes. It was built in 1920 and featured one of my favorite designs, the Italian Renaissance. It has two big ballrooms. They're both gorgeous, but I am more partial to the Gold Coast Room because it overlooks a stunning view of Lake Michigan and I love the ornately designed columns. Also, one of the hotel's main attractions is Afternoon Tea. I went there a few times with my friends and colleagues. I had such a wonderful time. However, I think the Peninsula is more modern and glamorous. I just went there with one of my friends."

"Good. We should have tea sometime," Sam replied.

Etta laughed, knowing that predominantly women go to Afternoon Tea.

Sam continued, "My brother and his fiancé rented the French Room. We're only expecting about three hundred guests."

"Only? That's a good number of guests."

"Yes. Are you interested in being my plus-one?"

"Oh, I would love to be your plus-one," Etta said without hesitation. Butterflies fluttered again. She was not sure if it was related to fear or because she felt elated about being Sam's date to his brother's wedding.

"Good! Since I will be busy helping out before and leading up to the wedding, would you like to go out to dinner and a show with me? I can get away on Friday of that week."

"Let me check my schedule," Etta replied, her voice loaded with anticipation.

"Sure," he said, anticipating her answer.

She switched the screen to her calendar and scrolled to see if she had plans for that day or week, but a mischievous glint sparkled in her eyes as she knew she would rearrange her commitments just to spend this special occasion with Sam. "I don't have anything during that evening, so I'm clear."

"Good," he said with relief and excitement in his voice.

12

ETTA, CHICAGO
AUGUST 17 & 18, 2018

The week flew by quickly, and before they knew it, it was Friday, August 17. Etta and Sam had a delightful evening, starting with dinner at the Purple Pig and then attending a show at the Lyric Opera. The entire experience felt surreal, like a dream. Etta wished the evening wouldn't come to an end, but time, as usual, slipped away when she was having fun. Her smile grew as she discovered her fingers interlaced in a tender dance with Sam's. Their steps harmoniously synchronized as they ascended the concrete staircase leading to her luxurious townhome. Upon reaching the landing, Sam, breaking the silence for the first time, uttered, "Well, here we are," his words resonating with reluctance, as if he shared her feeling of not wanting the evening to come to a close.

"Yes, indeed. Here we are," Etta echoed his sentiment, and her body turned to face him. Their grip of each other's hands remained tight and strong.

"I had a great time," Sam said, a smile gracing his lips. His eyes gazed into Etta's.

"Me, too," Etta said, with a soft smile of her own, her gaze locked into his enigmatic eyes. A strong sense of connection enveloped her.

They stood there, their eyes locked in a prolonged moment, Etta grappling with the decision of whether or not to invite him inside her home on only their third date. Inexperienced in the realm of dating, she felt a strong urge to consult Google for advice, regretting not doing so prior to their encounter. Seeking guidance from her friend Daron was also out of the question, as it would risk exposing her relationship with Sam. As the silence lingered, Etta found herself at a loss for words, not wanting to appear desperate or overly eager. Still, their gaze persisted, the unspoken tension between them growing palpable. With his right hand clasping her left, Sam delicately raised his left hand to caress her right cheek, with such softness it sent shivers down her spine. His expression remained impassive, yet his eyes delved deep into the depths of her soul. Her heart pounded like a blacksmith's hammer against an anvil, its rhythm matching the intensity of the moment. The allure of his pheromones left her breathless, her anticipation growing as he leaned closer and closer to her. Anticipation flooded her senses. Then, with a gentle touch, he lightly pressed his lips against her right cheek.

"It's getting late," he said, disrupting their tender moment. "I have a lot to take care of. I'll pick you up tomorrow at 6 p.m.?"

Etta smiled and nodded, understanding his duties but wanting so much for him to kiss her. She also wanted to be invited to the church ceremony, but he had expressed during their dinner that he was concerned about leaving her alone while he assisted with his brother's wedding. He assured her, however, that at the reception they would have more time together. Etta found his thoughtfulness endearing.

Six o'clock on Saturday did not come fast enough. When the time finally arrived, and Etta swung open her door, her heart skipped a beat at the sight of the dashing Sam wearing a sleek black suit and a crisp white bowtie. With her hair elegantly pinned up and her slender figure adorned in a long-sleeved, floral lace wrap-over mini-dress with jewel neckline, she exuded a modest yet stylish charm. She could see Sam's gaze lingering upon her, his eyes loaded with admiration.

"You look absolutely stunning," he said, causing a blush to grace her cheeks.

"Thank you," she replied, her voice soft, quiet, and hesitant. "You look rather handsome yourself."

His charming smile widened, illuminating his face. With a graceful gesture, he extended his hand toward her. In that moment, the air surrounding them felt light, warm, and invigorating, setting the stage for an unforgettable evening.

As they entered the French Room of the Drake arm in arm, the collective gaze of the well-dressed crowd turned toward them. It seemed as if the entire room fell into a hushed silence, allowing Etta to perceive even the faintest sound. She felt the weight of judgmental eyes upon her, particularly from some of the women, but she also detected a sense of relief in the majority, as they beheld Sam's happiness being with someone. Sam led her toward his sister, who was engaged in conversation with her husband and their esteemed guests. Etta's nerves fluttered as she observed Vida's impassive expression.

"Vida and Paolo," Sam said, his voice calm and gentle, "I would like to introduce you to Etta, my plus-one."

"Hi, it's a pleasure to meet you," Etta said, her smile radiant as she extended her hand toward Paolo and Vida, respectively, in a friendly gesture. To herself she noted, *So this is Vida. My aunt says she's uppity. I hope she's wrong about her.*

Vida's gaze remained fixed on Etta, a mix of intrigue and surprise evident in her expression. Hesitantly, Vida extended her hand and lightly shook the tips of Etta's fingers. Etta, accustomed to a firm handshake, couldn't help but wonder if she was being subtly slighted.

"How do you know my brother?" Vida said, her voice carried an aristocratic tone. Etta noticed there seemed to be similarities between Sam and Vida, not only in their enigmatic nature but also in their mannerisms and the way they carried themselves, with a certain air of mystery.

Before Etta could utter a word in response, Sam interjected, "Etta actually drove me and the kids to meet you in Chinatown."

"Oh, is this the woman you rear-ended?" a tall, slender woman with a melon-seed-shaped face inquired. She was dressed in a silk red gown, and her words carried an accusation. "Is inviting her to your brother's wedding your way of apologizing? You do realize you're not obligated to do so, as your insurance covers the damages. That's what insurance is for, in case you've forgotten," she added, maintaining a serious expression.

Etta maintained her polite smile in response to Tomi's scrutiny, as the latter scanned her from head to toe.

Vida, who seemed to be annoyed by Tomi's way of butting into the conversation, turned her attention to her husband and guests.

"Etta, this is my best friend, Tomi," Sam clarified, attempting to ease the tension. "She has a playful sense of humor."

"And he doesn't," Tomi retorted, a hint of amusement in her voice. "He's not much of a fan of idle chatter, I must say."

Sam chose to disregard Tomi's remark and redirected the conversation. "By the way, the gentleman behind her is her husband, Kevin."

Well, Sam does have a female best friend who embodies the kind of beauty that Asian societies around the world hold in high regard. Should I be threatened by her? Etta had witnessed firsthand how friendships between men and women frequently evolved into something more, like her high school boyfriend who slept with one of her female friends. Whether it was unrequited desire or the friendship naturally progressing into romance, she had observed that platonic relationships often morphed into love, physical intimacy, and commitment, though not always in that particular sequence. I shouldn't let myself feel that way. Daron and I have a strong friendship, and I don't sense any romantic interest between us, nor does he. Perhaps they're similar to us, genuinely caring for each other due to a shared bond.

Etta's awareness heightened with this contemplation, and she became conscious also of the need to make a favorable impression on Tomi. She considered the dynamics of friendships and how friends could be critical of the person their friend was dating. The thought crossed her mind that perhaps Sam had brought Etta along as a plus-one to win the approval of his family and friends. Etta couldn't help but contrast this situation with her friendship with Rochelle, Daron's wife, who seemingly didn't require her approval in the same way Sam required Tomi's approval of her. Etta recognized that Rochelle, as a mature and educated woman, never seemed concerned about impressing her or feeling threatened by her friendship with Daron. With that in mind, Etta maintained her composure and extended her hand, greeting each of them respectfully. "It's a pleasure to meet you," she said, offering a warm handshake to each person in turn.

Sam turned to more guests to introduce. "Etta, this is my older brother Daniel and his wife, *bang srey* Sopheap."

Etta smiled at Sam, proud of him for upholding Khmer mannerism by referring to his sister in-law as "older sister." Considering that both Daniel and Sopheap were older than her, and to show them her respect, as they seemed to adhere to Khmer culture, Etta clasped her palms together and brought them up to her heart with a little curtsy. As the younger person she followed Khmer custom in uttering the greeting, "Chum reap sour." Daniel and Sopheap reciprocated, appreciating her mannerism.

"You're a pretty young lady," Sopheap said, admiring Etta.

"Thank you and so are you," Etta returned the compliment. Sopheap laughed good-naturedly.

Tomi's gaze traveled from Etta's head to her toes as she also complimented her, saying, "Yeah. You're pretty. That must be why Sam chose you."

"Thank you," Etta said. "I must say, you are absolutely stunning." Lord, am I that desperate to seek her approval? Why do I need to ingratiate myself with her like that? Do I value the validation and acceptance from his best friend that much? Perhaps Daron was right when he reminded me I worry about what others think of me too much. Argh. This is the characteristic of me that I dislike. I need to change it. It's not my style As she turned her gaze toward Sam, her intentions blurred, captivated by the enigmatic depths of his eyes.

"Obviously," Tomi remarked, casually flicking back her lustrous, silky mane. Etta chuckled, unaware of the sincerity behind Tomi's words.

"You must know something about my wife," Kevin said, putting his free arm around Tom's waist and looking longingly into her eyes while he held up a drink in his other hand. "She has always regarded herself as a striking individual. Anytime someone compliments her, she sees it as a reaffirmation, an expected validation of her own stunning presence. And she's right. That's what I love about her: confident, stunning, and smart."

"Come on," Tomi said to Etta, brushing him off without being obvious, as she grabbed Etta's hand away from the group. "Let's find our table and have a chat." Etta, who had only one close female friend in Rochelle, felt a surge of excitement at the possibility of forming a new friendship with Tomi through Sam. *She must be a good person if Sam is friends with her.* However, she was wary of having too many friends due to people's gossiping nature, herself included. She was afraid she might catch herself gossiping, too.

She bid farewell to Vida and the others, waving her hand and saying, "It was nice to meet everyone," before

Tomi, like a high school girl, playfully pulled her toward a table situated near the bride and groom and their bridesmaids. Vida held her head high, briefly looking at the two women before she turned away again. Meanwhile, Daniel, Paolo, and Sopheap waved back, smiling. Etta glanced back at Sam, who genuinely smiled at her, while Tomi's husband shook his head, finding amusement in the situation.

"Tomi seems to like your girlfriend, Sam. She never had a female friend before. It would be a good thing if both of them hit it off. The four of us can all be good friends," Kevin looked excited at the prospect.

"Here is our table," Tomi said. "Sit." The women sat down next to each other. "So tell me about yourself." Etta's face lit up. Tomi seemed to be eager to delve into Etta's life, and in return, Etta yearned to uncover more about Sam. Etta believed that if Tomi was Sam's best friend, she must be privy to intimate details about him. Etta herself had no reservations about sharing her own life story and openly discussing her family's history and background. To Tomi she recounted the harrowing experiences of her grandfather, father, aunt, and mother who endured unimaginable hardship under the murderous Khmer Rouge regime before finding refuge in the United States with nothing but the clothes on their backs and no knowledge of the English language. "Through their unwavering determination, persistence, and adaptability, they not only survived but thrived in their new home, America. I'm grateful that my life is comparatively easier. I can't imagine the emotional torment my parents and my ancestors endured witnessing brutal deaths, enduring starvation, and suffering all kinds of abuse. I learned about their trials and tribulations through the many stories and references they shared at our family gatherings."

Before Etta went any further, Tomi stopped her by saying, "I'm not particularly interested in such stories. To be honest, everyone in this world suffers or is victimized by somebody or others."

"What do *you* want to know?" Etta said, masking her hurtful feelings by her sweet demeanor. She stared at her as if studying her, wondering if Tomi lacked empathy or if she desired to avoid engaging with difficult emotions or topics. Either way, Sam's friend came off as dismissive and rude.

"Well, what's your story? Have you always been single?"

"No. I was once engaged."

"Oh. What happened?" Tomi's ears perked with wide eyes.

"He cheated on me."

"Oh. Sorry to hear that," Tomi said. "So you've been single since?"

"Yes. We had been together for eight years. It took me a long time to get over it."

"So you've never been with someone since then?" Tomi asked, as she picked up her champagne glass from the table to take a sip.

"No. I guess I was waiting for the right man to come along," Etta said, looking for Sam. Her eyes finally landed on him, still talking to Daniel, Sopheap, and Kevin.

"Oh, really?" Tomi said, following her gaze. "So in total, how many relationships have you been in?"

"Two. Why?" Etta said, turning her attention back to Tomi.

"I won't beat around the bush. I genuinely care about Sam," Tomi admitted. "We've been friends ever since our days at St. Ignatius College Preparatory School, and I don't want to see him get hurt."

Etta's gaze shifted between confusion and contemplation as she locked eyes with Tomi. "Do you truly believe I would hurt him?" The question reverberated in her mind, leaving her torn between a sense of offense at Tomi's apparent lack of trust and a genuine attempt to understand the underlying concern and care that Tomi might harbor for Sam. It wasn't the first time someone had expressed reservations about her connection with Sam, who carried an air of mystery and had a complex past that seemed to intrigue and worry others simultaneously.

Etta's thoughts drifted back to a previous conversation she had shared with Daron. The memory of his expressed concerns about her connection with Sam resurfaced. Daron had highlighted Sam's emotional baggage and reserved nature, making it challenging to fully understand him and his intentions toward Etta.

As Etta reflected on both Tomi's and Daron's concerns, she realized their intentions were rooted in genuine care. They were simply looking out for their friends' well-being and trying to protect them from potential heartache. After all, both she and Sam had experienced heartbreak in their past relationships. While it was tempting to let offense take over, Etta chose to approach the situation with empathy and understanding.

She turned to Tomi and said, "I appreciate your concern. I understand you care about your friend's happiness and don't want to see him hurt. However, he knows everything there is to know about me. I have nothing to hide," Etta said, hoping Tomi would accept her sincerity.

"Hmm. We'll see about that," Tomi mumbled under her breath, as she turned to take another sip of her champagne.

Etta could still hear her and looked at her with confusion, as if not sure what to make of this woman. *Is she a foe or a friend?*

Kevin and Sam leisurely made their way to their seats next to their partners, and Kevin, with a warm smile, said to his wife, "I think you've drilled the poor woman enough."

Settling himself next to Etta, Sam reached out and gently clasped her hand, a gesture that met with a look of contentment from Kevin.

"I'm happy Sam finally finds someone special. Cheers to you, Etta." Kevin raised his glass of champagne to her. "I can feel at ease now that my wife no longer carries the burden of constantly worrying about her best friend or consoling him when he feels sad, lonely, or just needs help with the children. I appreciate she's trying to take a load off Vida, but I need my wife."

"While I appreciate Tomi's help, I told her not to worry about me and the kids. We're doing fine," Sam offered.

"Yeah, but she cares about you. You know, Etta, I have never had a true female or male friend. Everybody is either nice or afraid of me because of my money and influence. Actually, more like my parents' money and influence."

Etta looked at Sam. He gave her a blank look while Tomi looked at her husband with annoyance.

Kevin rambled on, "I find my wife's relationship with Sam intriguing. I acknowledge my limited understanding of such deep bonds, having never experienced a truly intimate friendship myself. You know, Sam is the closest I have ever come to having a best friend, and I cherish this honest connection. Sam is a good man. I trust in his integrity. If it was any other man, I would not trust him at all, not one bit. I wholeheartedly believe Sam's relationship with my wife goes no further than friendship."

Again Etta looked at Sam, wondering if Kevin actually was jealous of his relationship with Tomi.

"Etta," Kevin said, "I think you're an ideal life partner for Sam—you complement each other perfectly, both in appearance and personality."

"They're only dating, honey. Don't push marriage on them," Tomi said to her husband, sounding extremely annoyed. A man with a tray of champagne came by and before Kevin could reach for another, she grabbed his hand. "I think you have had too much to drink already, honey."

"But I'm having a good time. Anyway, what was I saying? Oh, yes! The prospect of having my wife all to myself makes me giddy. We can now start a family that we have been putting off—right, sweetheart?" Kevin playfully winked at his wife before he leaned in to kiss her on her cheek.

Tomi gently tapped him on his cheek and said, "All right, honey. The world doesn't need to hear about us starting a family." She picked up a glass of water for him to drink, to dilute his alcohol intake. When dinner was served, she made sure he ate to have something in his stomach.

Attention at the table turned to the bride and groom, as Vincent stood to offer thanks to all families, relativies, and guests. After the speech and toasting, the good-looking bride and groom gracefully glided onto the dance floor, their movements a symphony of love and devotion. Vincent's arm encircled Rima's delicate waist, his other hand intertwining with hers, and they appeared genuinely happy as they gazed into each other's eyes. In that moment, their bodies merged into a harmonious unity, swaying to the dulcet tones of a slow ballad.

Etta, an admirer of beauty and happiness, beheld the couple with awe. Their radiant joy was palpable, their gaze fixed solely upon each other. A genuine smile graced her lips as she reveled in their bliss, genuinely happy for the beautiful bride and handsome groom.

Thereafter, the MC called out and welcomed other couples to join the bride and groom. Captivated by the tender melody, they filled the dance floor, each couple's eyes locked on one other in their graceful movements.

Sam, smiling and seeming to be in a happy mood, extended his hand to Etta, his eyes kind and inviting. She placed her hand on her stomach as if she were feeling actual butterflies fluttering within her stomach, their delicate wings stirring a sense of anticipation she had not felt since being in the arms of her former love, Jack Edlin.

Sam's touch was tender, his hand cradling hers like a fragile blossom. With a gentle guidance, he led her onto the floor, his arm secure around her slender waist. Etta, her hand resting upon his shoulder, intertwined her fingers with his, a connection both tender and warm. Closer they drew, their bodies swaying in perfect harmony, attuned to the rhythm of the music.

Locked in a gaze of bliss, their eyes became windows to their souls. A soft flush graced Etta's cheeks, as she became aware of his intense gaze. A warm, tingling sensation covered her entire being, as if an electric current coursed through her veins. She wondered, in that precious moment, if Sam could sense the rapid vibrations of her heart, beating in unison with the music. *This feels so nice. Wow. How did I land this incredibly handsome man? I wish we could hold each other like this and gaze into each other's eyes forever.*

"Etta," he gently called out to her, his voice pulling her away from her daydream.

"Yes?" she swallowed, anticipating his words.

"Have I told you that you look stunning tonight?"

"Yes, you have."

"Well, it's worth repeating. You look stunningly beautiful tonight."

"Thank you," Etta murmured, her voice packed with gratitude and vulnerability. The effect of his admiration left her feeling weak in the knees, as she realized he saw her in the same light as she saw him.

He gazed deeply into her eyes, a vulnerable sincerity shining through his own. With a tender voice, he began, "You know, Etta, I've never been in a position to say something like this before. Perhaps it's the festive atmosphere surrounding us, or the profound love radiating from my brother for his bride, but..."

"Yes?" Etta said, her voice overlowing with anticipation and hope, yearning for him to utter something sweet and memorable that would linger in her heart.

"Etta Kem, I want to grow old with you."

The weight of those seven glorious words hung in the air, surpassing any expectations she had for this stage of their relationship. Coming from a man who seldom spoke his heart, the impact of his declaration struck Etta deeply. It was as if those words compensated for the silent moments of their past. She appreciated his aversion to idle chatter, and the fact that he chose to express such a profound sentiment meant he was genuine in his intentions. The sincerity behind his words touched her, and a warmth spread through her heart, knowing that he truly meant them.

"Yeah?" Etta managed to utter, her voice sounded pleasantly surprised.

"Yeah," he replied, his smile widening as he bundled her in a tight embrace.

Their bodies melded together, and in that moment, she could feel the rhythm of his heartbeat, or perhaps it was her own heart syncing with his. Resting her head against his strong chest, a contented smile graced her lips as she basked in the intimate affection they shared. Etta had never experienced a love so profound, so all-encompassing. The echoes of his words, "I want to grow old with you," reverberated in her mind, putting a smile on her face. She replayed his heartfelt declaration over and over, each repetition igniting a renewed sense of happiness and certainty in her heart.

13

As the night ended, Etta bid farewell to everyone she had been introduced to, expressing her gratitude, and exchanging warm goodbyes. She even got a chance to see Vincent and Rima driving off to the airport to take a private jet to their honeymoon destination. Sam, ever the gentleman, offered to accompany her home. Vida, Paolo, and Tomi were busy trying to help the intoxicated Kevin to the room at the Drake. The families of the bride and groom and some of their guests were staying there for the night.

Sopheap, smiling at Sam and Etta, said, "Don't worry about the kids, my parents are watching them. Daniel and I… I'm sure Vida will be checking in on them as well, so take your time."

"Thank you, *bang srey*," Sam said, appreciating her consideration.

Etta smiled at Daniel and Sopheap. "It was nice meeting everyone. I'm so happy to have met your parents, *bang* Sopheap. I should have expected that they would know my family. After all, we're a small community and all the old folks know each other."

"Yes; that's true. We, as the younger generation, should get to know each other like they do and be united like them," Sopheap said, with her gentle smile.

"I second that," Etta said.

"We're looking forward to seeing you coming over for a BBQ with Sam one of these weekends."

"Thank you. I'd love that very much. Have a great night," Etta said, offering a genuine smile.

"You, too," Daniel and Sopheap replied and waved goodbye.

"It's a beautiful night," Etta suggested, a glimmer of adventure in her eyes, as they exited out the main entrance. "Would you like to walk? It's only a fifteen-minute walk to my place, and I could use the opportunity to walk off the food we ate this evening. It was delicious, by the way."

Sam's smile widened, his eyes reflecting his fondness for her. Without hesitation, he reached out and took her hand, interlacing their fingers. It was a silent affirmation of their connection. The touch evoked a sense of warmth, comfort, and inner peace. She held tightly onto him, as just a touch of his hand weakened her knees. There was something about being in Sam's presence that made her deliriously happy. Walking hand in hand through the night streets of downtown Chicago, they made their way toward The Magnificent Mile, their path illuminated by the city lights.

Contrary to her hopes, the silence persisted throughout their walk, leaving Etta longing for more words from Sam. He remained lost in his thoughts, wearing a pensive expression, his gaze fixed on the distant horizon. Etta, not wanting to disrupt the delicate rhythm of their walking, hesitated to break the silence, but she could not help herself.

"What are you thinking about right now?" Etta inquired gently, her voice carrying a mix of curiosity and concern, as they reached her street at East North Water.

Sam turned to face her, his eyes meeting hers. "I was just thinking about my children," he admitted, a little regret in voice. "I haven't seen them all evening, and I missed out on putting them to bed. I hope they're not upset that I wasn't there to give them their bedtime kisses."

Etta gazed at him with a softened heart, understanding the weight of his parental responsibilities. She reached out and gently squeezed his hand, offering reassurance through her touch. "Aww. I'm sure they're all tucked in and sound asleep," she said, her voice packed with warmth. "You're such a devoted father; that is what I like about you. I know how much you love your children. You should catch a cab back. I can make the rest of my way home. We have many more days, months, and years to get to know each other. The kids come first," Etta said, with sincerity. Though she loved and felt a certain kind of way when he said he wanted to grow old with her, she did not think he would jump at it right away nor did she want him to do so.

"No. Don't be silly. You're almost home. I would like to make sure you get home safely," Sam said. "Besides, you're right. They're probably sleeping soundly. By the time they wake up I'll be back with them."

"Thank you," Etta said, reaching for his hand.

They made it to her doorstep. As they stood there, a moment of awkwardness hung in the air. As she parted her pink, full lips to say something, Sam gently pulled her closer, their bodies melding together. With a touch laden with longing, he cupped her delicate face, his eyes brimming with desire. Without hesitation, he leaned in, capturing her lips in a fervent kiss that ignited a fire within her.

Wide-eyed and flustered at first, she quickly surrendered to the intensity of his kiss and the connection of their touch. She responded eagerly to the movement of his lips and the warmth of his tongue, savoring the sweetness of his mouth. Their tongues entwined, sending sensations that made her toes curl and her head spin. Warmth rushed throughout her body. In that moment, desire eclipsed all inhibitions, and her mind ceased its rational thinking.

Still locked in their passionate embrace, Etta's right fingers instinctively entered the code to her house without needing to look. Muscle memory guided her movements, allowing them to gain access inside. As to who was leading whom, it was blurred as they both succumbed to the intoxication of sensuality and passion. They kicked off their shoes randomly, not caring where they landed. The distance to her bedroom was too far to get to in their current state of passion. As if Sam read her mind, he gently guided her slender body onto her cream Pawnee sectional sofa, their desire for each other consuming the space around them. He pressed his body against hers, their faces locked in a passionate embrace. His arm encircled her, holding her close as he pinned her against the sofa. Their kisses deepened, growing faster and more urgent with each passing moment. He swiftly discarded his suit jacket, tossing it carelessly to the floor. His bow tie came undone, and his shirt was unbuttoned in a haste. Etta could feel the heat radiating from his body, matching the warmth that surged through her own veins. Beads of sweat formed on his skin, mirroring the rising temperature between them. Her hand rested on his firm chest, a silent confirmation of their shared desire, just as he reached behind her to unzip her dress. With a swift motion, he pulled it over her head, revealing her cream satin slip. The layers of fabric seemed to frustrate him momentarily, but he wasted no time in removing her slip, leaving her in only her undergarments.

They were on the precipice of surrender, ready to indulge in each other completely, when a sudden, loud bang on her door shattered the moment. Etta's brows furrowed, eyes squinted, and jaw tensed. She thought it was her other neighbor whose husband often came home late and drunk, so she continued to kiss Sam fervently. She could feel they were going through the most sensual experience of their life. The knock sounded just as loud and just as strong. *How dare someone intrude upon our intimacy! There should be some form of punishment for a person who disrupts someone about to enter the throes of ecstasy. Oh, how I wish I could cast upon him or her the Kindama's curse.* A look of confusion mixed with irritation clouded Etta's features, as the voice grew louder, calling out Sam's name urgently.

Recognizing the familiar, girlish tone, Sam reluctantly pulled his face away from Etta's, their intimate moment abruptly halted. He swiftly moved to put on his shirt, while Etta hastily grabbed her slip, wrapping herself in a throw from the sofa. With a sense of trepidation, Etta opened the door to reveal Tomi's anxious and angry face, her eyes scanning Etta up and down with a judgmental air. Etta couldn't help but feel disapproval radiating from Tomi, as if she felt utterly disgusted at Sam and Etta's actions. After all, they were both consenting adults, unattached and free to explore their desires.

Sam finished dressing himself, buckling his pants, as Tomi entered the room. Sam asked, "What's going on, Tomi? Why are you here?"

"I wouldn't be here if you had answered your phone," Tomi retorted, her frustration evident in her tone.

"I didn't hear it," Sam replied defensively.

"Obviously," Tomi shot back, her eyebrows furrowed and mouth slightly agape as she glanced between Etta and Sam.

Seeking answers, Sam persisted, "What is it?"

Tomi's voice trembled in anger but she managed to spit out, "Wallace... He fell and broke his arm."

Before Etta could express her concern or offer any assistance, Sam dashed out of the door without a word.

Concerned for Wallace's well-being and wanting to show her support, Etta spoke up, "Is he taken to Northwestern? I would like to come and see him, too."

Tomi's response was laced with hostility, "I don't think you need to concern yourself with our family matters."

Etta felt a wave of hurt wash over her as Tomi's eyes bore into her, jam-packed with venom. Tomi turned on her heels and chased after Sam, leaving Etta standing there, bewildered and disheartened. She closed the door, letting her face drop as she pondered why someone as educated and accomplished as Tomi would react with such hostility. *What could I have done to unintentionally upset her? What exactly does she mean by saying "our family matters"? Has she formed such a strong bond with Sam and the children that she now considers herself a part of their family? Don't jump to conclusions, Etta. She's probably scared because Wallace broke his arm.*

Restless and consumed by frustration, Etta found herself unable to sleep that night. Tossing and turning in her bed, her mind replayed the events that had transpired earlier. Seeking some form of reassurance, she decided to reach out to Sam, sending him a text to inquire about his well-being. Anxiety gnawed at her as she waited for his response, but the minutes ticked by without a reply either by text or call. Doubt crept into her mind, as if the connection they had shared, the intense moment they had almost embraced, was nothing more than a fleeting dream. Yet, the sensations of his touch lingered on her body and in her memory, a bittersweet reminder of what might have been.

14

SAM, CHICAGO

AUGUST 19 & 20, 2018

It was three thirty in the morning when Sam stepped out of a Flash cab and rushed into the Northwestern emergency entrance. Tomi paid the driver and ran after Sam. He reached the front desk and said, "Hi, my name is Samuel Angk," sounding out of breath not because he was out of shape, but because his heart was in his throat, worrying about his child. "I understand my sister brought my son—Wallace Angk—here with a broken arm."

"How do you spell the last name?" the front desk lady asked.

"A-n-g-k," Sam said.

"Yes. He's in room seven. Go through the double glass doors and turn right, sir."

"Thank you." Sam rushed down the corridor and through the doors, Tomi following. The sound of a little boy crying in pain caught his attention and he followed it to room seven.

"Daddy!" Wallace cried out as soon as he saw his father. Sam stepped in front of the drawn curtain while a doctor and nurse attended to Wallace and the boy's aunt Vida tried to console him.

"Daddy is here, Wallace," Sam said, rushing to hold his son.

Tomi arrived and said, "See, Wallace. I promised to bring you your father. He's here now. Everything will be okay."

"Ouch!" Wallace screamed, as he tried to move to embrace his father.

"You must be Wallace's father. I'm Dr. Dawood," a tall, middle-aged man said, reaching out to shake his hand.

"What happened? Will my son be okay?" Sam asked, as he shook the doctor's hand.

"He's got a buckle fracture on his right arm. I'm told he tripped and fell," the doctor said, looking at Tomi as if to confirm what she had told him when he was brought in, before turning his attention back to Sam. "It seems he fell on his outstretched arm with force, causing the bone to compress on one side and creating a bulge in his bone. No worries. This type of fracture is stable and doesn't require surgery. We've managed it with a splint to provide support to his fractured bone while it heals. Wallace can remove it during hand washing and bathing. However, outside of that, he must wear it all the time, including sleeping. If this tough little guy needs it, you can get over-the-counter Tylenol, Advil, or Motrin for his pain treatment as well as to keep the swelling down. We have given him some Tylenol earlier. He's good to go," the doctor said, ruffling Wallace's hair.

"How long will he be wearing the splint?" Sam asked.

"For two to three weeks," Dr. Dawood replied. "He should be back to playing sports in six weeks. Meanwhile, I encourage Wallace to use his hand, whether writing, coloring, or using utensils to eat, so that his wrist doesn't become stiff. And remember to keep his arm elevated."

"Thank you, Dr. Dawood," Sam said, breathing a sigh of relief.

"No problem. Nurse Taylor here will work on his release papers and you'll be discharged. Take care," he said with a smile.

Sam, Vida, and Tomi thanked him as he walked out, to attend to his patient in the next room.

Sam sat in the back seat with his arm around his son and smoothed his hair while Vida drove Daniel's black SUV Mercedes and Tomi sat in the passenger seat. "How did you trip and fall, son?"

"She scared me," Wallace said, pointing at Tomi. Sam looked up at Tomi through the rearview mirror with confusion.

"Ha," Tomi let out a nervous laugh, looking back at Sam through the rearview mirror. "My fault. I'm very, very sorry. I heard you were away with *Etta*"—she pronounced the name with disgust—"and I went to check up on the kids on your behalf, to make sure they were okay. I didn't know he was awake and accidentally startled him."

Vida side-eyed Tomi. "You don't think my family and I are capable of looking after my brother's children? They were sleeping soundly when Sopheap and I took turns checking on them. Not to mention my twelve year-old niece, Lek, is staying in the same room."

"I'm sorry, Vida. I don't mean to offend you. I was trying to be helpful. You can never be too careful in this city."

"The room was very hot, Daddy. I got thirsty. When I opened my eyes I saw a ghostly woman. I jumped to run but tripped and fell. Lek got up to turn on the light and we saw her," Wallace said, pointing at Tomi with his good hand.

"Don't point at Auntie Tomi like that," Sam said, gently holding down his son's hand. "It's rude. She said it was an accident. I'm sure she didn't mean to startle you. I'm sorry I wasn't around. I'll never leave you alone like that again, okay?"

Wallace nodded his head and his father kissed the top of his head. Tomi turned to her side window and smiled, seemingly pleased at what she heard, and that Sam was not mad at her.

By late afternoon, the Angk and Rizzo families packed up and were ready to go back home with Kevin and Tomi on their private jet. After saying goodbye to their siblings' families, Daniel, his own family, and his in-laws drove from the Drake back to their home in Skokie.

Once Sam arrived home, he made dinner for his children and later put them to bed. Exhausted, he crashed on his couch and pulled his mobile phone from his pocket, scrolling through his call and text logs. Not seeing any new messages, he clicked on the old text exchanges between him and Etta, but before he could type something to her, an incoming call distracted him.

"Hi Tomi," Sam said. "No, please don't bring anything. We're fine. I made the kids sandwiches. They ate and are asleep now. I'm going to turn in as well. All right. Good night." After he showered and put on his pajamas, he looked at his phone again. Not seeing any new messages or incoming calls, he put it on his nightstand. He stared at it. Picked it up, clicking on Etta's number and profile. He stared at her image for a bit and put his phone back down on his nightstand. Instead, he walked over to his brown leather bag sitting on his reclining chair and retrieved a diary that had been in there since his Aunt Betty passed away.

He pulled back the covers and got into his cozy bed. Propping himself up with two pillows at his back, he took a deep breath before he opened the diary. The introduction already captivated him, as his eyes scanned from left to right with urgency to get to the next part. Before he knew it, it was three o'clock in the morning, and he was close to finishing. Finally done, he tossed the diary to one side of his bed. Then, sitting at the end of his bed hunched over, with his elbows on his thighs and hands covering his face, he began to cry.

It was Monday, August 20, 2018. Sam woke up to the bright light shining on his melancholy face. He put his hand up to shield his eyes.

"Rise and shine," Vida said as she pulled up the blinds. "I didn't expect you to sleep this late. Good thing I checked in on my niece and nephews."

"Vida, what are you doing here?"

"Would you prefer Tomi to be here?"

"I don't know what you mean by that," Sam said.

"She left as she saw me coming."

"She was here?" Sam asked. "I gave her the key for emergencies only."

"Apparently, every day is an emergency. Do you find it normal that she's here all the time? Since Sara left, she took it upon herself to come and go here as she pleases."

"I haven't noticed."

"Typical men. You don't notice anything. Does Kevin know she has the key to your house? It doesn't look good to her husband and outsiders if she is here all the time."

"I think Paolo is annoyed that you're here all the time. Plus, you have a two-year-old child."

"Oh, *that* you notice. I brought baby Lily with me. She's sleeping in your living room."

"That's not the point," Sam said, sitting up and looking at her dumbfounded.

"Well, my point is, you're my little brother. I have a duty to look after you and help you out; at least, until I don't have to worry about you and the kids anymore. Even if I have to carry my baby around with me. Look, I don't care if Tomi is your best friend, but she shouldn't be abandoning her husband to attend to you and your children all the time," Vida said while picking up his clothes from his chair to drop in his laundry basket. "I feel for Kevin. He wants children and she is running around like she's a single woman. Speaking of children, Jonny, Wallace, and Sopraffina all showered and dressed. I already fed them pancakes, eggs, and sausages." Sam's nostrils flared as he inhaled the sweet and salty aroma from his sister's cooking. Vida stopped tidying up his room to examine her brother.

"What?" Sam said, looking confusedly at his sister.

"Your eyes are red. Were you crying? Or did you not get enough sleep?"

He scanned his bed to find the black diary book sitting on the edge at the other end. He reached to grab it, examining it as if he realized it was not a dream, what he read regarding their Aunt Betty and their family roots.

"What is that?" Vida asked.

"I don't think you're ready for it," Sam said, looking at their aunt's diary. "Aunt Betty asked me to edit and publish it."

Vida extended her hand and said, "I'm not the sensitive one in this family. If you can handle it, I can definitely handle it. I've seen and been through a lot."

Sam got up and walked over to hug his sister. She stood frozen by his door, her face a picture of disbelief, as if she were not used to seeing this emotionally available brother of hers.

"Wow. Etta Kem has opened you up, hasn't she?"

"Thank you for everything you do for me and my kids," Sam said, ignoring his sister's statement about Etta. "Thank God Aunt Betty moved us away from that perverted man. She did it to protect you and all of us. I'm not sure if you're ready to read her diary."

She patted his back. "Don't worry. I'm a strong person." She pulled away and put out her hand to receive the diary. He handed it to her. "So this is what she wanted to talk to you about when she asked us to leave the room."

"One of the reasons," Sam said, softly.

Vida raised one of her eyebrows. "You're not going to tell me the other reason?"

"No," Sam said.

"All right. I bet I can guess what it is anyway." He eyed her curiously. "Go and shower while I check on the kids and read this. I left them in the living room with the baby. I left your breakfast on the kitchen table. Come down and eat when you're done."

Sam showered and dressed. Downstairs he was greeted by Sopraffina.

"Daddy, Daddy, I don't know what's happening with Aunt Vida. She's crying in our living room."

"She's fine. She's just reading something sad. Why don't you go read the books we bought in Chicago."

"Okay, Daddy." Sopraffina ran off to their family room.

Sam stood still with the word "Chicago" ringing in his ears. He pulled out his phone to check for text messages and phone calls. Nothing had changed, except for a few text messages and some missed calls from Tomi.

He walked into the living room to find Vida sitting next to her sleeping baby, sniffing and wiping her tears.

Jonny had left her a box of tissues. "Daddy, I don't know what Auntie Vida is reading, but it's making her cry. It's hard to watch."

"She's okay. Why don't you join your sister to read and practice your piano lesson? Wallace, how is your arm, son?"

"It still hurts, but I got lots of presents from Auntie Tomi," Wallace said. "I know she's making up for making me fall."

Sam noticed the opened Amazon packages in the living room.

"Look, Daddy. She got each of us an iPad."

"Yeah, we're getting rewards from Wallace's accident," Jonny said, his eyes wide with excitement.

"Boys, I don't really want you to use or play with those iPads."

"Oh, come on, Daddy. Everyone and their mama have one," Jonny said.

"We can read many books on them, Daddy," Wallace said.

"Fine. Let me set them up before you use them. Give them to me."

Jonny handed all three iPads to his father.

"May I open the rest of my presents?" Wallace asked.

"Sure. Take them to the family room."

After his kids left with all the packages, Sam asked his sister, "Are you okay?"

"Look at our beautiful mother and our handsome father, an Anglo woman and a Khmer man. I've forgotten how good they looked and how loving they were. I missed them so much," Vida said, crying. "Poor Mom. To know how she put up with the torrent of harsh criticism and ostracism from her relatives and community is just heartbreaking. And poor Dad, having white men taunt and harass him for daring to love a white woman. He was so brave. Thank goodness our grandfather was a policeman and accepted our father. He was their protector until his untimely death. We can't say the same about our grandmother. She was a weak woman. She chose her brother's side, after he sexually abused his own niece. But poor Aunt Betty. She gave up everything for us."

"Aunt Betty said her uncle had abused our mom, and her, and was about to do the same to you."

"I can't believe Steve Cotton is our great-uncle. That piece of trash. The vile things he does and says; talking about how there wouldn't be any population if there weren't rape or incest. He makes my blood boil. We better be careful. We need to consult Daniel regarding this publication. Cotton is a judge of the Supreme Court of North Carolina. He's powerful and has connections all over."

"That was a major reason she moved us to Uptown Chicago two years after our mom died after giving birth to me, following the death of our father," Sam said, with sadness in his eyes. "She told me not to blame myself for our mother's death—that I was not the unlucky child I claimed to be. Growing up, when I saw other children with their mothers and when the country celebrated Mother's Day, I tended to fall into depression. I often thought if she had not given birth to me, she would not have died. This broke Aunt Betty's heart. She had tried her best to convince me not to feel that way, as our mother was going through a very painful situation in her life. She reminded me that our mother loved me very much. She was heartbroken by our father's death but fought for my birth, and if she knew I was blaming myself for her death, she would not rest in peace."

"She's right, Sam," Vida said. "Our mother's death was related to the death of our father. I heard he went to Cambodia to find his parents and siblings. I did not know that he was murdered by the Khmer Rouge, along with a journalist. This is devastating news. We don't even know where his body is, as of today." Vida started to cry again, only quieting herself when her baby was stirring. "I'm so glad Aunt Betty kept this diary since she was a teenager to document her tragic life. It was probably the one thing that kept her sane for all those years. She had to put her family history and her trauma on paper; otherwise, it would have festered within her, every waking second. She confessed everything here."

A somber shadow took over Sam's and his sister's faces.

"She said that in 1981, when I was two, she decided to run away from Chapel Hill to Uptown Chicago. She heard that many immigrants from Southeast Asia had been placed there. She thought she would learn about them and expose us to our father's Khmer culture, language, and religion," Sam said, reflective.

"Yeah, it says here she bought a white and brown, three-story, German-styled home, built in 1896. I liked that house, but I hated the neighborhood," Vida said, as she read her aunt's diary.

"It was a nice house. I had great childhood memories there," Sam said.

"Not when those Cambodian gangsters bullied and beat you up," Vida reminded him.

"They were not gangsters. They didn't have a proper upbringing. They were finding their way in a new society that did not accept them."

"Look at you, all enlightened. I hated it back then when Aunt Betty would bring us to the Cambodian Association of Illinois at the old location on Lawrence Avenue and Winthrop Avenue. She was adamant about us learning the Khmer language, culture, religion, and history. When you turned eight years old in 1987, you got into fights with those Cambodian boys, who I presumed were gangsters. You had a bad cut on your forehead. I was livid. I was fourteen years old at the time, and I hated and was mad at everything. I hated the Cambodian community. I thought harshly of the people there. I begged Aunt Betty not to bring us to the community anymore."

Sam looked at his sister with judgmental eyes.

"Don't judge me. I was acting uppity. I, too, was a victim of my environment and was finding my way in society," Vida said to her brother.

"Anyway, where do you suppose she got the money to purchase that big house?" Sam asked. "We know her mother kept all the money when her father was killed in the line of duty. And our private school and college education; that is not cheap. Even if she worked, she needed another income to provide for us. "

"Aunt Betty left us a will. That might explain where she got it from. I left it with Daniel since he's the attorney in the family. We were supposed to get together to discuss it when Vincent comes back from his honeymoon."

Sam raised one of his eyebrows at his big sister.

"Yeah," she continued, "you were not the only one she spoke to separately. She said I'm the oldest, so I got to bring this news to all of you. I planned to tell you when you are free from the clutches of Tomi. That woman follows you everywhere. She's your friend, not Vincent's. He did not need to invite her to his wedding." Vida mumbled the last part.

"Vida, she's like a family friend now," Sam said.

"All right. I won't argue. Now go on and eat your breakfast," Vida said, as she continued to read the diary. Sam got up to go.

"Etta Kem?" Vida suddenly said.

Sam stopped and turned to his sister.

"No wonder she seems familiar to me," Vida said, looking up at her brother. "She's that young girl who smiled at you when we brought you back from the doctor. No wonder she seems familiar. Our house stood across from her and that chubby redhead boy she was always hanging out with. I think the Kems were one of the few Khmer families that resided on North Dover Street. There were more Cambodians on nearby Beacon, Malden, Lawrence, and Wilson streets. I remember when you stepped out of the car after having come back from the clinic, she was playing double dutch with her neighborhood friends on her front lawn. I remember she stopped to watch us across from her house. That girl was always looking curious at us, and always seemed happy. I was moody all the time and hated her sunny, smiley personality. I resented her being happy while I was feeling miserable."

Sam spaced out, as if vividly remembering that day when he stepped out of the car with a bandage on his right forehead. Etta cast a sympathetic gaze upon him and, as their eyes locked, her countenance blossomed into the most radiant smile. That smile ingrained itself deep within his heart, a memory he would forever treasure. It was a tender and sweet expression, full of warmth and kindness. Observing the young Khmer girl's cheerful wave and smile, his sister gently took his hand and guided him into the house. He recalled that his Aunt Betty, acknowledging her niece's impoliteness, turned to the little girl and waved, almost as if apologizing on Vida's behalf. Undeterred by Vida's behavior, the spirited Etta waved back at his Aunt Betty with a beaming smile, seemingly oblivious to his sister's ill-mannered conduct. That moment in time brought a smile to Sam's face at the current moment in time.

"Does she know you were that eight-year-old boy who had a crush on her when we lived across the street from her?"

Sam looked at his sister, embarrassed.

"Don't think I didn't know your eyes were following her every time she was outside playing."

"No, she has no clue."

"She doesn't remember living across from us or who we are?"

"No."

"Why didn't you tell her?"

"I didn't get a chance to," Sam said, regretfully.

"Are you going to tell her?"

"When the moment is right."

15

ETTA, CHICAGO

AUGUST 21, 2018

A few days had passed without any word from Sam, causing Etta's concern to deepen. She found herself trapped in a state of uncertainty, unsure of how to proceed. The idea of reaching out to him again weighed heavily on her mind, but she feared appearing needy or desperate. Etta understood that seeming too eager or clingy could potentially harm their relationship. However, her genuine worry for Sam and his kids' well-being tugged at her heart. Unsure of the next steps to take, she picked up her iPhone to consult Google. She typed in the search bar: "Should I call after not hearing for two days from a guy I dated?" The search results advised her to "move on" and that "life is too short to play guessing games in dating." The suggestion sounded reasonable to her. However, it was easier said than done, considering the connection they shared. Conflicting emotions swirled within her, leaving her feeling lost and unsure of how to navigate the situation.

She decided to text him one last time: "Hi, Sam. Is everything okay?"

She kept checking her iPhone while she worked, wondering why he hadn't reached out to her through a call or text. The silence felt disrespectful. Didn't he realize she was also concerned about what happened to Wallace? Especially since he broke his arm, wouldn't it be common courtesy for him to inform her about his well-being? Regardless of whether the boy was okay or not, didn't she have the right to know about his condition and what was happening with him and his family? How could Sam be so heartless? She believed they were on the path to becoming a committed couple, even discussing growing old together. What happened to those meaningful seven words he shared? Why was he ignoring her? Did his friend say something to him after she left? What had she done wrong?

A playful knock on her office door startled Etta, causing her furrowed brows to relax. "Daron, what's up?" she greeted him, grateful for the distraction.

"You tell me. We haven't seen or heard from you for a whole week. Didn't you get my calls and texts? Been busy, or what?" Daron quipped.

"I did get them, but I was too busy with work."

"Too busy to even text and say, 'Hey, I'm busy, asshole?'"

"Sorry," Etta let out a tired sigh, her exhaustion evident.

Daron's gaze softened as he studied her. "Are you going through depression or something? You look terrible."

Etta offered a sarcastic response. "Thanks."

Daron's concern deepened, and he leaned against her desk. "All right, what's going on? There's clearly more to it."

Etta hesitated, unsure of whether to confide in him. After a moment, she decided to open up. "Remember Sam?"

Daron's exasperation was palpable. "Oh, hell. Why am I still hearing his name? I thought we had settled this, Etta." Curiosity mixed with apprehension as Daron probed further. "All right, what happened? Spill it."

"I went on a…" Etta's voice trembled, betraying the fragility of her emotions. She paused, realizing how brittle she sounded. She straightened herself, consciously trying to regain her composure. Taking a deep breath, she willed herself to be strong and resist the urge to cry. She did not want to reveal her vulnerability to Daron, who often teased her. It was not something she was prepared to do.

"Did he hurt you?" Daron asked, his voice full of concern.

Etta remained silent, looking away.

"You have developed genuine feelings for this guy, haven't you?" Daron said, observing her.

Etta continued, her voice steadier this time, "I went on another date with him. And then, he invited me to his brother's wedding. I know it might seem fast, but I decided to go. I met his beautiful family, his glamorous female best friend, and her husband. Perhaps you know them; they're a power couple, big-shot real estate tycoons who mingle with famous and influential people, the Lims."

"Oh, yeah, we billionaires and influential folks all know each other," Daron said, rolling his eyes.

"I always thought you oligarchy assholes had a secret club where you meet up to decide who gets the last slice of the pie in the world!"

"Yeah, we know them. They are my parents' real estate competitors," Daron admitted.

"Anyway," Etta went on, "the wedding itself was stunning, and everyone looked absolutely beautiful. Sam and I danced, and we had an incredible time. That moment, as he gazed into my eyes, he said he wanted to grow old with me."

"That escalated quickly," Daron said.

"I thought it was a significant step, a sign that our relationship was progressing toward something more serious. How could he have gone from that to complete silence, as if our connection meant nothing?"

Etta paused, catching her breath, her voice laden with longing as she allowed herself to be transported back to that beautiful and tender moment.

Daron shook his head, a mix of empathy and concern broadcasted on his face. His words cut through the air, and Etta felt a bit uneasy as she heard his accusations. "Was he drunk when he said that?"

"No! That's what I like about him. He doesn't drink or smoke," Etta answered, sounding defensive. "It's hard to find a man who doesn't smoke and drink."

"That's because he's a loser."

"Can you stop being a jerk for a moment?"

"Sorry. Force of habit." Daron's tone softened, and he probed further, "Did you sleep with him?"

Etta's response was quick and firm, "No, I did not, but almost. We were in the midst of passion when his best friend came to fetch him. She said his son Wallace fell and broke his arm, so they both rushed off. I tried contacting him, but he didn't respond to me. It has been a few days now, and he hasn't responded to me at all. Not even a text to say, 'Everything is okay.' I don't understand him at all."

"I see why you have been ignoring my calls and texts. You've been busy dealing with your emotions about him.

You know what I think about all of this, though? You can't be so in love with this guy that you don't see him for what he is, a philanderer! You like to hear a guy say nice things to you, and those seven words alone got him into your house and in bed with you. That's what guys do. They have an ulterior motive. They say nice things to get you into bed with them. Why haven't you learned this?"

Etta felt her heart sink at Daron's words, but she was quick to defend her actions. "No, I don't think he's that type. He said, 'If I wanted to, I could have sex with anyone, but I feel connected to you.'"

"Oh, Etta, Etta! How can you let yourself be so easily deceived? That's the kind of line a guy uses when he's only interested in one thing. It's clear he lacks originality and experience in the dating world. I had hoped I had taught you better than to fall for such empty words."

"Wait a minute. Why would you have a problem with me sleeping with him when you made a Tinder profile for me? Those guys are strangers, too. I could just as easily end up with a philanderer or a serial murderer from Tinder as well. He could be pretending to be a normal person just to get into bed with me, too. Make it make sense."

"Well," Daron said, sweeping his hair back, "I was hoping you would find someone local, and we could check his background."

Etta raised her left eyebrow, showing her skepticism toward his excuse and her lack of conviction in his reasoning. "No amount of intimidation and questioning by friends and loved ones would deter a philanderer or murderer from doing what he does," Etta suggested. "Just like friends and families can't always be there to protect their loved ones from abusive partners."

"I would do anything within my power to protect you if I know you're in danger. But fine. Fine. Point taken. Let's not dwell on it. It's happened, and we can use it as a learning experience. Forget about him entirely. Erase him from your mind, as if he never existed." But that was just the thing. Etta found it impossible to get Sam out of her mind. She believed there was a connection between them, a shared feeling that couldn't be ignored. It seemed unlikely that he could be so cold, distant, and unkind without reason. He wasn't capable of that. There had to be some explanation for his silence, something that could shed light on why he hadn't acknowledged her attempts to reach out.

"It's time to put an end to this, Etta," Daron advised, as if he could discern her innermost thoughts. "Continuing down this path will only leave you with lasting emotional wounds, as you've experienced in your previous relationships. It's best for you to distance yourself from this situation and move on. He's unreliable and unworthy of your time and energy."

Etta looked at her friend, realizing he was giving her the same advice as Google—which confirmed her belief that she didn't need to ask friends for advice. She decided she would be better off searching online without judgment. She would simply ignore the advice if she didn't like what she heard.

"You deserve to be with someone who genuinely loves and values you," Daron added.

"Perhaps you're right," Etta reluctantly acknowledged. Yet, deep down, she didn't truly believe it. In her heart and mind, she held onto the hope that her connection with Sam would eventually prevail. She firmly believed he harbored genuine feelings for her, and she couldn't shake that conviction. Despite the doubts and uncertainties, Etta clung to the belief that somehow, against all odds, their paths would meet again.

"What do you mean, 'perhaps'? You know I'm right. Why don't we go out for a meal and take a look at your Tinder profile? Huh? I bet there are plenty of guys eagerly waiting for your response as we speak."

She gave him a side-eye look. "Yeah, about that. I actually deleted my account the very same day you created it."

"What? Why?"

"You know why."

"Fine. If you're not comfortable with it, we can find another way."

"No. It has to be on my terms."

"All right. Whatever."

Etta and Daron sat across from each other, enjoying their lunch at River Restaurant. As Etta glanced toward the bar, her fork paused midway to her mouth, her gaze fixed on the television screen. Intrigued, Daron followed her line of sight and witnessed a fervent protest unfolding, with the news ticker mentioning the University of North Carolina–Chapel Hill. The scene showed demonstrators forcefully removing a Confederate statue named *Silent Sam* on Monday night. Then it cut to a reporter questioning a sympathizer of the Confederate statue and then an opposer.

Daron turned his attention back to Etta, a mix of concern and warning in his voice. "You better not be going there."

"Ha! What reason would I have to go there?" Etta noticed Daron was studying her, but her gaze was fixed on an empty void, and she had been responding with monosyllabic answers like "yes," "no," and "I guess" to his attempts at conversation.

It was clear her mind was consumed by Sam's absence. "Etta," Daron called out to her.

"Yeah?"

"Remember your relationships with your high school boyfriend, Thomas O'Donnell, and college fiancé, Jack Edlin."

"Yeah? What about them?"

"You went on like this for a long time. It's hard to see you this detached," Daron said. "I remember how time healed your wounds back then. I hope it comes just as fast this time, because I want you to move on and be happy again."

But Etta's connection with Sam seemed to evoke a deeper longing, despite their brief time together.

She went back to the office after her lunch with Daron. Work kept her occupied, until the day had passed and Daron had come to walk her home from work. Now she had not heard anything he had been saying as they made their way to Michigan Avenue.

"Do you remember that?" Daron asked.

"Huh?" She turned to look at him as they walked.

"You haven't been listening to anything I've said since we left your office, huh?"

Etta looked at him with confusion.

"Just as well. I'll pretend to be your bodyguard and not say anything anymore. You can walk in peace," Daron said.

They strolled along the streets north of Michigan, and just a few shops away from reaching Wacker Drive, Etta gazed at the intersection where Sam had crashed into her car.

Out of nowhere, a woman in her forties, dressed in black pants and a rocker's T-shirt, called out to Etta, "Miss, you look like you could use a reading."

"Oh, hell no. This could be potential trouble. Come on, pick up the pace," Daron urged Etta.

The woman pressed closer, her tone earnest. "A man you're in love with hasn't called you back."

Intrigued and taken aback, Etta halted her steps. She slowly turned to face the woman and responded, "Excuse me?"

"Oh, come on, Etta. Let's go," Daron urged. "She's just trying to make a buck. That's just a generic line she's using on every woman passing by. Hell, half of the women in the greater Chicago area haven't heard back from their dates."

The woman persisted, claiming, "A man you're in love with hasn't called or texted you back. He has a good reason."

Full of curiosity, Etta asked skeptically, "And what reason could that possibly be?"

Daron interjected, frustration evident in his voice, "Seriously, Etta? It's just a sales tactic. You know better than to fall for this." He turned to the woman pestering them. "Go away. Stop taking advantage of a woman in a vulnerable state," Daron firmly expressed. "Come on, Etta. Resist the temptation to fall for a scam."

The woman, undeterred, extended an invitation, saying, "Why don't you come inside, and I'll offer you a free reading. I can tell you why this handsome man can't reach out to you at the moment."

Daron gave Etta a disappointed look, recognizing she was being drawn in despite his warnings. "Oh boy, she's reeling her in now," he muttered, his concern mounting. Daron continued to voice his feelings, "You're going to find this to be a waste of time. Stop giving in to people who tell you what you want to hear, for fuck's sake. When will you learn, Etta?"

Etta countered, "It's free. What have I got to lose?"

"Time, Etta. Valuable time."

"I've got time."

Daron sighed, looking frustrated by Etta's persistence. "Nothing is truly free, Etta. She'll want money after she leads you into the next phase of her reading."

"I don't believe you," Etta dismissed his concerns.

Daron, looking helpless, tried one last time to reason with her. "Look, I'm skeptical of any predictions based on cartomancy. You should be too."

Etta chose to ignore his warnings, her curiosity overpowering his cautionary words.

Daron, exasperated, threw his hands up in frustration, as if realizing he could not prevent Etta from proceeding with the reading.

The woman's smile widened as she guided Etta up the narrow stairs and into her room, which featured a round table placed in the center. Daron reluctantly followed. Contrary to the clichéd portrayal of reading rooms in television shows and movies, this space exuded a serene atmosphere. It was tastefully decorated, devoid of excessive trinkets that supposedly connected to the spiritual world. The air was teeming with a pleasant aroma of incense and candles, creating a soothing ambiance. Daron took a moment to explore the room, examining the photographs and paintings adorning the walls.

Meanwhile, the woman motioned for Etta to take a seat at the table. With a graceful gesture, she pulled out a deck of cards and began shuffling them. The woman spoke gently, "Please take a deep breath and try to relax your body and mind."

"What is this, yoga class?" Daron remarked sarcastically.

Etta intervened, trying to defuse the tension. "Please ignore him," she said to the woman.

The woman continued, "Now, clear your mind of all other thoughts and focus solely on the question you want to ask," she instructed Etta.

"Yeah, she's convinced she's in love with a serial killer," Daron interjected, his tone full of cynicism.

Maintaining her composure, the woman responded calmly, "Would you like to wait outside, sir?"

"So you can take advantage of her vulnerability? No," Daron said.

"It's just that the reading is more effective—that is, insightful, helpful even—if she is relaxed and focused on the issue. It's a function of synchronicity, if you will," said the woman in a soft, soothing voice.

Daron rolled his eyes, but did not utter another word. Etta picked her six cards. The woman took and laid them before Etta. She turned the first one over.

"Ah, card one is Temperance," the woman said.

"What does that mean?" Etta said, anticipating her explanation.

"It reveals how you feel about yourself, my dear. You want peace and harmony in your life," the woman said.

"Doesn't everyone," Daron chimed in, picking up a scented candle and smelling it.

"You have been through some rough times…" continued the woman. As if sensing that Daron would make fun of this general statement, she and Etta turned to tell him with their eyes to zip it, which he gestured himself, zipping his lips as if to allow this woman to indulge Etta, "but peace will be restored."

The woman flipped over another card and said, "Card two is The Devil."

"The Devil?" Etta asked.

"It suggests what you want most at this time you can't have, but its forbidden nature only makes you want it more. You want passion and gratification, but you must be careful where you get it," the woman said.

"You don't need a psychic to tell you that, Etta," Daron chimed in again.

The women ignored him. She turned over another card and said, "Card three is The Hanged Man. It indicates your fears—fears of letting go and making decisions."

"Yeah, I'll give you that one," Daron said. "She tends to be very indecisive when it comes to her social life. Her idea of making decisions is consulting Google. Which is free, by the way," Daron cupped his hands around his mouth to form a makeshift megaphone with his hands as if to amplify the "free" advice from Google. "I don't think she'll ever get by without it."

If Etta wasn't so focused on what the woman's answer was to her problem with Sam, she would have bantered with her friend. *I'm not indecisive, I just can't make my mind up.*

The woman continued, "Sometimes we must have the strength to let go to attract new positive possibilities in our life."

Daron stopped reading one of the books on divination and metaphysical topics, which he picked up from the bookshelves behind Etta. His ears perked up.

"You are in a place of limbo and indecision right now. It's time for you to decide."

Etta nodded her head as if the cards spoke to her.

The woman turned another card. "Card four is The High Priestess. It reveals what's going right for you—that all lines of communication are open. It has always been with you. You just need to tap into it. Your intuition is your guide. Listen to it—listen to it carefully and the secret you want will be revealed to you."

Daron's thick eyebrows knitted together and he said, "Her intuition can't be all that good if she insists on chasing after a philanderer, or a serial killer for that matter."

"Ah, behold card five, The Chariot!" The woman continued without missing a beat. "It seems to be a formidable force opposing you, my dear. This card serves as a gentle reminder to steer clear of arrogance and prevent your ego from expanding. After all, no one likes a know-it-all. It's a reminder to watch your temper. Engaging in aggressive bullying behavior will only send you hurtling backward on your journey. However, if this description doesn't quite resonate with you, then exercise caution, for there may be someone lurking in the shadows who embodies these traits and poses a potential setback for you. So, stay vigilant and keep those chariot wheels on the right track!" The woman and Etta turned to look at Daron.

"What? You're not believing any of this shit, are you?" Daron said, dumbfounded.

The seemingly wise woman pressed on, her voice carrying a sense of purpose. "The Chariot beckons you to embrace a period of movement and transformation. It signifies that conflicts, my dear, shall ultimately yield to triumph. So, do not surrender! It is of utmost importance that you stay resolute in your pursuit of dreams. Remember, giving up is not an option. Let The Chariot propel you forward on your extraordinary journey!"

The woman continued, "And now, finally, behold card six, the illustrious Judgment card! It signifies a crucial moment of reflection, where you take stock of your life and bid farewell to an era or phase. But fear not, for this ending brings forth a wondrous array of fresh opportunities. Among them lies the prospect of uniting with your handsome man. But unfortunately, some pesky hurdles and barriers currently impede his connection with you. However, for the mere price of five hundred dollars, I can liberate you from this obstacle, paving the way for you to be with your soulmate."

"And there it is," Daron said, as if he had been waiting to get to what he had said all along. He dragged Etta's hand out of the chair and out of that building quicker than the woman could yell, "Okay. Four hundred.

Three hundred. Two hundred. I'm not going lower than a hundred." They kept on walking and never looked back. Etta suddenly slowed her pace as she experienced a pang in her heart when she reached the intersection of Michigan and Wacker, where her fateful accident with Sam happened. She stared at the location where she stopped her car, a place where she came face to face with the handsome Sam. Daron pushed her along before the light turned red.

That evening, Etta received a call from a man named Adam Brent who claimed he was the father of Suzan. "Oh, she was one of the students in my friend's class when I substituted. How are you, sir?"

"I'm doing very well. Listen. I'm an executive director of planning and design services at a university. We are looking to recruit great talents to meet our donor's expectations. My daughter told me you are one of the up-and-coming architects in Chicago, and that I should reach out to you."

"Oh? Thank you. Thank you very much. I take it your department doesn't have its own architects and engineers?"

"We do. Our team here is diverse and innovative; but unfortunately, our greatest donor is very particular about the design of this building. She doesn't like any of the designs our internal architects have offered, so we are thinking outside of the campus."

Etta laughed at his intended joke, thinking he must be from one of the universities.

"As it says on the engineering and construction website of our university, our vision is to preserve, create, and transform the campus environment to enhance our state's experience. So we would like to invite you to visit the campus for one day and offer your pitch the next day. The donor will be present to see your pitch. How does that sound?"

"That sounds great! I would be delighted and honored."

"My daughter said you have great artistic skills and are an expert in your field. I understand you own your design firm. That's impressive. Do you do modern as well as classic designs?"

"Yes."

"We are looking for a great pitch. I haven't mentioned... our donor is a billionaire alumnus who wanted to add a historical building to house books, arts, and other artifacts relating to specific areas of our history. Would you be able to meet with us on the morning of August 23rd?"

"Sure," said Etta, realizing she said yes too quickly. But then again, she never said no to a business opportunity.

"Fantastic. I'll have my secretary book a flight, hotel, and rental car for you. She'll send you a travel itinerary and details of the project."

"That sounds great," Etta said with excitement in her voice.

"I'm looking forward to meeting you and what you have to show us."

"I'm grateful for the opportunity. I can't wait to visit the campus and show you my ideas," she said with genuine enthusiasm.

Etta felt excited about keeping her mind occupied with work to take her mind off of Sam—that is, until she received the itinerary and project details. Her body tensed up. She put her hand on her chest, as though holding onto her heart from leaping out. "What? Chapel Hill-

University of North Carolina?" she found herself saying out loud.

Her heart beat faster than before. If she hadn't already sat down she would have fallen on her chair. Many thoughts ran through her mind. *So much for not thinking about Sam.* Not only did she have to focus on putting on a great pitch to win this project, but also she was afraid of running into him. She was on tenterhooks regarding both situations. *What am I going to do if I run into Sam? I don't want him to think I was stalking him. Should I back out of this project? No. I made a commitment to Mr. Brent. After all, personal integrity and honoring my promises are values I uphold.*

"Oh my God!" Etta said out loud, slapping her forehead with her eyes wide open and jaw agape. Could the cartomancer be correct? Is this the "new positive possibilities" and "wondrous array of fresh opportunities" the woman was interpreting from the cards? Nah. Etta shook her head dismissively. This is just a coincidence.

Considering how she had always clung to the belief that somehow, against all odds, their paths would meet again, this was simply the law of attraction. What she put out in the universe was coming back to her. She did not actually believe in cartomancy or psychic reading, as it lacked scientific evidence. She noticed the woman used card reading to make general statements that could apply to anyone; and most of all, she relied on the subject's own confirmation bias to give the illusion of accuracy of whatever she was feeling or going through. Etta and Daron were on the same page with that one all along, and she told herself now that she only went through with it for a distraction and entertainment.

Etta contemplated her dilemma about taking the job and the possibility of not knowing what to say or how to react in case she ran into Sam. Most of all, she did not want him to think she was stalking him. She wondered if she should confide in her friend Daron, but anticipated he might advise her to withdraw from the situation altogether, assuring her he had enough business clients and connections to sustain her firm indefinitely.

With a mix of hesitation and determination, Etta reached for her phone and dialed a 773 area code. Randy answered on the first ring, his voice brimming with curiosity.

"What's up, Etta?" he greeted her. "I've not heard from you for a while."

"Hi, Randy. Are you busy?" Etta asked, her voice uncertain.

"Nope, I'm in yoga class, shooting my YouTube videos," Randy replied.

Etta took a deep breath and gathered her thoughts. "What do you think about taking a trip to Chapel Hill, North Carolina?" she finally asked.

Randy's playful tone emerged. "Oh my. Are we stalking a certain someone?" he teased.

Etta quickly clarified, "No, we are not. Listen, a father of one of my students, whose class I had substituted for, asked me for a pitch. He's an executive director of planning and design services at the University of North Carolina–Chapel Hill."

"Nice. Congratulations. But don't they have their own architects and engineers?" Randy inquired.

"They do, but the donor doesn't like any of their ideas. Anyway, listen, I said yes before I found out it was at UNC–Chapel Hill," Etta explained.

"Hmm," Randy contemplated the situation. "Can you back out?"

Etta sighed. "You know I can't do that. Being indecisive in life is one thing, but when it comes to business I can't. I must march on and do what I have to do."

"I see," Randy sympathized. "Oh well, you're stuck then."

Etta expressed her concern, "I'm afraid that a certain someone might get the wrong idea and think I went there on purpose. Well, I kind of am, considering I put the idea out there in the universe through my prayers."

"Really?"

"Yeah, I kept saying in my mind that I want to see him again."

"Hmm," Randy said, as if trying to gauge the situation. "What are the chances of you bumping into him?"

"I don't know, but I don't want that awkwardness if I do run into him," Etta confessed.

"Wow. You want to see him but don't want to bump into him. You don't really know what you want, do you?"

"I want to see him, but not this way," Etta said.

"Say no more. You want me to be your wingman?"

Confused, Etta asked, "What?"

Randy corrected himself, "I meant your alibi. But who cares? You have to make a living, don't you?"

Etta hesitated, contemplating the potential consequences. "Well... anyway, don't tell Daron or Rochelle, not until we get back."

"Etta, don't you ever notice that you do whatever the hell you want, regardless of what other people tell you? Even if you are a people pleaser and want everyone to like you?"

Etta paused, realizing the truth in Randy's words. "I guess," she admitted.

"I like that in you. Let's do it," Randy declared, offering his support.

"Great! I'll ask Kristina to arrange a room for you at the same hotel and book you on the same flight. While she's at it, she can also upgrade my flight to first class so that we can sit together," Etta replied, feeling relieved to have Randy's support.

"I'm excited!" exclaimed Randy. "I've never been to Chapel Hill before."

Etta smiled, sharing in Randy's enthusiasm. "Yeah, you and me both," she replied, feeling a sense of anticipation for the journey ahead.

16

SAM, CHAPEL HILL
AUGUST 22, 2018

In the early morning, Sam pulled into his sister's driveway beside a grand, brick-exterior home. Vida emerged with baby Lily on her hip, her rosy cheeks stretching into a smile as she saw her uncle and cousins stepping out of the van. Sam gently lifted Sopraffina down from her seat. He greeted his sister and little niece by kissing them on their cheeks.

"Hey, baby Lily!" her cousins called out as they approached her, squeezing her chubby cheeks and legs while clutching their iPads and carrying their backpacks. Baby Lily reached out eagerly, kicking and screaming with excitement.

"All right, kids, head inside. Your cousins are having breakfast, if you want to join them. I'll come in shortly after I speak with your father," Vida said, watching them walk toward the house. "They seem glued to those iPads, don't they? So much for not allowing devices to babysit your children, eh?" She turned back to her brother.

"It's all thanks to Tomi," Sam said, sarcastically.

"Yeah, I was there when they opened the presents. You're giving that woman too much freedom with your children," Vida remarked.

Sam ignored her comment. "Could you watch them today and tomorrow? After teaching, I'll be meeting with some candidates at the nearby coffee shop, and then return to pick them up. I'll let you know when I am done."

"Be careful out there. Stay clear of McCorkle Place. It might become a place of violence following the toppling of *Silent Sam* on Monday night. Confederate apologists are extremely upset and may cause trouble in the area. I would hate it so much if we were to find out that the

Canadian sculptor John A. Wilson shares our family tree on our mother's side," Vida said.

It was bad enough sharing the same first name as *Silent Sam.* "I'm sure they wouldn't like us half-breeds either," Sam said, waving at his sister. "Anyway, it was fine yesterday. I'm sure it's fine today."

"About your interviews, I don't see why you need a nanny when I'm available and capable of helping out," Vida called out after him, as he was about to get into his van. "They are in class most of the time anyway."

He stopped and turned back around to face his sister. "I appreciate your offer, but you have three children and a husband," Sam reminded her. "Besides, I might not get out of the university in time to pick them up from school. I need someone to collect them, watch them at home, and feed them."

"Three extra children won't be a problem," Vida insisted. "There are too many crazy people out there."

"Family members are just as crazy. You just never know," Sam quipped, referring to their mother's uncle.

"Not our new generation families. That reminds me, did you discuss the potential publication issues of Aunt Betty's diary with Daniel?"

"He was busy. We agreed to talk about it later," Sam replied.

"I see. Also, I've been meaning to ask you. How's Etta?" Vida inquired. "You haven't mentioned her since the wedding. I notice you're talking and spending more time with Tomi than with the woman you're dating." Sam stayed silent. "Remember the woman who made you smile and happy? Don't think I didn't notice the way you looked at her at the wedding. Something never changed," Vida said, smirking, as she recalled the eight-year-old Sam looking out the window at the six-year-old Etta.

He hesitated before replying, "I don't know. I haven't spoken to her since Wallace's accident." He extended his hand to baby Lily, who reached for him in return. He held her up to the sky. She cooed and laughed, and he lowered her back to chest level to kiss her on her cute cheek before handing her back to her mother.

"What? What happened? Did you two have a fight?" Vida asked, placing her little toddler back on her hip.

"I'm not sure."

"What do you mean you're not sure?"

His face dropped and he didn't say anything.

"Sam?" Vida asked. "She didn't text or call you?"

"No."

"That doesn't make sense. She seemed to be smitten with you as well. That's not an action of someone who cares about you. Why didn't you reach out to her?"

"I was busy. I tried calling her the other day but…"

"But you got distracted?"

"Yes."

"Is Tomi one of your distractions?"

"Vida," Sam said, looking at his sister with annoyance.

"What's going on between you and Tomi? Are you two having an affair?" Vida fumed.

"Hold on. Please don't cheapen me or her like that."

"I take that as a no?"

"No. We're definitely not having an affair. How could you possibly even think that? She's my best friend."

"That is good to know. I don't know about her, but at least I know you're not having an affair with her. I've never had a best friend of the opposite sex before, so I'm not familiar with the dynamics. Do male and female friends typically act this closely and talk this frequently?"

"She is a friendly person, Vida."

"She's awfully too familiar with you. I don't see her acting like that with her other male friends. But what I wanted to know is, are you interested in her romantically?"

"No!" Sam said, sternly.

"Then you need to set boundaries with her. For goodness sake, she's a married woman. Back to Etta. What is going on between you and her, then?"

Sam stood quietly, lost in thought.

"Look, if you're not interested in Etta anymore, you need to be frank with her and let her know before she falls any deeper. Sopheap told me the poor girl has got her heart broken twice. For God's sake, if you're breaking up with her, let her know."

"That's just the thing," Sam said, his arms wrapped over his chest and looking down at his feet, as his back leaned against his car.

"What thing?" Vida asked, switching baby Lily to the other side of her hip.

"I'm crazy about her, but I think I moved too fast, to the point of neglecting my son."

"That is very drastic, moving quickly to not moving at all. Are you feeling guilty because of what happened to Wallace?"

"It scared me. I think I scared her, too. With my confession."

"What confession?"

"That I want to grow old with her," Sam said, embarrassed.

"Aww. You are already seeing yourself with her and imagining yourself spending your life with her. That is very romantic. What did she say in response to that?"

"She was receptive and joyful," Sam said.

"Did she say you were moving too fast?"

"Not in those words," he replied.

"In what words then?"

"That we have many more days, months, and years to get to know each other."

"Was this after your confession?"

"No, it was in response to me thinking about the kids as I was walking her home that night after the wedding."

"Oh, you silly goose. She said that to protect her heart. Also, she was just letting you know that the last thing she wanted was to come between you and your kids.

She doesn't expect to be your number one priority over your children."

"She did mention she liked that I love and care for my children."

"See? So she's saying that regardless of days, months, or years, she'll be there. She knows you love your children, and about the children having to adjust to her being in your life. She accepts that she'll always come second, third, or whatever, but you got scared because you were opening up and expressing your love to her quicker than expected. You didn't do that with Sara Berg, your ex-wife. And Wallace's accident made you feel guilty for including Etta in your heart. You're afraid she might dominate it. Since Sara had already abandoned the children, which she did not fight for in the custody hearing, you're afraid that a new woman in your life might mess up your children's minds. Am I right?"

Sam averted his eyes to baby Lily, who was cooing and laughing as if she was in on the conversation.

"You can love Jonny, Wallace, and Sopraffina and still have a place for Etta in your heart. By the way, what took you so long to get back to the hotel after you walked her home anyway?"

A faint pink color spread across his face and neck.

Vida gasped, "You did not…"

"No, but we almost," he said, shyly.

"Tomi stopped you, didn't she?"

Sam didn't say anything.

"How did she know where to find Etta's home anyway? Did Etta tell her where she lives?"

"No, I think I said in passing that Etta lives in one of those townhomes in the Riverview neighborhood. She probably asked the front desk for her address."

"Hmm. I am wondering if Wallace's accident was done on purpose."

"Vida, that's a wild accusation. You must have evidence to back that up. I know her. She wouldn't do that."

"I guess a woman's intuition doesn't count, considering when I saw her busy freaking out with you walking Etta home rather than helping her drunk husband to their room."

Sam didn't say anything in response, but looked pensive.

"For heaven's sake. You need to call Etta and straighten things out. How long has it been?" Vida said, starting to count the days after the wedding with her fingers. "Nineteen, twenty, twenty-one, twenty-two. Oh, Sam! The poor girl is probably wondering what she did wrong to warrant this long silent treatment. What do the young people call it, ghosting? You need to call her. Rectify this now!"

Sam's eyes, not focusing on the road ahead, seemed distant, lost in reveries of all the moments he shared with Etta. He did not even notice that he had arrived at the school parking lot. He pulled into his spot and paused for a moment. He took a deep sigh before gently banging his head against his wheel, muttering, "Stupid, stupid," as if to punish himself for his action or inaction with Etta. He looked up from the wheel of his car through the windshield with sadness and longing in his eyes—longing to hear Etta's voice and feel her presence once again. He knew he needed to explain himself for not calling her. At the same time, why hadn't she called or texted him? Was she mad at him for running from her home abruptly?

He exited the van and slung his messenger bag over his shoulder. As he made his way to the campus, he pulled out his phone and began typing, "Hi, Etta. Can we t..." when a call from Tomi interrupted him. He stared at

Tomi's number and furrowed his eyebrows, wondering if his sister was right that Tomi was trying to sabotage his relationship with Etta. Surely this was just a coincidence. She wouldn't know that he was in the process of texting Etta. Furthermore, she couldn't possibly have romantic feelings for him. If anything, she might feel jealous or fearful of being abandoned due to a potential shift in the friendship dynamic now that Etta entered the picture. That must be it, he thought.

"Tomi, I can't talk right now. I'm on my way to class," Sam said.

"It'll only take a minute," Tomi insisted from the other end.

"Okay, if it's quick."

"I have been thinking about this since you told me you were hiring a nanny slash maid to look after the children. My maid can pick them up and drop them off at my house," Tomi offered. "She can cook for them and help them do their homework. You can come and get them whenever. This way, you don't have to worry about their well-being and time while you are teaching."

"No, I can't ask you to do that," Sam replied.

"I'm happy to help," Tomi insisted.

"While I appreciate your offer, I need to handle this myself," Sam responded firmly.

"Come on, Sam," Tomi urged in a nagging voice.

"No, Tomi. I really have to go," Sam said, and he ended the call.

Before he knew it, Sam passed by the pedestal of the statue called *Silent Sam*, which was commissioned by the United Daughters of the Confederacy. He stopped to look at it. This was the first time he had gotten a good look at it without the armed soldier perched on top, which, according to its apologists, had been a symbol of the South's "noble heritage," honoring veterans of the war. The day before, while reading UNC–Chapel Hill's Twitter post regarding the removal of the Confederate monument by protesters, he saw a commenter suggesting that *Silent Sam* symbolized young men from the school who joined the army to protect "their home and family from the threat of invasion from the North." However, the general consensus viewed the statue as representing violence, hate, and racism—a symbol of white supremacy and caste system propaganda. It conveyed a message to black Americans that, despite the abolition of slavery, those in power could still assert dominance and terrorize them through means such as Jim Crow laws and systemic racism, reinforcing a social order that had no place at a university that prided itself on inclusion, diversity, dignity, equality, and justice for all.

That chapter of America's horrific history weighed heavily on Sam's mind. As he continued to make his way to Greenlaw Hall, his thoughts of Etta shifted his emotions. Concerned about the long silence that had strained their relationship, he felt nervous about whether she would still speak with him as he reached for his phone in his pocket. He pressed on Etta's number to call her; however, it kept ringing. It just kept ringing with no option to leave a message. Confused, he texted her. His message was simple: "Hi, Etta. I hope you are doing well."

At that moment, he arrived at the Old Well, a symbol of beauty as envisioned by Edwin Alderman, the university's president, whose own life was marked by grief and loss, having endured the passing of his wife and children. In 1897, he undertook the transformation of the "squalid and ramshackle" wooden hut that once covered the campus water source into a grand rotunda with columns and a copper dome, inspired by the Temple of Love in Versailles. The Old Well has been a subject of discussion and writing throughout its history, undergoing various reconstructions over the years. However, its beauty and magic remained, drawing students to drink from it for good luck as they began their university journey and upon graduation. As Sam stopped by the fountain, his gaze was intense and concentrated, indicating his wish to meet and speak to Etta again.

17

ETTA, CHAPEL HILL

AUGUST 22 & 23, 2018

It had been three days going on four and Etta still had not heard from Sam. Her friends and colleagues could not understand what she saw in him in the first place. Google agreed with them: best to cut her losses and move on. It was easier said than done; after all, they did not feel what she felt, and they did not know what she knew about him, which was not much. But he seemed to have feelings for her and they had a spiritual connection. Her heart told her he probably was busy being attentive to his children. That was one of the qualities she found admirable in him—his devotion to his children. To see a man taking custody of his children, loving, and caring for them unconditionally warmed her heart. It made him sexy. If she had to come second to them, she'd be fine with it. As Etta's mind wandered, she couldn't help but think about Tomi, his best friend, and the strange incident that occurred between them. The memory of the night Tomi showed up at her door, banging on it like a maniac and giving her a venomous stare, played in her mind. It was an odd encounter that she hadn't shared with anyone. Etta had dismissed it as Tomi's deep concern for her best friend's child. Perhaps Tomi didn't handle stressful situations well. After all, a child had broken his arm, which was undoubtedly a distressing experience. On top of that, discovering that the child's father was in the process of making love to a woman whom he has just met may have further complicated matters for Tomi. Despite the confusion, Etta couldn't understand why Sam hadn't reached out to her. She longed to know if Wallace was okay and if their relationship was still intact. Before allowing frustration to consume her, Etta found herself making more excuses for Sam's silence, trying to rationalize his lack of communication.

After a smooth flight from O'Hare International Airport, Etta and Randy landed at Durham International Airport in Raleigh, North Carolina on the evening of August 22. They quickly collected their luggage and proceeded to pick up a rental car for their stay. The hotel they had chosen was conveniently located near the university, allowing them to settle in quickly.

Since they had arrived late in the evening and Etta had an early morning meeting with the executive director of planning and design services, they decided not to venture far from the hotel. Instead, they opted to have dinner at a nearby restaurant, enjoying a relaxing meal before calling it a night. Etta wanted to ensure she was well rested and prepared for her important meeting the following day.

Etta found herself unable to sleep, her mind preoccupied with a whirlwind of thoughts and emotions. Anxiety dominated her. It could have been the unfamiliarity of the bed or the mounting nervousness surrounding both her personal concerns with Sam and the upcoming pitch she had to deliver. Instead of lying in bed, restlessly tossing and turning, she decided to channel her energy into something productive.

Etta dove into her work, preparing for the upcoming meeting. Etta already understood the client vis-à-vis the university's background, vision, and goals for the project, based on her emails and conversations with them over the phone. She had conducted her market research, and with the help of her team, they armed her with information and data to develop her design inspiration, budget, and feasibility analysis, as well as sustainability and green building practices. Her team with their expertise supported her in this endeavor, and she had already meticulously listed their titles, biographies, credentials, and experiences in one of the presentation slides. Although she conducted some Google searches of the site, her team provided her with a site analysis based on their research and physical site visits. Her upcoming visit and walk-through would further enhance her understanding of the project site, including its location, surroundings, topography, climate, and relevant regulations or restrictions, enabling her to create her presentation with high-quality visualizations that would bring her concepts to life.

The hours slipped away, and she completed her work, but she was able to get a few hours of sleep.

As the morning sun began to illuminate the city, Etta found herself energized by adrenaline. She took a refreshing shower and carefully selected her two favorite attires for the meeting. After calling Randy to see if he wanted to join her for breakfast and help her pick out her outfit, she placed an order for room service.

The hotel staff delivered their breakfast orders just as Randy walked over to Etta's room. Etta generously tipped the man and sat down to enjoy her breakfast with Randy. After they finished eating, they left the trays with empty plates and glasses outside Etta's door. The lingering aroma of coffee, saltiness of sausages, and sweet pancakes still lightly wafted through the cool room.

Etta picked up her two outfits, still on their hangers, and held them for Randy to see. "What do you think? Should I go with ankle length pantsuit or pencil skirt suit?"

Looking up from the couch where he was sitting and reading the hotel magazine, he said, "The pantsuit says elegant but powerful."

"That's why they call it a power suit," Etta said, smiling and running into the bathroom.

"So how do I look?" Etta asked after coming out of the bathroom.

"Perfect," Randy said.

"Thanks. So what are you going to do today?" She asked, walking over to grab her thin laptop to place inside her black tote bag.

"I want to come to the university with you," Randy stated, while reading something from the hotel magazine. "Chapel Hill campus looks pretty and historical," he said, lifting up the section of the magazine to show the stunning image of the iconic Old Well surrounding by greenery and azaleas in bloom.

Etta paused, considering Randy's proposal, as she put on her pearl-studded earrings. She pulled out two pairs of shoes, contemplating her options. "Why? Don't you want to take the SUV to explore the city, try out some local cuisine, and vlog about our experiences to your followers when we return home?" she questioned, curious about his change of plans.

"I already gave them a taste of where we went last night," Randy mentioned, causing Etta to pause in her shoe selection.

"Oh, no!" Etta exclaimed, looking at Randy with concern.

Randy shrugged it off casually. "Don't worry about it. Rochelle and Daron never watch my vlogs. They're more into Facebook. Facebook is for old people," he quipped, trying to put her mind at ease, as he nonchalantly flipped through the magazine. He got bored and pulled out his iPhone.

Etta couldn't help but point out, "We're practically in our forties."

Randy chuckled confidently. "Don't you know thirty is the new twenty? We've got more than a few years to go. But whatever; you and I age well. People even say I look twenty-something. Anywho, don't worry. I won't post anything while we're here. I don't think they follow me on Instagram, Twitter, Snapchat, or YouTube, so we're good."

Etta held up a pair of blue pumps in her left hand and tan ones in her right hand.

"Tan will give your blue ankle pants power suit a chic look," he said. She took his advice and put on the tan pumps.

"You're right," she said as she twisted and turned in front of the full-length mirror.

"Oh, no," Randy said.

"What is it?" Etta said, turning to Randy.

"Something is going on at the campus. We are going to have to be careful," Randy said, as he looked at his app that warned people not to visit or go to certain areas. He then started scrolling through his Twitter feed.

"Oh, you mean the protests. That's sweet of you to be concerned," Etta remarked. "You don't have to walk with me there if you're scared."

Randy smiled. "Shouldn't you be concerned as well?"

"Well, I have a job to do. I was told that I would be escorted through the campus," Etta explained.

Randy pondered the situation. "Isn't it typical of humans? We create apps to warn us about dangerous areas, but then we use them to march right toward them," he mused, scrolling through tweets.

"Yeah, like a moth to a flame," Etta remarked, agreeing with him. She couldn't ignore the fact that he might be referring to her and Sam. The idea of coming to Chapel Hill had weighed heavily on her mind—how Daron would pass judgment on her decision to venture into a forbidden town and grow intimately connected to someone who had distanced himself from her for four days now. "Nevertheless," she continued, "I had anticipated the protests would have subsided by now."

"No. There's still tension there. Seriously, though. Security or not; you shouldn't be going there by yourself. I'll be brave and walk with you to the university."

"Again, that's sweet of you," Etta said, as she picked up her Canon camera to put in her tote bag. His concern touched her, and she acknowledged his sweetness with a soft smile, as they walked out the door.

Randy, catching the sentiment, responded with a playful yet sincere comment, "I know I'm sweet."

Etta playfully rolled her eyes, appreciating his attempt to lighten the mood. She replied, teasingly, "All right, don't turn into Daron on me. I can only handle one Daron."

Randy chuckled, as they made their way down the stairs, assuring her, "I'm nothing like that meanie.

Anyway, the people you're meeting with would call you if they sense danger, right?"

"Right," Etta said.

It had been three tumultuous days since the protesters successfully toppled the controversial *Silent Sam* statue. The repercussions of this act had reverberated throughout the University of North Carolina, as discussions and debates raged on regarding the statue's fate. The university's boards found themselves under immense pressure, grappling with the decision of whether to reinstate the statue with proper historical context, replace it with a monument honoring a significant black figure, or consign it to a museum.

Etta, ever the avid reader and seeker of knowledge, had diligently followed the developments surrounding the bronze Confederate soldier. She was well aware of the nationwide movement to remove Confederate monuments, as well as the fierce resistance from those who believed their history and heritage were being erased. However, she also couldn't ignore the disheartening reality of individuals who took pleasure in sowing discord and animosity. The desecration of the Emmett Till Memorial and the unsettling act of placing a noose around the statue of James Meredith—someone who had triumphed over racism and blazed a trail for minority students at the University of Mississippi—served as painful reminders of the lingering racism and prejudices that persisted in the current American society.

James Meredith's resilience and courageous efforts to champion civil rights and overcome adversity had left an indelible mark on Etta's consciousness. She recognized the invaluable contributions of those who had paved the way for her to thrive in a more inclusive society. Gratitude swelled within her for the individuals who had made her journey easier, allowing her to forge friendships and connections across the diverse tapestry of America.

Lost in her thoughts, Etta couldn't help but wonder about the possibility of being invited to contribute her expertise in the construction of a museum dedicated to housing Confederate monuments, though they did not mention that the museum they were asking her to design was to specifically house them. *What if the donor is one of the descendants or members of the United Daughters of the Confederacy? If so, they wouldn't be calling on me or consider hiring me for the job. Right?* She asked herself.

Etta and Randy strolled through McCorkle Place, the symbolic entrance to the university. The atmosphere seemed relatively tranquil, with only faint traces of the recent upheaval lingering in the air. Etta couldn't help but yearn for a resolution that would bring about a sense of harmony and understanding on campus. However, she couldn't shake off her apprehension, considering the deep divisions prevalent in American society.

The nation's social and political climate had become increasingly polarized, and the actions of its leader seemed to exacerbate the chaos rather than heal the wounds. Etta sighed, recognizing the tactics of fear-mongering and appeals to base human instincts that had contributed to this state of affairs. She knew all too well that in such an environment, finding common ground and fostering empathy could be a daunting task.

Etta and Randy approached the area where the Confederate statue *Silent Sam* had once stood, now cordoned off by the police with yellow crime scene tape. The space was adorned with various signs, each carrying its own message. Among them, a striking sign in bold red letters caught their attention: Hands off Sam.

Randy, catching sight of the sign, turned to Etta with a playful grin and said, "Too late." They shared a hearty laugh. In that moment of lightheartedness, it seemed like a harmless joke. However, a flicker of unease passed through Etta's mind as she pondered the sign's underlying meaning. Was it a subtle reminder for her to distance herself from Sam, the person she had fallen deeply in love with?

Suddenly, a surge of anxiety washed over her as a vivid image of Tomi's hostile face materialized in her thoughts. The memory served as a stark reminder of the complications that entangled her connection with Sam, and which the fortune teller had warned her about. Could Tomi be one of the "pesky hurdles and barriers that currently impede" her connection with him? The conflicting emotions within her—love and fear—clashed fiercely, leaving her with confusion. Which path should she take: move on or go to him to find closure?

Etta's widened eyes betrayed her inner turmoil, and for a moment, she felt a wave of vulnerability. The image of Tomi's venomous expression lingered, serving as one of the challenges she faced in going after her heart's desires. *Could it be? Could she have given me the hands-*

off-Sam look? Her face and that sign sync up so well. But why? Why would she have a problem with me dating Sam? Was she being protective of him just like Daron was being protective of me? Does she think I'm not good enough for Sam?

Randy woke her troublesome thoughts. "Good riddance. It's about time we stop putting racism on a pedestal. I mean, literally." Randy's ancestors on his father's side were victims of slavery and cruelty, while those on his mother's side were landowners and slaveholders.

"You're funny," said Etta. They laughed again like young adolescents.

"I think they should get rid of that pedestal as well. It's all part of that evil statue. Why not root it out?"

The jovial laughter of Etta and Randy abruptly dissolved into a perplexed silence as their eyes beheld an unexpected sight. Their gazes briefly locked, with shared bewilderment came across their faces, before they turned their attention back to the figure standing on the opposite side of the pedestal. There, like a bizarre apparition defying logic and reason, stood a black man donning a Confederate uniform, clutching a Confederate flag.

"Someone is feeling nostalgic. That just boils my blood. I wonder if he knows about that despicable Julian S. Carr who spoke at the unveiling of this odious statue in 1913, talking about 'horse-whipping a Negro wench until her skin hung in shreds.' What a deplorable, disgusting piece of shit. And Carr claimed he had done that just one hundred yards away from here." Both Etta and Randy turned in every direction of the campus to see where that hundred yards would have been. "Argh. I am getting goosebumps thinking about this."

Etta eyed Randy. "Hmm. Someone read up on *Silent Sam*."

"Yeah, I did when I saw protesters roping it down on its face, in the news. I cheered. I breathed a sigh of relief. I don't understand why that guy over there doesn't get why this statue is a symbol of hatred, exclusion, and violence. What does he like about this dark period, as a black man? Let me ask him," Randy said, charging toward the man.

Etta yanked him back. "Forget about it," she said. "A brief exchange would only get each of you riled up. Can you do anything in one exchange? We haven't got time for this. Let's think of doing something for the community instead. Come on."

Etta and Randy bid farewell to one another as he left her at the office of the director of planning and design. While Randy headed to the library to delve deeper into the history of Chapel Hill and its surroundings, eager to "drop" his newfound knowledge with his social media followers, Etta embarked on a meeting with the executive director and university architect. She was introduced to another talented architect and designer, who accompanied her on a fascinating tour in a luxurious golf cart adorned with dark green and black leather seating.

As they explored the university grounds, the architects shared intriguing historical insights about the buildings on campus. Although Etta had already studied the university's history, she couldn't help but be fascinated by the insider tidbits shared by her guides. The director emphasized the importance of the new building harmonizing with the existing structures and the overall campus aesthetic. Etta listened intently, absorbing every sight, sound, and sensation that surrounded her.

The director informed her that the following day she would be presenting her pitch to the donor, the chair of the board of trustees, and other influential individuals. Etta's face lit up with a radiant smile, brimming with enthusiasm. Their journey led them to a square, brown brick building, adorned with slender windows and a beige metal frame. Etta's smile wavered slightly when the director confirmed that it was the Department of English and Comparative Literature building, known as Greenlaw Hall. *Great. Of all of the buildings, one of our stops is here.* Etta's gaze swept from the foundation to the rooftop, taking in every detail of the building before her. *So Sam works here and traipses around this area. I wonder what he is doing right now. Oh my God. What if he enters or exits the building at this moment? What would I do or say?* She was unsure of how such a meeting would unfold. Feeling a surge of emotions, Etta instinctively placed her hand on her heart, attempting to steady the rapid beating within her chest.

"Etta? Are you okay?" asked the director, with genuine concern in his voice.

"Oh, I'm fine," Etta replied, realizing that her pensive expression had momentarily distracted her hosts. She swiftly composed herself, eager to engage in conversation. "Is this building named after Dr. Edwin Greenlaw, the scholar and teacher in English and Literature?"

The director's face lit up with delight. "Yes, indeed," he confirmed. "Are you familiar with Dr. Greenlaw?"

Etta's eyes sparkled with enthusiasm. "He was a native of Illinois, much like myself. I discovered his works during my exploration of literature. I enjoyed his notable works such as *Literature and Life* and *Selections From Chaucer*."

The director nodded, clearly pleased with Etta's knowledge. "Dr. Greenlaw made significant contributions to UNC–CH, both as a professor and an administrator. He not only brought literature and culture to the South but also played a pivotal role in shaping the university. His boundless energy and passion for literature left a lasting impact on his students, instilling in them a hunger for knowledge. Thanks to his efforts, UNC–CH has become a renowned research institution known worldwide."

Etta, appreciating the significance of the department being named after such an influential figure, remarked, "How fitting it is to honor Dr. Greenlaw in this way."

As the day progressed, Etta found solace in the fact that she was being productive and hadn't encountered Sam, which allowed her to focus on the present moment and the conversations she shared with her hosts.

18

ETTA, CHAPEL HILL
AUGUST 24, 2018

With her pitch successfully delivered and a sense of relief, Etta gracefully descended the steps of the prestigious Giles Horney Building. The weight of the moment lifted from her shoulders, leaving her with a great sense of accomplishment. As she approached the waiting sleek black SUV, driven by Randy, a contented smile graced her face. Though the university was within walking distance from their hotel, Randy picked her up, so they could venture out of the area for a late lunch.

As she settled into the passenger seat, Randy's eyes sparkled with excitement, unable to contain his curiosity any longer. "Well, how did it go?" he asked eagerly, his anticipation palpable in the air.

"I did great!" Etta replied with confidence. "However, it's hard to say for certain. While I felt confident and received positive feedback from everyone else, I couldn't gauge the donor's reaction. She remained impassive, not giving away any positive or negative indication of her thoughts." Etta paused for a moment, reflecting on the situation. "But overall, the others seemed genuinely enthusiastic and receptive to my pitch."

"She's not a descendant of one of the Daughters of the Confederacy, is she?"

"I don't know. It's possible. She said three generations of her family attended UNC."

"I bet you anything she is related to one of them."

"I don't know. If she is one, she hides it well. Oh well. I did my best; that's all that matters." She cast a reassuring smile toward Randy, knowing that she had given it her all.

"Good enough for me. Let's go explore this dandy town now that we're here!"

"Let's go," Etta said, feeling happy and relieved for a job well done.

As Randy navigated the streets, Etta's attention was abruptly captured by something she spotted ahead. "Stop! Stop!" she exclaimed, her voice bursting with urgency and excitement.

"What is it?" Randy said.

"There it is, the university's landmark. I want to take a closer look at it and capture more pictures, especially since I didn't want to take up my hosts' time by taking many photos of it the other day. Now that I am on my own, I want to photograph it from all angles."

"I've seen it."

"Okay. I'll be gone for a moment."

"All right. I'll wait here."

Etta swiftly retrieved her camera from her tote bag and stepped out of the vehicle. With an artist's eye, she captured the famous landmark, framed by vibrant flowerbeds, majestic trees, and timeless brickwork, from a distance. Eager to capture every detail, she briskly made her way toward the neoclassical rotunda with its striking copper dome, getting a closer look.

The afternoon sunlight bathed the scene in a warm glow, revealing a vivid image of the enduring symbol against the backdrop of the historic Old East Residential Hall. As Etta focused her lens, her mind raced, trying to recall where she had seen a similar architectural style before. Memories of Greece, Italy, and France flitted through her thoughts, and then it clicked—France, specifically the Gardens of Versailles.

Before she could delve into the depths of her own memory—her resource of choice besides Google—as to when she had visited the Temple of Love, a silvery voice resonated from behind her. "The Old Well was modeled after the Temple of Love in the Gardens of Versailles," the voice confirmed. Etta turned around, her eyes widening in surprise, to find the square-faced man with melancholy eyes standing there. Her heart stirred, and her stomach dropped, overwhelmed by a mix of anticipation, familiarity, and a touch of fear. Was she hallucinating?

In that moment, time seemed to stand still as Etta locked eyes with the man she had both longed to hear from and feared encountering. He appeared more handsome to her than she had ever remembered, but a little bit gaunt and skinnier than when she last saw him in

Chicago. Words eluded her, dissipating into thin air, as she stood there, transfixed, almost forgetting to breathe.

"How are you, Etta?" he greeted her courteously, as if they had parted ways on good terms and were now joyfully reunited. His words stirred up emotions within her that she had thought were buried.

Excuse me? How am I? Can you even begin to comprehend the depths of my emotions? Do you have any idea what you've put me through? I can't sleep. Food has lost its taste. Endless days were spent questioning why you haven't called or texted me. I believed we were in a meaningful relationship. I envisioned a future where we would grow old together like you said. How could you vanish without a trace, without even offering a simple goodbye? And now you have the audacity to inquire about my well-being, as if we casually decided to part ways? Etta's emotions swirled within her, teetering on the edge of tears. Frustration, love, and anger intertwined as she faced the man who had both captured her heart and caused her immense pain through his physical and emotional absence.

Feeling the weight of her conflicting emotions, Etta took a deep breath, consciously centering herself before responding. "I... I'm okay, I guess," she managed to say, her voice betraying her vulnerability. As she spoke, he flashed her that familiar warm smile that had always held the power to make her weak in the knees. The sight of it momentarily melted her defenses, offering a mix of nostalgia and longing within her.

Sam continued, "Did you know that students have a tradition of having a drink of water from this well on their first day of class? It's believed to bring luck and good grades. And, on their graduation day, they do the same to symbolize a brighter and more successful future."

"Yes, I recall reading something similar somewhere before. Wh-what are you doing here?" she said, uncertainty in her voice. Her emotions were a jumble of nervousness and confusion, torn between feelings of love and hate for him, considering what he had done to her. A nervous laugh escaped her lips as she attempted to dismiss her unease. She instinctively placed her palm on her forehead as if checking her temperature, while clutching her camera in her other hand. "Hah. That's a lame question. Given that you work here, it's only natural for you to be passing by the area."

Caught in the midst of her internal turmoil, her mind volleying back and forth like a fierce Ping-Pong match, she became aware of his intense gaze, his brows furrowed in contemplation. His unwavering stare made her feel self-conscious and uneasy.

She felt compelled to offer an explanation for her unexpected presence at the university. "You must be wondering why I'm here." He remained silent, his eyes abounding with admiration and joy as they locked onto hers. "I'm here to do work for the university," Etta volunteered.

"You were called to pitch for the museum? Congratulations! I'm sure you did well. Did they offer you the project?"

"I don't know. The donor was hard to read. They said they'll let me know. They have other pitches to consider."

"I can imagine," he said. "She's very picky."

"Oh. You know about the woman."

"I heard of her through other staff members."

"Oh, I see," she said, her nervousness escalating and mingling with a growing sense of anger toward him, exacerbated by his seemingly oblivious demeanor. She resented the idea of appearing foolish in his presence.

Determined not to subject herself to that vulnerability, she made up her mind to retreat. "Well, it was... nice running into you. Goodbye," she uttered hastily, turning away and walking off, a subtle ache piercing her heart as she distanced herself from him.

"Etta," he called out, his voice filled with urgency and longing.

Her instinct was to keep moving, to not give in to his call, but she couldn't help but feel a tug of curiosity. In her mind, the waiting SUV seemed close yet distant.

"Etta, please wait," he pleaded, his voice full of desperation.

The words echoed in her mind, triggering a wave of conflicting emotions. *Wait? Wait for what? What could you possibly have to say that would make me want to stop and listen?* She was unsure if she was ready to open herself up to whatever he had in store.

"Am sorry," he said.

She stopped and turned to witness his pathetic look of contrition. That all-too-familiar "am" without its trusty sidekick, the letter "I," was his signature linguistic quirk. As an English professor, she expected better from him. She couldn't help but ponder the mysterious absence of the honorable and important "I" following the word "am." It seemed like his vocabulary had always been "am" this, "am" that, but never "I am." Perhaps he was just a victim of the modern-day epidemic known as laziness! People these days, they'd rather type "am" instead of "I am" or "I'm," saving those precious microseconds of effort. It's as if modern technology has unleashed a wave of linguistic shortcuts, turning us into masters of abbreviation and champions of laziness. Why bother with two whole letters when you can get the point across with just one? Who needs proper grammar when you can have speed and brevity? Soon enough, we'll be communicating in grunts and emojis, reducing conversation to a simple "LOL" or "OMG." But this was not the time for her to nitpick on him dismissing his sense of self.

He apologized. The unexpectedness of his words caught her off guard, and she fought back the tears that threatened to escape her eyes. With a determined effort, she lifted her head and took a deep breath, steadying herself. Something within her compelled her to give him a chance, to hear him out. With a glimmer of hope mixed with caution in her eyes, she said, "Excuse me?" She heard him the first time but wanted to hear it again.

"I'm sorry."

Oh, the apology must be sincere because he's using "I'm." Regardless, I'm not going to give in so easily. "What do you have to be sorry about?" she questioned, her voice containing a mixture of confusion and frustration. His silence in response only served to amplify her exasperation. It seemed he had a habit of avoiding comment on obvious matters, and this reticence only further fueled her irritation. Once more, she made the decision to walk away, her steps represented a renewed sense of disappointment.

"I'm sorry for leaving so abruptly," he finally spoke up, his voice teeming with sincerity. "I'm sorry we went on without speaking this long." As she heard his words, she paused in her tracks, her curiosity piqued. Turning around, she fixed him with a gaze brimming with knitted brows, waiting for further explanation.

"That's it?"

"What else is there, Etta?"

Oh. My. God. What is wrong with you? Her frustration and hurt spilled out in her words to him: "You left me abruptly, and that alone was difficult to handle. But what truly hurt me was the fact that you never responded to any of my texts or phone calls." Her voice quivered with anger and disappointment.

"You called and texted me?" he said, with a surprised look.

"Excuse me?" she fumed.

"I never received your calls or texts."

"Please stop playing games with me. We're both too old for this." She attempted to walk away again.

"I honestly don't know if you texted or called me," he replied, his innocence evident in his voice. She halted once more, facing him with frustration and disbelief.

"Even if you didn't receive them, wouldn't you have had the common decency to call and let me know that your son was okay?" Etta said with anger. "Don't I deserve to know that?"

"I tried calling you the other day, but it kept ringing. I even texted you, granted it was later than I wanted, but I did text and call you, Etta," he replied.

"First of all, why would you wait that long to call me?"

"There was a lot going on with me: school, children, and then my aunt's diary...," he said, stopping as if he did not want to open up about his aunt. "But when I was ready I called and texted you."

"It's impossible that I did not see your text or phone call. Please don't lie to me. If you didn't or don't want to see me anymore, just say so," she retorted, her voice sounded hurt. "I hate mind games."

Her statement hung in the air, leaving him momentarily speechless. Finally, he responded, "Why would you think I didn't want to see you anymore?"

"Oh, my God! Seriously?" she exclaimed, her voice exasperated from the emotional turmoil she had endured. "You went completely silent for the past week. How was I supposed to interpret that?"

"I thought you might be angry."

"You knew that but didn't have the common courtesy to let me know that you were busy and that you would speak to me when you were ready?"

"I was hoping your anger would subside and we would talk again," he explained, a hint of vulnerability in his voice.

"That is ridiculous. You left me to think all kinds of thoughts and expected me to calm down? When would that right time be when I didn't know what happened?"

"On Wednesday. Like I said, I tried calling you and texting you. I can prove it," he said, pulling out his phone. According to his log he called her at seven thirty in the morning; she also noticed her calls had not made it onto his log. He then showed her his last text to her, which she never received.

"This is ridiculous," Etta responded. Her frustration mounted, when all of sudden Daron's words seeped into her mind. She could hear him telling her that Sam was lying: "That's what philanderers do, they lie." She began to doubt Sam and felt a surge of irritation, sensing that he was evading responsibility for his own actions.

"Etta. Listen. I'm sorry for leaving you abruptly and for not calling you. I should have known better. But since you're here, can we talk about this? Please give me a chance to explain my side of the story."

Etta's mind swirled with conflicting emotions, leaving her at an impasse. Uncertainty hung heavy in the air as she grappled with the tangled web of her feelings. On one hand, the bitter taste of disappointment lingered, reminding her of the way their relationship had unraveled. Yet, on the other hand, an ember of affection still burned within her, refusing to be extinguished.

As Etta stood there, caught between longing and apprehension, the blare of a car horn jolted her back to reality. Turning away, she saw Randy waiting. "My friend is waiting for me," she murmured softly, torn between the desire to stay and confront her turbulent emotions, and the practicality of escaping this tumultuous moment.

"Can I see you tonight?" he pleaded, his voice loaded with longing, hoping for a glimmer of possibility. He impatiently waited for her response.

I don't know, can you? Etta asked, sarcastically in her head, as if mocking him. Her mind raced, searching for her own answer. The weight of indecision pressed upon her, making her footsteps falter as she began to walk away, lost in her own thoughts.

"I assume you're staying at The Carolina Inn," he called after her. Etta did not say anything but kept walking. Too many conflicting thoughts whirled in her mind. Since she did not correct him, he continued, "I'll be waiting in the lobby at seven, if you're interested in meeting again."

Etta bolted toward the car where Randy had been waiting, and with the grace of a furious tornado, she slammed the door shut behind her. Desperation filled the air as she buried her tear-stained face in her hands, letting out a soft cry.

"Oh sweet Jesus, tell me it isn't who I think it is," Randy exclaimed, his voice packed with concern and curiosity.

"Please drive away," she pleaded, her words muffled by her trembling hands.

"Okay. Okay." Randy replied, his brows furrowed in confusion. With a mix of bewilderment and a heavy foot on the gas pedal, he kicked their getaway vehicle into high gear. Through the rearview mirror, he stole a glimpse of Sam, standing there like a statuesque sentinel, observing their hasty departure. "He's quite the dashing scoundrel, isn't he? I see the conundrum you're facing, Etta," Randy said, as he continued down the road.

Etta's cries grew louder, echoing through the car like a forlorn siren in distress. All the emotions she had suppressed came out at this very moment. Randy put his hand on Etta's shoulder. "Aww, Etta. Let it all out. It'll make you feel better. Sometimes, we must let it out. I won't judge you. I understand what you are going through. I'm here for you, if you want to talk about it."

She shook her head and pulled out a packet of tissue to wipe her tears.

"Okay. Whenever you're ready or if you want to let it all out, I am here for you."

Etta nodded her head in understanding. She wiped her teas. Just then, they drove past *Silent Sam*'s pedestal. Etta was staring out the window, lost in her own world, and Randy looked her way. He shook his head. "Oh, Lord. There is a white man dressed in black with a straw hat, holding a Confederate flag. I wonder why the black man from yesterday did not stand next to him. He's nowhere to be found. Are they taking turns guarding the pedestal? How do they know to avoid each other? I wonder if they even spoke. After all, they are fighting for the same cause: *Silent Sam* and the Confederacy. I have a mind to find that man and grill him, but one thing at a time," he said, as if to distract Etta. She didn't repond, so he asked, "Are you okay?"

Etta took out more tissues from the packet to wipe off her never-ending tears. "I'm sorry. You must think I'm a mess."

"Hey, I understand."

Just then the Darth Vader ringtone came on. "Oh no. It's Daron," Etta said.

"Crap," Randy said.

"I'm putting him on speaker." Etta wiped the last of her tears, propped herself up, and answered the call.

"Hey, Etta."

"Hi Daron," Randy said simultaneously with Etta, but louder, to drown out her cracked voice.

"You're together? Where are you guys off to?" Daron asked.

"We're looking for something to eat. And where are you?" Randy asked, to put the focus back on Daron.

"I'm in Florida, driving to some crazy little town to meet a client. Etta, I just finished listening to a podcast that reminds me of you."

"What?" Etta said, trying to sound normal.

"You've got to listen to it. This is so about you."

"What are you talking about?"

"The show is called Dirty John. Listen to it. This will make you think twice about that psycho Sam."

"Please don't call him that. He's a nice guy, just reserved and quiet, that's all," Etta said, feeling offended by her friend's name calling.

"Reserved. Quiet. They are code for crazy, Etta!"

Etta and Randy exchanged impatient looks. "Maybe Sam is loving and passionate in his quiet way," Etta said, defending her love interest and challenging her best friend.

"Stop building him up to this ideal person he's not, Etta! I can assure you, he's no Mr. Darcy."

"You don't know what that story is about," Etta said, rolling her eyes and feeling impatient with Daron's rhetoric.

"Sure I do. In her wounded pride and her prejudice due to her wounded pride, Elizabeth Bennet confuses Darcy's quiet love and passion with aloofness, pride, and arrogance," Daron said.

Etta's raised eyebrow conveyed a sense of intrigue. "You were paying attention in class," she remarked, her voice sounded surprise. "You actually know the plot of Jane Austen's *Pride and Prejudice*."

"The price I pay for going to a liberal high school." Etta could picture Daron rolling his eyes. "In your situation," he went on, "you're confusing Sam as loving and passionate when in actuality, he is more of an aloof, psychotic type. Understand this, Etta: Sam is no Mr.

Darcy. Don't think you can change him, either, the way Eliza changes Fitzwilliam and vice versa. *Pride and Prejudice* is just a fairy tale. I know girls like you are hopelessly romantic about finding your Mr. Darcy. But you're living in the real world. So get real. Move on. Find someone who suits you. In the real world. Stop wasting your time finding Mr. Darcy. He doesn't exist. And for the love of God, stay away from this Sam guy!"

"Sam is not psychotic," Etta murmured.

"Okay, clinically depressed."

"Oh, stop! Just stop it, Daron," Randy said, seeing how upset Etta looked.

Daron ignored him. "Your aunt is right. By the way, if you tell her I said that, I'll deny it. Anyway, there are two types of guys on this earth: one who likes you and one who values you. I don't have to tell you which one you need. Anyway, after listening to Dirty John you will recognize lines guys like him use to get what they want. You'll understand the type of guy to stay away from, Etta."

"What is it about?" Randy asked.

"Etta will have to listen to it herself."

"Can you give us a synopsis?" Randy said.

"All right. Warning. You're going to be very annoyed with the girl in it, with her valley girl, California way of speaking; but if you could just get past that, the story is very good and you can learn a lot from it. I feel bad about what she went through but damn, the up-talk. Maybe the story can save you from this crazy Sam guy, Etta."

Etta and Randy looked at each other wanting to roll their eyes but did not.

"It's about a woman—the mother of the valley sounding girl—looking for love, but she ends up with a con artist who knows how to say *sweet* things to her to get what he wants. In actuality, he's a lying, manipulative, and abusive son of a bitch. I'm not going to give away the ending. Listen to it yourself. I'm almost at the client's site. I'll catch up with you and talk to you about it later."

Etta downloaded the Dirty John podcast on her phone. "What the hell. There are seven episodes, about forty minutes each."

"Well, we can tune in to the first episode while we're driving to our restaurant. That's thirty minutes right there," Randy suggested.

As they listened to the podcast's introduction, a young woman's voice filled the car. Randy and Etta exchanged cringing glances. "You know, you occasionally speak like that," Etta pointed out.

"Yeah, sometimes. Anyway, are you ready to talk and fill me in on what happened back there?" Randy asked. They let the podcast continue playing in the background.

"That was Sam," Etta began, her frustration evident in her voice. "He greeted me as if nothing happened. And then he had the audacity to say I was mad at him because he did not hear from me. He said he had decided to wait for me to calm down before calling me. But when I questioned why it took him this long, he said he was busy with school, his kids, and something about his aunt's dairy. He is so wishy-washy. That's what bothered me the most. He was warm and inviting before his son's accident, and then after that he was cold and distant."

"Maybe he's bipolar."

"Maybe."

"So what did he say about not responding to your texts and phone calls?"

"He said he never received them."

"You're kidding."

"I kid you not."

"So now what?"

"He wants to see me tonight. He wants to talk, I guess."

"What's there to talk about? It's so weird that he said he never received your calls or texts. Is he lying?"

"I don't know. When he showed me his phone log of the time and date he called me and texted me, I did not see any of my calls or texts reaching his phone. I don't know what happened, unless he blocked me."

"That is strange."

"Yes, it is strange," Etta agreed.

"You're conflicted because you want to see him and hear what he has to say, don't you?"

"Am I a glutton for punishment?" Etta pondered aloud.

"Nah, you're only human," Randy replied.

Etta gave him an uncertain glance.

"I say, go for it. Why not? We're here, aren't we? Take the chance and seek closure. Maybe something positive might come out of it. Whatever happens, I'm here to support you," he encouraged.

"Thanks," Etta said, feeling gratitude and a glimmer of hope in her heart.

19

Etta paced back and forth in her room, her restless energy rivaling that of a caffeinated Pomeranian. Randy had ventured off into the night to catch up with an old friend he stumbled upon at the local tavern. Meanwhile, Etta, dressed in a refined sophistication—a navy blue, floral sheath dress, looked out her large window with black shutters, to see guests walking in and out of the main entrance. Emotionally, she found herself facing the one thing she wasn't prepared for—meeting Sam after a long four-day absence from each other. The man who had shattered her heart into a thousand tiny heart-shaped confetti pieces. Why should she grant him a second chance?

He had audaciously declared he would meet her in the lobby at 7 p.m., and she had left him hanging without a single response. She was certain he wouldn't bother showing up, either. And yet, here she stood, ten minutes past seven, plagued by an incessant nagging feeling that Sam was undoubtedly waiting for her in the lobby. She tapped her fingers on the windowsill, watching people come and go, a departure from her usual nervous habits. Uncertainty and vulnerability dominated her, like a floundering fish caught in a net. She placed a hand over her midsection, as if trying to nudge the butterflies, figuratively speaking, in stomach to settle down.

Conflicting emotions swirled within her like a tempestuous whirlpool. Was she about to embark on a perilous journey that would scar her forever, or was this the chance for a lifetime of happiness? Amidst the maelstrom of emotions, one thing remained steadfast: Etta was unequivocally, madly in love with Sam. She yearned to fight for their love, and now, he was extending an invitation for them to reconnect. Taking a deep breath, she inhaled determination and exhaled uncertainty.

Etta's resolve solidified. That's it, she declared to herself. He might be telling me the truth after all. I should be more understanding. He was preoccupied with his job, children, and possibly still deep in grief over his aunt's passing. There must be a reason why he never received my phone calls or texts. "I should cut the guy some slack," she said out loud, trying to give herself a reason for her desire to see him again.

Etta glanced at her watch, only to be greeted by the hands showing forty past seven. Panicked, as if she had not expected herself to be mulling over the meeting so long, she burst out of her door, descending the stairs with the swiftness of a startled gazelle.

Her keen eyes darted around the lobby and the cozy lounge areas, where guests engaged in idle chatter. Alas, no sight of that tall, svelte gentleman, meticulously dressed, loitering or lounging about. It seemed her impulsive nature, usually a harbinger of trouble, had done a complete flip-flop, leaving her with a missed opportunity for bliss with the man who had ignited all sensories in her body.

Her shoulders drooped like a deflated balloon, as her head hung low and her hands retreated into her dress pockets. She decided to saunter around the hotel, unknowingly meandering her way toward the hotel's restaurant known as Crossroads. What to do now? Etta found herself standing at the crossroads of her own emotions, yearning for a path to redemption.

When she walked past Crossroads a familiar voice sounded her name: "Etta." She quickly turned in every direction and saw her happy friend, Randy. "Hey, Etta. I want you to meet my friend, David. David, this is my good friend Etta."

Etta and David smiled at each other and exchanged pleasantries.

"So?" Randy craned his neck to see if Sam was around. The disappointment on her face said it all. "Oh, Etta. Want to join us for dinner here?"

"No. I want to go out and get some fresh air. You two go ahead and enjoy yourselves."

"Okay. I promise to check up on you later."

"Thanks."

"It was nice meeting you," David said, looking back and forth between the two friends, confused.

"Etta is supposed to meet a guy here but it doesn't look like he showed up," Randy told David.

"Oh, I see. Well, you're welcome to join us," David said.

"It's sweet of you two, but I'll be fine," Etta told them.

Her head hung low again as she walked away and stepped outside of the hotel on the street.

"Etta," a voice called out in surprise. She looked up to find a dashingly handsome man standing before her with his hands in his pockets, eyeing her with a sense of relief that she finally showed to meet him.

"Sam. Hi. Um. Hi." She kept moving her hair to the back of her ear out of nervousness. Her heart almost leaped out of her chest. She put her hand over it to calm herself, feeling equally relieved that he had not lied to her about showing up, nor had he left after waiting for her. "You've just arrived?" she asked, as if to confirm her wonder.

"No. I've been here for about an hour. I just stepped outside to talk to my sister to make sure the kids were okay… and to tell her I might be home either early or late." He raised one of his brows as if asking her.

"Oh. I'm sorry. It was just… I… um… I…"

"That's okay. I understand."

"You do?"

"Say," Sam said, with one hand in his pocket and another sweeping his hair back, perhaps, Etta wondered, a nervous tic of his own, "would you like to have dinner? Or have you eaten already?"

"No, not yet. Sure, I would love to." Etta said nervously. She surprised herself by yielding to him so quickly. *Man, I'm such a sucker!*

"Would you like to stay here at the Crossroads or venture outside?"

"Outside would be nice. I'm not feeling the name."

He let out a laugh, as if finding her sincerity humorous. "I needed some fresh air anyway." He gazed at her with a gentle smile.

And so, they picked up where they left off at a nice, cozy restaurant called Elaine's On Franklin, which was only a fifteen minute walk from The Carolina Inn. The waiter sat them by the windows. Etta stole a glance at Sam. Her forehead furrowed. She did not understand how he never received her texts and phone calls. *Is he toying with me? The only explanation would be someone blocking my number. What if I asked him if my phone number was intentionally or accidentally blocked?* Knowing he did not like to argue about the same thing over and over, she bit her lips, literally. She had never yielded so easily to someone before. Nevertheless, her mind often came back to how he blew her off and waited too long to call her back. Considering whether or not he received her texts or calls, he could have at least found a way to let her know everything was fine with Wallace or that he missed her; because she certainly missed him. Did he not miss her? This annoyed her.

His gaze searched her face, as if he sensed she was still soured about the situation he left her with. "I miss you. I'm sorry I ruined everything," he said.

"I beg your pardon?" Etta thought her ears were deceiving her, because she was busy arguing with herself internally.

"I left abruptly and I should have called you regardless of whether you called me or texted me. I was busy with everything and by then I had not heard from you…"

"You thought you did not hear from me, so you decided to let go of what we had?" Etta said, feeling vulnerable for revealing how much the relationship meant to her.

"I'm sorry," Sam said, averting his eyes from hers as if feeling shameful.

Feeling like they were going in circles, Etta changed the subject and asked, "So, how's Wallace?"

He looked up at her and smiled. "He is doing better now. Thank you for asking."

"May I ask what happened?" Etta said, taking a sip of her water.

"He said he woke up thirsty and was startled by Tomi who was checking up on him. He got up to run and fell on his outstretched arm. He should be fully recovered in five more weeks," Sam said, also taking a sip of his water.

Oh, so she was the reason Wallace broke his arm. Etta's radar went up. She wondered if Tomi would have had access to Sam's phone and erased her messages from the night of the accident and blocked her number. *Should I ask him if my number was blocked?* Just then a waitress came to take their order; and when she left, Etta asked Sam how Jonny and Sopraffina were doing.

Sam smiled at her, as if he thought of something. "What?" she asked.

"Oh, nothing."

"Come on, spill it."

"I was thinking about what Vida said about you."

"What did she say?" Etta asked, curious about his sister with whom she had had less interaction than his other siblings.

"She said you genuinely care about my children."

"She's right. I do."

"Again, I'm sorry for not letting you know how Wallace was doing after he was released from the hospital."

Etta smiled with her own internal thought. "What?" he asked.

"You must be really sorry because you said it for the third time," Etta said with a smile. She knew he seldom repeated himself and dwelled on things. She knew he knew he had made a mistake. Her heart melted, and she wanted to forgive him.

After enjoying their dinner and freshening up in the restrooms, they paid and left the restaurant. "It is a beautiful night," Sam said. "Would you like to walk around town?"

"I would love to," Etta said.

"Good. It's my turn to show you my hometown," Sam said with a teasing smile.

With her hands in her pockets, Etta looked up to the sky, admiring the bright stars sparking on the blank canvas of Chapel Hill, wondering what the fortune teller said about there being an obstruction that kept her from being with Sam. Could Tomi be her obstruction? Could Tomi possibly delete her texts and calls from the night of the accident and then block her number? The fortune teller said she could remove the obstruction for a fee. How would she do that? *And why would I believe what the fortune teller said?*

"What are you thinking, Etta?"

"Hmm?" Etta said, waking up from her reverie. "Oh, nothing."

"Really?" He raised his thick eyebrows.

"Yes." See? I can be reserved, too. How do you like that?

He smiled at her, his expression seemingly able to decipher her thoughts. His captivating smile sent a wave of weakness through her knees. "So have you heard back from the donor or the university?"

"No, not yet," she said, sounding disappointed.

"Oh. Don't worry. You'll get it."

"Thank you for that vote of confidence. By the way, can I ask you something?"

"Sure," Sam replied.

"Do you know if the donor is a member of the Daughters of the Confederacy?"

"Her mother was, but I don't think she is."

"Really?" She stopped walking to look at him.

"You don't think you'll get the job because of that?" Sam said, looking into her eyes.

"Possibly." Etta turned away from him and kept walking.

Sam and Etta leisurely strolled along Franklin Street and other bustling parts of Chapel Hill. It was now Sam's turn to play the role of tour guide, regaling Etta with the city's history and sharing anecdotes from his own upbringing there. He proudly pointed out the diverse range of small businesses and shops that thrived in the vibrant town. Some of these establishments held sentimental value to Sam, especially those he frequented with his sister Vida.

"So, how is your sister Vida?" Etta asked.

"She's doing well."

"Is she watching Jonny, Wallace, and Sopraffina while you're with me?"

"Yes, she insisted. I don't know how she does it with her three children and a husband," Sam said. "And then taking care of me and my three children."

"She's a superwoman," Etta said.

"Yes. She's very family oriented."

As Sam continued the engaging tour and sharing of his family background, Etta couldn't help but compare their current stroll to the ones they would take back in Chicago, where they would intertwine their fingers, laugh, and playfully tease one another. Although they walked side by side, their hands remained separate. Etta longed for that physical connection with Sam, yet his animated lips kept moving, describing the quaintness of Chapel Hill and the array of entertainment options it offered, such as live music, museums, and theater shows. Unbeknownst to Etta, Sam occasionally stole glances at her and smiled.

A ten-minute stroll brought them to a busy part of town. They walked past people standing in line to purchase tickets to shows at the Varsity Theater. "We need to cross here," Sam said, pointing to the corner of West Franklin Street and North Columbia Street. Etta nodded. She trailed behind Sam, the steady rhythm of their footsteps harmonizing with the gentle evening breeze. Suddenly, a dark car with tinted windows materialized out of nowhere, hurtling toward them with a menacing roar. The piercing sound of its engine ripped through the tranquility of the moment, jolting Etta from her thoughts of wanting to touch and hold onto Sam. Instinctively, she glanced up, her eyes widening in alarm as she realized the imminent danger barreling toward her.

In a swift and deft motion, Sam sensed the impending danger and pulled her close, shielding her fragile form from the oncoming car that whizzed past in a hair-raising blur, barely grazing the folds of her dress. Etta found herself held in the safety of Sam's embrace, just as she wanted, her racing heartbeat blending with his own. It was as if their hearts had synchronized, pulsating in perfect unison, reminiscent of their tender waltz at the illustrious Drake Hotel in Chicago. However, this time, Sam could feel her body trembling with fear and shock, amplifying his concern for her well-being. As the adrenaline began to subside, a concerned middle-aged couple approached the shaken pair.

"Oh my God, are you okay?" the woman asked. Etta, still dazed and disoriented from the close call, struggled to comprehend what had just happened. To her bewilderment, the woman urged Sam and her to contact the authorities, convinced that the incident seemed to be a deliberate act of malice. "Whoever that person is, I think they did it intentionally. You should call the police."

"And tell them what, honey?" her husband said.

"I'm sorry I didn't get a good look at the car, though," the wife said.

"Nor the person inside, for that matter," the husband added.

Breathing deeply to steady her nerves, Etta mustered the strength to meet Sam's worried gaze. Her pallid complexion mirrored the remnants of her terror, while her eyes showed a mixture of disbelief and gratitude. She turned to the couple and said, "Um. That's okay. I'm okay." Yet Sam and Etta still clung to one another.

"Be careful. Look left and right always. Keep your wife close to you, young man," the husband said.

Neither Sam nor Etta corrected him. All they could say was: "Thank you."

As soon as the couple walked past them, Sam let her go; instead, he slipped his hand into hers. Before they knew it their fingers laced together like intertwined vines. She felt the warmth of his strong hand. He brushed his thumb against her thumb as if to confirm the sparkle in their touch was real. Her heart raced—whether from fear of nearly being run over, or what was to come in their relationship, she did not know. Whatever it was, she took great comfort in knowing he cared. To hold the hand of someone she was enamored with exhilarated her. Butterflies fluttered a familiar and good feeling. Everything seemed like a dream, but the tactile sensation of his touch would last forever in her mind.

"I'm sorry you had to experience that. Must be a drunken person or something. Chapel Hill is a nice town, full of nice people. I can't imagine anyone would want to hurt you."

"You saved my life," Etta said. "Thank you."

He glanced her way and smiled that gentle smile that she had come to know and love. He held onto her hand tightly. "Yes, but I still have not made up for the time I rear-ended you," he said. They both laughed that good-natured laugh.

Sam stopped. "What is it?" Etta asked.

"I have a confession to make," he said.

Etta swallowed, wondering if he was going to ruin the beautiful moment they shared. "Go on," she said with hesitation and worry.

When he pulled her closer to him with one arm wrapped around her and his other hand caressing her smooth face, he said, "Etta Kem, I was falling for you fast in Chicago. When Wallace got hurt I felt I was neglecting my son. I didn't know what to do. I got scared that I completely shut myself off from you. I fought the strong feeling off by telling myself that I refused to be the kind of father who forsakes his flesh and blood in pursuit of love for a woman whom I just got to know."

Etta opened her mouth to speak, but he caressed her lips with his thumb, suggesting he already knew what she wanted to say.

"I was a fool," he went on. "I know you understood my duties as a father. My kids are young and I used that as an excuse, thinking they might be confused or it might mess up their mind if they see me in a serious relationship with you. The truth of the matter is, I love you. My love—

deep love for you—doesn't negate the love I have for my children. Vida made me see this."

"I'm sorry. What did you say?" Etta asked.

"You're going to make me repeat it, aren't you?"

"I have to be sure."

"Okay. Be sure of this. Etta Kem, I love you."

"I love you, too," Etta responded, smiling and loving to hear the three words coming from Sam's lips, and appreciating that Vida was on her side. But then she looked at Sam with disappointment and said, "So if Vida hadn't put some sense into you, you wouldn't have called me?"

"I would have. I would find a way to connect with you. I'm sorry I was an emotional mess... between you, the kids, and my aunt's diary."

Etta raised her arch eyebrow.

"Am not ready to share that with you yet," he told her, as if sensing her curiosity.

"Okay."

"I had hoped when things settled down and my dark mood did not dominate me I would come to you. You probably would not believe this, but I made a wish to see you again in front of the Old Well, and sure enough, a few days later, I met you right there."

"Amazing. The Old Well is magical after all," she said, smiling.

"Or coincidental," he said, moving his right hand to caress her soft cheek.

"I still don't get how you never received my texts or phone calls. Did you block my number?" Etta asked.

"That is not possible. I would know if I had blocked your number." He pulled out his phone to look, went to Settings and then selected Blocked numbers, only to find Etta's as the latest number being blocked. Both of their jaws dropped, as they both looked up from the screen and at each other. "I promise you, I did not do that," Sam said. "This is very strange."

"Does someone else have access to your phone?"

"No. It's always by my side and on my nightstand when I shower or sleep. And the kids would never touch my phone."

"That is weird," Etta said. Hmm. I wonder if Tomi visited his home and found a way to mess with it.

"What are you thinking, Etta?"

"Oh, nothing. Just wondering, why would my number be blocked?"

"I would have to tap and hold your number and select Block, but I did not do that and would never ever do that in a million years. I'll have to look into it, but now, let's get back to us." He joined his hand with hers.

She was so curious about her number being blocked that she forgot to play over and over in her head what he had said to her moments ago. *I can't believe he actually said those three words, 'I love you.'* He held tight on to her hand as if he did not want to let her go. She smiled as they made their way back to The Carolina Inn, as it was getting late.

They made their way into the lobby, where Randy and David, laughing and flirting with each other, crossed paths with them. Randy saw how glowing Etta was with Sam. "My, my, aren't we cozy and crazy in love," Randy said, seeing how Etta and Sam were clinging to one another.

"Hey, Randy. You're still up," Etta said.

"Indeed we are," David said. He looked at Randy and they both laughed.

"Oh, I'm sorry. Sam, this is my friend from Chicago, Randy. He accompanied me on this trip. And that is his friend David, who lives here." The three men shook hands.

"You were the person driving the SUV and parking by the Old Well."

"Yes, that was me. Well, we better get going," Randy said, as if to give Etta and Sam their time and space.

"He's a good friend, accompanying you here," Sam said, after Randy and David walked away.

"Yes, he is."

Their intertwined hands remained tight as they ascended the staircase, each step bringing them closer to Etta's room. A familiar warmth spread through her, causing delicate butterflies to awaken within the confines of her stomach.

Finally, they reached the door to her room, standing before it as they shared the feelings of familiarity and intimacy. Etta's heart skipped a beat, mirroring the delicate flutter of the butterflies within her. *Okay. Now what?* She softly uttered, "Thank you for a lovely evening,"

"Thank you for seeing me," Sam murmured, his voice tinged with gratitude and vulnerability. His eyes, laden with longing, searched Etta's face, and then, driven by an irresistible impulse, Sam leaned in, his breath mingling with hers as his thin, soft lips met her luscious, full lips. The world around them faded into insignificance as their passion for each other ignited into a fiery blaze. They kissed.

Their kiss was emotionally charged, expressing their love, longing, and connection. But before their fiery passion could fully consume them, a jarring ring shattered the delicate bubble of intimacy, its sound echoing through the hallway of the hotel. Reluctantly, Sam pulled away, his eyes lingering on Etta's face, a mixture of desire and regret swirling within their depths.

With a sigh, he reached into his pocket, retrieving his phone. The weight of responsibility settled upon him as he hesitantly answered the call. "It's my sister. I'm sorry." Etta nodded her head in understanding. "Hello. We are done with our dinner. Yes, we talked. No. Don't worry. I'm on my way home." Etta knew their night had now ended. "I'm sorry," he said, looking at her and caressing her soft face. "My daughter needs me. She skinned her knees…"

"No. Say no more."

"I…"

"No. I completely understand," Etta said.

"I'm so…"

"No. No. Don't be. I had a great time."

"When are you leaving?"

"Tomorrow."

"What time?"

"8 a.m."

"Do you have to leave? Do you think you can change your flight and extend it for a few days?" He almost sounded boyish.

"Why?" Etta said.

"Because I want to spend more time with you. And I was hoping you could spend time with Sopraffina and me tomorrow. I had to take her to the doctor to get her checkup and fill in medical paperwork for her school. You don't have to be with us during the doctor's visit and paperwork, but I'm hoping you could be with us afterward for lunch or something."

"Oh, wow. That is a big step. You want me to meet Sopraffina. Are you sure about that?" Etta asked, worried.

"Well, she has met you before. I would like to slowly introduce you to the children, so you can get to know each other. Do you think it's too fast? Are you ready for it?"

Etta smiled and nodded her head, remembering Sopraffina was the most pleasant child out of the three. "Sure. I would love to meet her again. But do you think she still remembers me? Will she be okay about meeting me?"

"She has a great memory. I'm sure she remembers you. I'll talk to her about it and see how she feels about it."

Sam and Etta gazed longingly into each other's eyes. He kissed her passionately again and forced himself to pull away to leave. The kiss left her breathless.

All she could think about that night before she fell asleep was their kiss and the way he pulled her into his arms when a car nearly ran her over. Most important of all was when he declared, "Etta Kem, I love you." She recalled that moment over and over in her mind. It made her heart smile, loving the way he called her name and surname. Love and happiness made her forget about everything else.

Randy decided to extend his stay as well. He and David were in a getting-to-seriously-know-each-other phase.

20

Etta, Chapel Hill
August 25, 2018

Emotions flared at McCorkle Place, Chapel Hill campus, as supporters of *Silent Sam*, holding Confederate flags, and anti-*Silent Sam* protesters yelled at each other and got into each other's faces. "Racists go home," yelled the anti-*Silent Sam* protesters. The situation turned ugly when pushes and shoves ensued. About a hundred people participated in the protests. Etta stood watching on her hotel room TV, with a cup of coffee in her hand, the footage of the protesters clashing with the opposite side and one of them stomping the Confederate flag. The anchor announced that seven people were arrested for assault, destruction of property, and inciting a riot.

A knock on the door broke her attention from the screen. She walked over to look through the peephole and then opened the door.

"Randy, you're extra fine looking this morning."

"David is taking me all over town. I want to look my best, as I will be taking lots of videos and pictures."

"Nice."

"Where is your handsome man taking you?" Randy asked.

"I don't know. I can't imagine far. He has his little girl with him."

"Ooh. You're meeting his kid. Things are getting serious, eh? Did you and him… you know?" he winked and nudged her.

"No. But I take it you did."

"Why else would I still be here? Girl, what are you two waiting for?"

"He was called home."

"See, that is the thing with dating a man with children; his kids come first."

"I wouldn't have it any other way. It showed he's moral and responsible."

"Whatever you say. I'm going to be with my boo. When is he picking you up?"

"Around eleven or so. I figured I would get some work done before he comes to pick me up."

"All right then, I am off. Have a fun day."

"Thanks. You do the same."

"You know I will." They both laughed.

Etta could sense herself smiling at every passing scene of Sam's hometown. The minivan's cool air kept everyone comfortable from the outside humidity. The midmorning sky remained partly cloudy as if it was a sign of bad things to come, but the feelings within Etta remained upbeat like sun rays on a field of sunflowers. She had been pleasantly surprised when Sopraffina ran to hug her at her hotel lobby. She felt touched that the little girl not only remembered her but bonded with her.

Etta and Sopraffina sat quietly as Sam made a right turn from Raleigh Road onto an entrance to Glenwood Square. He pulled into the parking lot between The Fresh Market and the FedEx Center, just down from the Thai Palace restaurant.

"Is this where we are going, Daddy?" Sopraffina asked.

"Yes, dear." Sam turned to look at Etta. "I hope you don't mind coming to a Thai restaurant. It's the closest to having Khmer food."

"Not really that close, but I do love Thai food," Etta said.

"Well, you must show me how to make Khmer food one day," he said, with a smile.

"Oh, you like Khmer food?" Etta said, surprised because she didn't think he was in touch with his Khmer side.

"That is a silly thing to say. Have you forgotten that my father was Khmer? I'm proud of who I am and so are my siblings. We're proud of our Khmer heritage just like our Anglo side. Every time we visit my oldest brother Daniel in Skokie, his wife and her mother always make authentic Khmer food for us. They're great cooks. We love their food."

"Oh," Etta said, feeling bad for judging him, as she was uncertain if he was looking down on his Khmer side when they first met at Le Cafe. Now that she knew he was proud of his Khmer heritage, she broke into a silly grin.

"What?" he asked, raising his eyebrow.

"Oh, nothing."

They opened the car doors. The humidity felt unbearable, but people paraded in and out of nearby shops and restaurants with pleasantries. Sam stepped out of his minivan and lifted his daughter out of her car seat. Residents and vacationers alike took their sweet time striding to and fro on the plaza.

"Thank you, Daddy."

Etta smiled, admiring the doting father and his adorable daughter. She glanced over to the father and no longer focused on the daughter, watching his every move as he closed and locked the door. She wondered how happy she would be to have a husband who was so loving and attentive to his kids. She was already seeing their wedding and living happily ever after doing mundane things together. He made sure his doors were locked and checked to make sure his windows were all rolled up. Then he stopped what he was doing and looked around. "Sop, Sop, where are you? This is not funny."

Etta looked left and right. She started to panic realizing Sopraffina was nowhere in sight.

Her father heard a giggle on the side of a Ford truck next to his car. He walked over. He picked her up and raised her up in the air as she kicked her feet and continued to giggle. Etta noticed a black and red birthmark on her right arm shaped almost like a butterfly. He gave her a disapproving look before he put her back down on the ground.

"Oh, thank God," said Etta. "I'm sorry I was not more aware of the surroundings. I didn't know she would disappear like that."

"That's okay. She has been playing hide and seek with her auntie Tomi. She thinks it's funny to have people searching for her. It's a phase. I'm hoping she will get over it soon."

"It must be hard raising your children on your own," Etta said, as she looked at the little girl holding her father's hand and smiling, as she skipped and bopped up and down alongside him.

"It's not that bad. I just have to be very alert with my kids. Plus, I have my sister and Tomi to help out."

Etta found herself pondering the thoughts of Vida and Tomi when it came to her dating Sam. An uncertainty lingered in her mind, suggesting that Tomi harbored some level of dislike or disapproval toward her. Aside from hearing about Vida confirming her caring nature toward Sam, she did not know her well yet. Vida was like a blank canvas waiting to be painted upon.

Entering the casual dining establishment, Etta, Sam, and the child were greeted by a warm and cheerful waitress. With partitions separating the tables, each group enjoyed a sense of privacy. The waitress led them to a snug table meant for four, where Sam and his daughter settled against the wall, and Etta took her seat opposite them, with her back to the aisle.

Etta's eyes skimmed the menu, and a flicker of concern crossed her face. "It doesn't seem like they offer a children's menu," she observed, scanning the options available.

"Actually, they do, but you'll have to ask them to make it. They'll make whatever the kids like," Sam said. "Sop likes rice noodle soup. Doesn't she?" He turned to his adorable daughter.

"Yes, I like noodles with chicken," she said, in her cute voice.

Etta's smile radiated with adoration as she gazed at Sam. The coziness of being in the company of a loving man and a child offered her a glimpse into the joys of family life. The thought crossed her mind: *I could easily become accustomed to this*. Sam reciprocated her smile, his eyes conveying an unspoken understanding and shared agreement. A blush crept onto Etta's cheeks, compelling her to delicately tuck a stray lock of hair behind her right ear. She glanced downward, feigning interest in the menu before her.

"So, I would like to order the chicken larb, which is similar to what my sister-in-law Sopheap used to make," Sam said, looking over the menu.

"Hmm. I see Massaman Curry here. That is similar to Khmer; however, I don't see papaya salad on the menu. That would be similar to Khmer, too," Etta said, flipping through the menu.

"Yeah, Southeast Asian patrons often ask about that dish, but they don't have it on the menu, which is strange for a Thai restaurant."

The lunch proved to be a delightful experience for all involved. As they prepared to leave, Sam approached Etta with a request. He kindly asked if she wouldn't mind keeping an eye on Sop while he made a quick trip to the restroom. Etta felt a surge of warmth and was touched by

Sam's trust in her to care for his beloved daughter, the apple of his eye. A wide smile graced her face as she assured him that she was more than happy to look after the six-year-old darling.

"Of course, let's go wait for Daddy outside," Etta cheerfully proposed, her tone filled with happiness and confidence.

The little girl, Sop, exuded an infectious energy as she hopped, jumped, and skipped ahead of Etta with carefree abandon. It was the vibrant hour of lunchtime, and the plaza teemed with people of all ages.

Etta matched Sop's enthusiasm, her eyes never straying far from the child. "Let's wait right here for your daddy, Sop," she suggested, her voice filled with warmth and affection.

"Why can't we wait in the car?" Sop inquired, her gaze fixed upon Etta with a pair of captivating honey-colored eyes framed by curled lashes.

Etta returned Sop's gaze with a smile, her voice gentle. "Your father didn't give us the key."

Sop's innocent expression softened as she absorbed the information. "Oh," she responded simply.

"He won't be long," Etta reassured her.

"Okay," Sop replied, her trust in her father's timely return evident in her tone. Just then, Etta's mobile phone rang with that Darth Vader ringtone, causing her to release Sop's hand and delve into her purse to retrieve it. The caller ID displayed Daron's name and profile, triggering a wave of nerves within Etta. She couldn't help but feel anxious, fearing he would give her a hard time if Daron discovered she was in Chapel Hill.

"Etta, what the fuck?"

"Excuse me?" she said.

"What the fuck are you doing in Chapel Hill?"

"Hey. Can you please not use that kind of language?"

"Did you put me on speaker?"

"No, but your voice is bombastically loud."

"Why does it matter? We're adults. Are you with him now? Do you want to get hurt again? Did you listen to *Dirty John*? I guess not. If you did, you would know better."

"If you must know, I am here because of a job."

"Why did you take that job, so that you could run into him?"

"I had no idea that I would run into him…" Etta said, as she looked down from her phone. She started to look around her. "Sop, Sop, Sop. Where are you? Sop. This is not funny."

"What? Who is Sop? Where are you anyway? What are you doing?"

"Sop, Sop!" Etta called out, her voice filled with worry. She scanned the expanse of the vast parking lot, but there was no sign of Sop. It perplexed Etta as she hadn't expected Sop to wander so fast, considering she had only briefly looked away for a few seconds—or so it seemed.

With a growing sense of concern, Etta surveyed the entire plaza, her eyes darting from one corner to another. Finally, she made a decision and hurried into the adjacent Subway restaurant, hoping to find a trace of Sop's whereabouts. She dashed into the restroom, hoping that Sop might have sought refuge there. She approached the women inside, anxiously inquiring if they had seen a six-year-old girl. Their responses were unanimous: no one had seen Sop. Some regarded Etta with judgmental eyes, while others empathized with the distress of a mother losing her child.

As the realization sank in that Sopraffina was nowhere to be found, panic surged through Etta's veins. "Sop, please show yourself," she pleaded, her voice trembling. Hastily, she dashed back outside, scouring the walkway of the plaza, desperately searching for any sign of Sop. With a glimmer of hope, she even ventured into the nearby FedEx Center, located to the left of the Thai Palace restaurant, hoping to find Sopraffina there.

"Etta, Etta, Etta," Darren's voice echoed through the phone before abruptly cutting off, as the area seemed to have poor cellular service. Despite his attempts to call back, Etta was too consumed by her distress and preoccupied with her search for Sop to care.

Just as Etta emerged from the FedEx Center, her heart pounding and her mind racing, she was startled by Sam's sudden appearance. He had been frantically searching for both Etta and his daughter, sensing the urgency in the situation.

Sam's panic was evident as he confronted Etta, desperate for answers. His voice quivered with fear and anxiety as he demanded to know, "Where is my daughter?"

Etta's own distress was palpable as she tried to gather her thoughts and find the right words. "I... I don't know," she stammered, her voice trembling.

"What do you mean you don't know?! I asked you to watch her."

"I was with her, but... she disappeared. I looked away for just a moment, and... she was gone."

Her words hung heavy in the air, the weight of her guilt and uncertainty pressing upon her. She felt the weight of Sam's accusatory question, knowing that she had been entrusted with the responsibility of looking after Sop.

"I was just on the..." Sam rushed toward The Fresh Market, desperately calling out for his little girl, before Etta could finish her sentence. She watched him frantically search, his voice full of anguish and hope, scanning every corner, from the parking lot to the surrounding bushes and trees. A glimmer of hope flickered in the depths of Etta's mind, willing herself to believe that Sop might just be playing a game, hiding somewhere nearby, as her father had said before they went into the restaurant.

However, as time wore on and the search continued fruitlessly, a chilling realization began to dawn on Etta. The possibility of abduction crept into her thoughts, a haunting notion that sent shivers down her spine. The idea that Sop might have intended to play hide and seek but had been snatched away seized her mind, almost paralyzing her with fear. Her heart sank, and her stomach twisted into a hollow pit. How could she be so negligent? Maybe she was not ready to take care of someone besides herself.

"No," Etta whispered to herself, her voice filled with disbelief and anguish. Tears started to form at the thought of Sop being abducted. "This can't be happening. Abductions, disappearances... they happen to other people, far away." The weight of her carelessness, of momentarily letting go of Sop's hand, bore down on her with a crushing guilt. Regret flooded her thoughts as she questioned her lack of focus and vigilance.

In her desperation and despair, Etta turned to a higher power. "Oh, Lord," she pleaded in a whisper between her and God, her voice trembling with desperation and faith. "Please bring Sopraffina back to us." As if using telepathy, she called out in her mind: *Sop, please. No more games. Please don't scare us like this. Let us know if you're okay. Come back. Please.*

After an exhaustive search around the plaza, parking lot, and even his car, Etta could see that Sam's desperation was reaching its peak. He ran tirelessly, calling out Sop's name and describing her as a six-year-old with a peach and cream complexion, honey-colored eyes, in a sunflower dress, to anyone who would listen, desperately hoping for a glimmer of information. As each minute ticked by, Etta's anxiety amplified.

Finally, overwhelmed by the gravity of the situation, Sam made the decision to dial 911. His voice trembled as he provided the operator with Sop's name, a detailed description, and the clothing she was last seen wearing. Amidst the chaos and distress, he glanced at Etta, acknowledging her presence as he spoke to the person on the other end of the line. "She was last seen with a friend who is with me now," he relayed, emphasizing Etta's involvement in the search.

Friend? Are we really just friends now? Priority, Etta! Priority! We are in the middle of a crisis. Don't let a mere label consume you. It was hard to discern whether the ache within her stemmed from the absence of Sop, who had gone missing, or the sting of her father reducing their connection to mere friendship.

Shortly after, a patrol officer arrived on the scene, and Sam immediately provided him with all the details about Sop's disappearance, including her physical description and what she was wearing. The officer then turned to Etta, asking her what she was doing when Sop went missing. Etta felt numb as she recounted the events, explaining how she had let go of Sop's hand and briefly lost sight of her.

As the officer conducted his preliminary investigation and spoke with witnesses in the area, Etta sensed Sam's disappointment and anger toward her. He turned away from her, refusing to look her in the eye. The weight of his silence was deafening. With her downcast eyes, and rubbing of her forehead as if to ease the pain she felt, Etta showed a deep sense of shame and regret.

Eventually, the officer concluded his initial report and asked Sam and Etta to meet up with him at the police station. Etta followed Sam to his car, hoping he wouldn't mind her riding with him. However, as they sat in silence, Etta could sense Sam's anger and disappointment, and his Silent Sam mode only reinforced her sense of guilt and shame.

"I take full responsibility for my carelessness. I understand that mere words like 'I am sorry' hold little weight in your eyes at this moment," Etta confessed, her voice heavy with remorse. As she looked into his furrowed brow and the tight seal of his lips, his silence bore deep into her soul. The profound disappointment she had inflicted upon the father and the possible immense loss of a precious human life, his daughter, weighed heavily upon her heart.

How do you lose a human being, especially a child? Poor Sop. She must be trapped somewhere or kidnapped by someone.

The thought of the little girl being harmed felt like the ultimate violation of the rules of life. Her chest constricted, suffocating her with each labored breath. The intense heat emanating from her flushed face and trembling body mirrored the intensity of her guilt. It was she, with her actions, who had brought harm upon Sop, and that realization weighed heavily upon her conscience.

Why was I so careless? Oh, Sop. I'm so sorry. I'm so, so sorry. I'm a terrible adult.

The overwhelming urge to break down and release a flood of tears consumed her, but she remained numb, consumed instead by the relentless replay of the scene in her mind. She was consumed by the desperate need to retrace her steps and unravel what had transpired during those fateful moments when her gaze had strayed from Sopraffina. Together with the police officer who arrived on the scene, they had scoured every inch of the surrounding area, combing through hidden spaces and even the tiniest crevices to find any trace of her.

Sop, where could you have gone?

As she glanced at her phone, Etta propped her right elbow on the car door panel, pressing her forehead with her fingertips in a desperate attempt to piece together the exact moments she had taken her eyes off Sopraffina. The vibrant red numbers indicating missed calls on her iPhone went unnoticed, as her mind was consumed by a whirlwind of thoughts. Lost in her own world, she failed to notice Sam parking the car and silently departing without uttering a single word to her. He texted someone, and by the time she finally stepped out of the vehicle, he had already briefed his sister Vida of the devastating incident, ended the call, and opened the door to the police station without holding it for her. Etta harbored no resentment toward him for this slight; in fact, she believed she deserved such treatment. The weight of her own actions left her anticipating the worst treatment from

Sam, and she held no blame toward him whatsoever, for she knew she had let him down in the gravest of ways.

21

The police swiftly separated Sam and Etta, directing them to separate conference rooms where they would be individually interviewed by officers of their respective genders. Each of them diligently recounted the events leading up to Sopraffina's disappearance, as well as any conversations or interactions they could recall. Both provided a meticulous description of Sop's attire and any personal belongings she had carried at the time she went missing. Sam, with a heavy heart, mentioned the black and red birthmark on her right arm that almost looked like a butterfly, while also sharing endearing details of his daughter's sweet nature. The mere thought of anything sinister happening to his beloved little girl threatened to shatter him completely, leaving him on the verge of emotional collapse. He held up a close-up headshot of Sop on his Galaxy phone, clinging to the image as a bittersweet reminder of her innocence.

Sam and Etta cooperated fully with the law enforcement investigators, providing them with all the information they had initially told to the officer at the scene. After the interviews concluded, the officers left them alone in their respective rooms. Etta's phone incessantly rang with a barrage of incoming calls, but she paid them no mind, her gaze fixed on an empty space as if her soul had vacated her body.

After what seemed like an eternity, they were finally reunited. Etta's knees trembled, though not in the way that brought comfort. She yearned for something or someone to anchor herself to, to provide stability amidst the chaos. The investigators informed them that they had gathered surveillance video recordings from the surrounding areas. They advised Sam to restrict access to his home until law enforcement arrived and had the opportunity to collect any potential evidence. Although Sopraffina had not gone missing from home, but rather from the neighborhood plaza, precautions needed to be taken to ensure the integrity of the investigation.

"Please do not touch or remove anything from your child's room and home in general. We've given you the name and telephone number of the law enforcement investigator assigned to your case. Keep his information in a safe and convenient place, we'll be in touch."

Just then tension filled the air, as a thin, ghostly pale woman abruptly approached Etta, unleashing a venomous scream, "You stupid bitch!" Her hand rose, poised to strike Etta, but before the blow could land, Randy swiftly emerged from a different entrance, intercepting the woman's wrist in mid-air.

"If you lay a finger on my friend, I'll knock you out and pay a fine," he warned the woman.

Standing next to Randy, David interjected, "Hey, Randy. Need I remind you we're currently at the police station?"

Tomi, the pale woman, spun around in astonishment, her eyes fixing on the source of the voice.

"How dare you! Do you know who I am?" she retorted, attempting to free her wrist from Randy's firm grip.

"Look, lady! I don't care who the hell you are. You don't run up to a person throwing hands, especially at my friend. As far as I'm concerned, you're just a crazy person," Randy responded, his voice unwavering. "Etta is the kindest and sweetest person on this planet. I'm not about to let you hurt her."

"Let go of me! So you're one of her hoodlum friends," Tomi said. She yanked her hand away and ran over to hold onto Sam's arm. He stood in silence not saying anything.

"Hoodlum? Bitch, who are you calling hoodlum?" Randy said, fuming.

Etta and David ran to pull him away before he got himself in trouble. "It's not worth it. We have a bigger issue to solve," Etta said softly, shaken by what was happening. "I appreciate you standing up for me."

"Do you see that, officers? He threatened me and dared to come at me. Have them arrested. They have something to do with little Sop's disappearance." Tomi's accusatory words pierced the air, her trembling fingers pointing directly at Etta. "Officers, did you hear me? She deliberately lost a child, and her friend had the audacity to threaten me. Arrest him! Arrest them! They're involved in Sop's disappearance." The desperation and anger in Tomi's voice echoed throughout the room.

"We can't just arrest people without any evidence," Captain Miller said.

"I'll find you evidence," Tomi said with confidence.

Etta stared at Tomi, a mix of disbelief and confusion showed on her face. It was as if she was witnessing someone who had completely lost touch with reality. Her gaze then shifted to Sam, who stood in silence, his disappointed eyes fixed upon her. At that moment, Etta felt her heart shatter into a million pieces. The weight of the accusation, coupled with Sam's disapproving gaze, crushed her spirit.

Vida and her husband Paolo arrived next on the scene, with annoyance and surprise evident on Vida's face at Tomi's presence. She couldn't help but comment, "You managed to get here quickly," her voice sounding vexed. Tomi, however, remained locked arm in arm with her silent brother, displaying a possessive sense as if Sam belonged to her. He made no effort to free himself from her grasp, his vacant stare fixed upon nothingness.

Vida, her expression now stoic, turned toward Etta, with disappointment evident in her piercing eyes. Speaking with a sense of superiority, she addressed Etta with grave disappointment. "How could you be so careless? She's just a child."

"I'm so, so sorry, Vida," Etta said, in tears. "I have no excuse for what I have done."

"How could you let your eyes wander away from her? If anything were to happen to her…" Vida's voice trailed off, the unspoken implications hanging heavily in the air.

"Vida, she lost the child on purpose," Tomi said. Then she pointed to Etta. "I swear, if anything happened to her you are going to pay for it. I'll make sure of it!"

"'Lost the child on purpose'? For what reason?" Randy asked, flabbergasted.

"It could be jealousy," Tomi said, "because of how much Sam adores his little girl."

"Do you hear yourself? How does that even make sense?"

"Who knows. She could resent his children, have mental issues or some other personal motivations."

"The only mental person I see here is you," Randy shouted.

"You better watch who you are talking to," Tomi said with a hand on her hip. "She is responsible for this nightmare. I'll get all the evidence you need, officers," Tomi said to the officers standing watching the commotion.

"Look here, chicky-poo! You are batshit crazy!" Randy said.

Etta, overwhelmed by the weight of her own guilt, chose to remain silent throughout these exchanges. Typically not one to shy away from speaking up, she found herself unable to defend herself.

"All right. Just stop!" Captain Miller's commanding voice resonated through the room. The tall, bearded man in his early fifties held a commanding presence as he addressed the distraught adults. "I understand the overwhelming emotions you're experiencing, but dwelling on blame won't aid our efforts. Rest assured, we are taking swift action to locate the missing child," he said.

Turning his attention to Sam, Captain Miller addressed him directly. "Mr. Angk, I want to assure you that we are taking every necessary step to locate your child. Our investigator has entered your child into the National Crime Information Center Missing Persons File, and we have issued a Be On the Look Out bulletin. Additionally, at your request, we have involved the Federal Bureau of Investigation in the search."

The captain's words carried a sense of determination and empathy as he continued, "We have gathered all the information we need from you and Ms. Kem at this time. Before we classify your child's disappearance as an Abduction by Non-Family Members," we will intensify our efforts to locate and question your ex-wife. We are fully committed to leaving no stone unturned in our pursuit to find your daughter."

"I doubt she knows anything," Sam managed to say.

As if understanding the anguish and anxiety that Sam must be feeling, Captain Miller gently urged him, "In the meantime, I implore you to return home and wait for our call. It is essential that you take care of yourselves and find solace in the knowledge that we are doing everything possible to locate your child. Your cooperation and patience will greatly assist our investigation."

With a reassuring nod, Captain Miller concluded, "Please remember that you are not alone in this ordeal. We are here to support you, and we will keep you informed of any updates or developments. Have faith, and we will work tirelessly until your little girl is reunited."

Tomi's voice trembled with anger as she spoke out, "We know who is responsible for this! Why don't you question her? Investigate her!" Her frustration was evident as she demanded that the authorities take immediate action. "I know she did it! I just know it. She and her friends are responsible for kidnapping little Sop!"

Captain Miller maintained his composed demeanor, understanding the intensity of the situation. He responded calmly but firmly, attempting to pacify Tomi's anger. "Ma'am, please allow us to do our job."

"We'll gladly cooperate, Captain, and to further demonstrate our commitment, we are willing to undergo a polygraph test," Randy declared confidently.

Etta remained silent, already having completed her polygraph examination as per the standard protocol.

Vida weighed in with her own suggestions. "Have you reached out to the National Center for Missing and Exploited Children and other reputable nonprofit organizations? It might be worth considering assembling a dedicated search team as well. Additionally, contacting the media could significantly amplify our efforts." Her desperation was evident as she recognized the urgency of every passing second in locating her beloved niece, Sop.

"Vida, please try not to worry," Tomi responded. "As soon as I learned about Sop's disappearance, I allocated funds toward employing skilled search teams and private investigators to expedite the search. I will personally handle the role of the family's spokesperson, and my assistant will promptly contact the media. However, in the interim—" Tomi's gaze shifted toward the captain and the accompanying officers—"it is crucial that you thoroughly investigate this woman. I have a strong intuition that she is involved in Sop's disappearance, and we demand that a report be filed against her. We implore you to investigate her for kidnapping or any other potential harm inflicted upon my innocent child." Though Etta did not notice, but Sam and Vida were glancing at Tomi with confusion.

Etta's eyes narrowed with intensity at this crazy woman. *Her innocent child?* she thought, her confusion mounting. The woman's behavior toward her had been consistently cruel ever since their first encounter. Etta believed that one could be protective of a friend and their family without resorting to illogical and hurtful behavior. Unless…

Etta lifted her face and directed her stare at Tomi as she finally connected the dots: the disruption of her lovemaking with Sam, the venomous look she gave her that night, Wallace's broken arm, the speeding car, the blocked phone number, and her relentless unkindness. Tomi seemed to get more and more desperate as she and Sam grew close. Maybe her accusation of her being responsible for Sop going missing was a confession. Etta internally gasped, as her eyes widened. *So the card-reader was right! The formidable force, the pesky hurdles, and barriers that currently impede Sam's connection with me is this woman, Tomi. She must be crazy in love with him to do all of these things. Perhaps she is responsible for kidnapping Sop. According to Sam, Tomi taught Sop how to play hide and seek, possibly for this reason. I need to contact a private investigator of my own to investigate her. Jack Edlin knows all the great detectives.*

"This woman is batshit crazy. I need to make a phone call," Randy declared, concerned by the situation unfolding before him.

Tomi's mind raced with suspicion. "You must trace his call. He's likely one of her accomplices, trying to alert their co-conspirator to move Sop to another location.

Dear God, I hope we're not running out of time. Every moment is vital. Captain, you must take immediate action," she pleaded, recognizing the urgency of the situation and the need for swift intervention.

"Are you Mr. Angk's wife?" inquired Captain Miller.

"No, but we share a very close bond. We're like family," Tomi replied, with an air of arrogance and superiority. "But you must know who I am. I'm Tomi Lim."

"Oh, Mr. Kevin Lim, the real estate tycoon."

"That's right."

"Mrs. Lim, we have followed all the proper procedures, so I kindly request that you go home," responded the captain.

"No, you don't understand. You need to hold her, arrest and charge her," Tomi shouted.

"That's enough," Vida interjected, seeming to be growing weary of Tomi's craziness.

Overwhelmed by the events that had transpired, Etta sank into one of the chairs, feeling the life drain from her body as she tried to process the situation. She thought about calling her ex-fiancé to suggest a good detective to look into this woman who was determined to create problems for her.

"This isn't over. I will gather a team of legal experts and investigators to ensure that you pay the ultimate price," Tomi declared, her voice dripping with anger. "You will suffer the consequences, never to see the light of day again. I'll expose your actions on social media, and mob justice will descend upon you swiftly and mercilessly. You will be unable to work or show your face in public. You will deeply regret ever entering our lives," Tomi berated Etta with the vehemence of a sworn enemy.

Before Etta could defend herself, an unexpected voice thundered across the room.

"Enough, Tomi!" Sam's voice boomed, releasing Tomi's arm from his.

"What? How... what? You've never raised your voice at me before. She—she lost our Sop. How could you..." Tomi stammered, her confusion evident.

"It's about time someone silenced you. I'm glad it's him," a voice resonated through the room, and Etta immediately recognized it as Kevin's. Her gaze dropped, only to discover his hand intertwined with a tiny hand.

Surprise, relief, and unbounded joy surged through her heart at the sight.

"Sop, my sweet child!" Sam exclaimed through tears as he rushed to embrace his little girl. He showered her cheeks and forehead with kisses, carefully ensuring she was unharmed. Vida, his sister, hurried over to join them, feeling as if a dark cloud had lifted from their lives.

"Sop, my sweet Sop," Tomi said, her voice filled with relief. "You're here. You're okay," she said with a look of confusion as if wondering how Kevin found Sop.

"You should know. You kidnapped her," a voice resounded, one that Etta hadn't heard in years.

"Jack," Etta and Randy both uttered in unison.

"What K-drama is this and who is that hot man?" David asked, fanning himself.

"That's Etta's ex-fiancé who cheated on her. He's not that hot," Randy said, with a bit of jealousy in his tone.

"What's going on?" Etta asked, her confusion mirrored by Sam, Vida, Randy, and David. The turn of events had left them all looking perplexed.

"I'll explain to you later," Jack stated, his gaze fixed on Etta. Then he turned to Captain Miller and other officers involved in the case. "The woman standing before us," he pointed toward Tomi," is a malevolent person. She has developed an unhealthy and obsessive infatuation with Sam, according to her husband here, and she is willing to resort to any means necessary to eliminate her rivals. She thought she got away with it the first time. She played a significant role in driving Sam's ex-wife into a profound state of depression, ultimately pushing her into the arms of another man. Shockingly, just the other day, she even attempted to intentionally run Etta over using a rental car. No one who tries to harm Etta will get away with it." The room erupted in a collective gasp as Jack's words settled in. Sam and Vida turned their heads toward Tomi, their expressions a mixture of revulsion and disbelief.

"I knew I wasn't going crazy," Etta murmured, her words almost a soliloquy. It became evident to her that a woman wouldn't exhibit such intense possessiveness without reason. Jack had just confirmed her suspicion. Everything suddenly fell into place, although she grappled with the realization that someone who came from a respectable background and held a professional demeanor could harbor such vindictiveness and irrationality. However, she quickly came to terms with the truth. It was a stark reminder that individuals with wealth, influence, and authority would stop at nothing to fulfill their selfish desires and cravings.

"You're crazy. You make all of this up to protect this woman," Tomi said, as she side-eyed Etta with disgust. "You have no proof."

"I've got surveillance video to prove it. And I have video footage of the kidnapping, which you thought you had cleared. And just as importantly, I have witnesses," Jack pointed to Kevin and her hired accomplice.

"How could you do this to me? I'm your wife," Tomi said.

"You haven't been my wife since the day you married me," Kevin expressed with sorrow and anger. "It has become painfully clear to me your intentions were solely driven by greed, fixated on acquiring my family's wealth and influence, but the love you have is for Sam. I should have recognized the signs when you began incessantly shadowing him, going out of your way to be near him and his children. We uprooted our lives solely for his sake! You said you didn't want to live with my family in Chicago, because you wanted privacy for the two of us. You adamantly refused to bear children with me, taking advantage of my unwavering love and admiration for you."

His voice brimming with a deep-scated resentment as he recounted her malevolence. "You stooped so low as to deliberately scare Wallace at the Drake hotel where he stumbled and fell, because you found out from Sopheap that Sam was walking Etta home; and when he took so long, you had to find a way to get him back, knowing nothing makes him return faster than his children. You would do anything to lure Sam away from Etta's side. You even orchestrated a treacherous game of hide and seek, enticing Sop to chase after you and look for you in a concrete backyard, secretly hoping Sop would stumble and injure herself when running. To your twisted delight, she tripped on an object you left in front of her on purpose, so that she fell and scraped her knee. You were well aware of Sam's boundless love for his children, and you exploited that knowledge to manipulate him to cut his time short with Etta. I had no idea what you were doing with his phone at the hotel, but—" he turned to address Sam—"I bet you anything she erased Etta's calls and texts to you, Sam."

"Wow," Randy and David said simultaneously, as they looked at each other.

"How did you know Kevin? And how did you become involved in all of this?" Etta asked, in a whisper to Jack.

"I'll tell you later," Jack responded. "After all, we billionaire assholes all meet to decide who gets the last piece of the pie," he said, winking at her.

"Oh, you and Daron spoke," Etta said with a grin.

Kevin's words dripped with contempt as he continued. "When your previous schemes failed to separate Sam from Etta, only to bring them closer, you resorted to hiring a ruthless accomplice to kidnap Sop, imprisoning her within one of our abandoned properties slated for demolition. Thankfully, he has a conscience and contacted me. Anyone with an ounce of sense would recognize this as an act of attempted murder—kidnapping with the intent to kill."

Sam and Vida looked at Tomi with contempt.

"Hey, man. That's my line," Jack said, attempting to lighten the mood when the situation got too hostile.

"That is beyond messed up," Randy exclaimed, his words resonating with the collective sentiment amid the unfolding drama. The room fell into a heavy silence, as Kevin exposed the depths of her malevolence and the extent to which she was willing to go to achieve her love.

"Stop! This is not true. I love you." Tomi's voice trembled with desperation as she tried to salvage the remnants of Kevin's one-sided love for her, as if clinging to a sliver of hope that she could still appeal to his deep affection for her.

"No. No!" Kevin cried out, his voice choking with sorrow. "I cannot continue to be trapped by your spell. You always use it to distract and get your way. Even in our most intimate moments, you think of him."

Etta and Randy exchanged a significant glance, of horror and disgust. The gravity of the situation was not lost on them, and they understood the profound impact it would have on everyone involved. Sam, in particular, looked devastated upon hearing the revelations. Etta knew from their casual conversation that his feelings for Tomi had always been akin to that of a protective older brother, and the idea she had hurt his children and deceived others probably left him betrayed and mortified.

Kevin continued, "As much as I love you, I can no longer avert my gaze from the truth. I simply cannot tolerate it any longer, to wait for you to come to your senses!"

"This is all a misunderstanding, darling," Tomi proclaimed, as if desperately clinging to the hope that she could somehow refute the damning accusations against her.

"No, there is no misunderstanding here," Jack asserted firmly, his voice carrying a sense of finality. Then, he called out, "Ms. Sara Berg, please come in."

As everyone turned their attention toward the entrance, Sara walked into the room, her presence eliciting gasps of surprise from the gathered crowd. She approached Sam and their daughter, a mixture of emotions playing across her face. The room fell into a tense silence, as the significance of Sara's arrival elicited the revelation that would follow.

"Who is she?" Randy and David asked in unison.

Etta's heart sank. "That's Sam's ex-wife," she whispered to Randy and David, her voice filled with confusion. If Sara had been forced or misled to leave her family, then Etta knew she had to morally give up her love for Sam.

"What?" Randy asked.

"He told me she was suffering from postpartum depression after she gave birth to Sopraffina. She was allegedly abusing her prescribed pills and wanted to commit suicide. She was getting help for it but then she met a man, probably at that clinic, and he helped her to get better and they, allegedly, fell in love. Sam said she fell out of love with him and left him and their children to be with the mystery man."

"I get it now. It was all Tomi's doing. I wonder how she did it though," Randy said.

"Who knows. Evil and conniving people have their ways," Etta said.

Randy and David exchanged glances, their expressions overflowing anticipation and unease for Etta. "I'm sorry, Etta. I guess you have your closure now. My dear friend, this relationship can't go any further," Randy said, putting his arm around her shoulder.

The realization hit Etta like a wave of sorrow and disbelief. Tomi's actions had shattered Sam's family, and now the return of Sara, prompted by an Amber Alert for her little girl, added another layer of complexity to the already tumultuous situation. As Sara stood before them, Etta could see the confusion on Sop's face. It was evident that the passage of time had changed her appearance, making it difficult for her young child to recognize her mother, as Sara had left her when she was a baby. The woman standing before her seemed like a stranger to her.

As the mother reunited with her daughter and ex-husband, Jack took a moment to confer quietly with the captain and the officers involved in the case. Their amicable expressions conveyed a shared understanding, and their gaze shifted toward Etta.

Jack approached Etta and cloaked her in a comforting embrace. Etta wanted to cry but held herself together. "I'm sorry you have to go through yet another heartbreak," he whispered, his voice full of tenderness and genuine empathy. Sam looked on with confusion.

"Don't look back, Etta. Go home," Jack advised, triggering Etta to remember that she had not looked back when she left him. His voice brimming with care. "I have to turn in evidence and make sure your good name is clear. I have a few days to finish taking a few depositions for my patent infringement case. I'll call you when I return to Chicago."

"Thank you," she uttered softly, her emotions still raw and overwhelming.

"Oh, it's nothing. I was a jerk when I was your fiancé. Let's just say I'm trying to make up for it," he admitted, with regrets in his voice. "Good thing I was in town for a deposition before you arrived and Daron asked me to do some investigation and look into *a special someone*. Who knew his best friend was the nutty one."

"How did you find out?" Etta asked, curious.

"I headed to the links the other day and met Kevin at Chapel Hill Country Club. We got to talking and one thing led to another. He wanted legal advice on some real estate matters, but I told him I'm not a real estate lawyer. Then he wanted some male advice and I gave it to him. Who knew, eh? I'll tell you more about it when I am back in Chicago. Go home." He kissed her on the forehead.

"It's nice of you to help our girl," Randy said in a sarcastic tone, his voice filled with resentment and animosity. Etta gently elbowed him to be nice, because she no longer held grudges against Jack and appreciated his help. After all, he was a well known litigant in Chicago.

"How did Daron know you were taking depositions in Chapel Hill?" Randy's voice dripped with disdain as he confronted Jack. "I know he doesn't like you," Randy said, giving him the evil eye, crossing his arms, and tapping his foot.

"Since you guys like to hang out at Monk's, I thought the food must be good, so I took my client out for a drink there, and that's when I ran into Daron," Jack explained. "He made it clear that if I wanted any chance of gaining his favor, I needed to dig deeper into this enigmatic figure called Sam and uncover his true intentions with Etta. I need to clear some paperwork with these officers. Take Etta home. I'll fill in whatever gaps later. Daron knows most of it. He'll tell you on the plane home."

Etta left the police station, her thoughts and sorrow swirling around her like a tempest. She did not even notice she was inside the SUV and unconsciously put on her seat belt. Lost in her world of emotions, she failed to notice Sam had chased after the car in a desperate attempt to reach her, only to be left behind as Randy accelerated away. Sam tried calling, but his phone faded into black. He had used up all the power and had not thought to recharge it. Some things never changed.

After bidding farewell to David, Randy and Etta boarded Jack's rented, luxurious private jet. As they settled into the comfortable surroundings, Etta sat by the window and reflected on what had transpired that long day. It had become somewhat of a routine for her—delving deep into the intricate labyrinth of her heart, dissecting the twists and turns of love gone awry.

Etta felt an overwhelming sense of relief and joy as Sop, the missing child, was finally found and reunited with her parents. The weight of worry that had burdened her during the search, with the possibility that Sop could have been killed, dissolved, replaced by a profound gratitude that the child was safe and sound. Amidst the prevailing emotions of happiness and relief, another sentiment quietly crept into Etta's consciousness—guilt.

The incident had served as a stark reminder of the dangers lurking in the world, and Etta couldn't help but blame herself for the temporary loss of the child. She questioned her own actions, replaying the moments leading up to Sop's disappearance, and chastising herself for what she perceived as carelessness. The knowledge that Tomi, someone who had harbored ill intentions, had almost taken an innocent life only compounded her guilt and anger. She wanted to reach out and give her a good slap. Knowing Tomi would get her day in court and imprisonment satisfied her; but then again, her money and power might buy her way out of prison. She'd be living freely among other citizens of the United States, like most wealthy American criminals and powerful politicians.

The thought of the distress Sop's parents must have experienced during those agonizing hours haunted her. Etta battled with self-doubt, questioning her ability to fulfill the responsibilities entrusted to her. She didn't blame Sam one bit for being angry with her.

However, within the depths of her guilt, a glimmer of hope emerged. The fact that Tomi's hired kidnapper had a change of heart and ultimately decided to release Sop was nothing short of a miracle. Etta found solace in the knowledge that her captor had been moved by compassion or a change of conscience, allowing the child to be safely returned. It reminded her that even in the face of her own perceived shortcomings, there were elements beyond her control, and the outcome wasn't solely determined by her actions.

To reconcile her feelings of guilt and self-blame, Etta embarked on a journey of self-forgiveness and acceptance. She acknowledged that mistakes happen, even when trying to be vigilant. Etta resolved to learn from the experience, embracing the lessons it offered.

As the jet whisked them away to Chicago, Etta found herself at a crossroads in her relationship with Sam. The events she had experienced and the introspective journey she had undertaken had brought her to a critical juncture—a point where she needed to address and rectify her feelings for him. His wife had returned. Due to Tomi's meddling, Sara broke away from Sam. And now, she, too, had to break away from Sam, because of Tomi. She bowed out for Sam and Sara to reconnect. *Maybe the love is still there. Maybe they worked things out and found their way to each other again. I must let him go; no matter how much I love him.*

22

TANGLED HEARTS, CHICAGO
NOVEMBER 25, 2018

Three months had passed since Etta walked away from Sam without saying goodbye or looking back. She blocked and erased his number, so that there was no temptation on her part to expect his call or to call him. Her once vibrant spirit had been dampened, leaving behind an empty shell that merely went through the motions of existence. The sparkle in her eyes had dimmed, and the laughter that once danced from her lips had grown silent.

Day by day, she mechanically carried out her responsibilities at work and at home, but her heart remained adrift in a sea of melancholy. The world around her seemed dull and colorless, as if drained of all its vitality. The family, relatives, and friends who came by to check up on her became mere strangers passing by, their conversations fading into distant echoes. Her friend Daron understood but still checked up on her now and then. Their friendship remained strong, because he genuinely cared about her. However, Daron learned to be a good friend by no longer intervening in her emotions or imposing his views on her.

Life had become a monotonous routine, devoid of the joy and purpose that once fueled Etta's every step. Despite accepting that Sam was not meant to be a part of her destiny, the embers of her love for him stubbornly refused to be extinguished. Like an indelible mark etched upon her soul, the memories of their brief time together danced vividly in her mind, while her heart continued to beat with the rhythm of their shared affection.

This severance of the relationship was a journey she had taken before, with her past two relationships. The wounds inflicted by her high school sweetheart had taken a year to heal, while the mending of her heart after the dissolution of her engagement with Jack Edlin had required five long, arduous years, because he was her first real relationship. It was hard on her also because older-generation Cambodians, especially her aunt, were old-fashioned and intolerant. To them it was a big deal when a woman lost her virginity before marriage, as she would never be taken seriously or be considered marriage material to a good man from a good family.

This time the pain of separation felt different. The ache was deeper; therefore, she felt it would last longer and more profoundly. The previous relationships had left her wounded and betrayed, no doubt, but the love she had felt for Sam transcended them all. It was a love that resonated in every fiber of her being, defying logic. However, she was still sane and lucid enough to control herself and not let herself become what Tomi was: obsessive and feeling so entitled to what she wanted that she did not care whom she hurt in the process.

As Etta searched for answers, she couldn't help but wonder what it was about Sam that had imprinted such an enduring love upon her soul. Was it his sexy smile that made her weak in the knees? The way he looked at her?

The way he touched her that had the power to turn Etta into a puddle of mush—a touch that evoked a cascade of emotions and invited her to let go of her defenses and surrender to the depth of their love? Or perhaps the chemistry they shared? Their presence complimented each other. Could it be some kind of spiritual connection?

A loud knock did not move Etta from her standing position with her back to the door. It was then pushed open. Daron watched her standing and staring out her large window overlooking the river. "You need to pull yourself together, Etta. Here, I got you your favorite *banh mi* sandwiches. Actually, Rochelle stopped by Eden Center at Falls Church before she flew back home from her business trip. I know you were complaining about how Chicago's banh mi sandwiches are not as good as the ones in Virginia. Eat something to keep your strength up. It's going to be a long trip. And I'll grab a bottle of water so you can eat and drink on the go." He walked to her kitchen and came back out with a bottle of water, which he placed in a bag for her. "My family and I will join you in Cambodia during the last week of your trip to celebrate you getting the building project. You didn't find love in

Chapel Hill, but hey, at least you get to build a museum in his school. Talk about a plot twist, eh?"

Etta was not amused. She stood there, looking at the Riverwalk, kept revisiting her tender moment with Sam when he said, "Etta Kem, I love you" and "I want to grow old with you." These words lingered in her mind like a sacred proclamation of deep affection that she forever held in her heart.

Etta—like any woman, a romantic—clung to those words for dear life. In moments of vulnerability or when faced with loneliness, she would revisit that cherished memory, drawing strength and reassurance from Sam's heartfelt confession. At least, she knew the love was reciprocated and not just one-sided like Tomi's.

A text came through Daron's phone and he typed back and then called out, "Come on, Etta, your parents are waiting with your grandfather. You need to get to O'Hare two hours in advance. Hell, with the way Chicago traffic is, you better get moving."

Etta picked up her carryon while Daron grabbed her heavier luggage. She looked around her house and her eyes stopped at the couch where she and Sam almost made love. "I'm glad your grandfather is taking you on a trip to

Cambodia. Maybe visiting the motherland for the first time might open you up to something. Hey, just consider it your Eat, Pray, Love awakening thing that you women travel the world to do."

Etta ignored him.

Stay tuned for the enchanting sequel, *Christmas in Chapel Hill*, where new adventures await!

**Meanwhile, here is a teaser from
Christmas in Chapel Hill.**

Stay Tuned for Christmas in Chapel Hill!

1

Etta, Pochentong International Airport
November 26, 2018

Etta, having accepted the end of her relationship with Sam, trudged forward in the line at Pochentong International Airport as if she were merely going through the motions. Her memories of leaving O'Hare airport were as hazy as a distant dream, and now she found herself in the sweltering, humid climate of Cambodia, unsure of her purpose. Her best friend Daron had suggested she embark on her own rendition of *Eat, Pray, Love*, but she felt no inclination toward the latter. She approached the customs official at the passport control counter, her mind preoccupied. Unbeknownst to her, a supervisor of the customs agents had separated her grandfather and directed him to another counter.

"Welcome to Cambodia, *che*," the thin man in a uniform greeted Etta with both politeness and cheer. "Is this your first time here? I've never seen you before."

Etta scrutinized his face and then glanced at his name tag, which read "Vuthy Chhay." She regarded him with a perplexed expression. Aware that Cambodians of Chinese descent often used Chinese kinship terms such as *ma*, *kong*, *gu*, *yi*, and *che* (depending on the age difference to one's own parent), to address each other and to distinguish and acknowledge themselves as having Chinese blood, she found it confusing when he referred to her as "che," meaning older sister. A thought crossed her mind: Had China completely conquered Cambodia?

"Are you Khmer?" she inquired.

His cheerful response was immediate, "Yes, I am, che."

Coolly but firmly, she asserted, "I am Khmer too. Say, since we're both Khmer, you can stop calling me che."

With a seemingly affable smile, he acquiesced, "Yes, che. I mean, *bang srey*. You're very pretty, *bang srey*."

Etta sensed an ulterior motive behind his complimentary remark, and she did not like it one bit. "Thank you," she replied, trying to be as polite as possible.

"All right, now just look into the camera and smile. There we go, perfect!" he exclaimed as he stamped her passport and held onto it. "Whew, it's a scorcher out there, isn't it? You must be melting in this heat," he added with a smile, trying to maintain a veneer of friendly banter.

Etta, eyeing Vuthy suspiciously, responded, "Yes, it's quite different from what I'm used to," her thoughts drifting to the gratitude she felt for the four beautiful seasons of her home state of Illinois. "Thank goodness there's an air conditioner blowing through here." *Why am I engaging in small talk with this man when I know he's working an angle?*

In a casual tone, Vuthy remarked, "I can imagine. You know, it's been a really long day for me today. A little 'tea money' would certainly brighten my day."

And there it is! "Seriously?" Etta retorted, clearly annoyed by the suggestion.

Grinning, Vuthy persisted, "Ten dollars, twenty dollars. Any amount is appreciated. Though the more you give, the happier you'll make me."

Flabbergasted, Etta replied, "It seems you've already set the amount."

Vuthy's attempt at soliciting "tea money" left Etta feeling taken aback and incredulous at his casual corruption.

Etta's heart raced as she found herself thrust into an unsettling and bewildering situation, which Khmer of the diaspora who had a conscience had complained about whenever they checked in and out with customs agents at the Cambodian airport. The air was thick with tension and humidity. In a desperate bid for solace, her eyes darted across the room, searching for the steady presence of her grandfather, seeking his wisdom. She found him standing on the distant side of the counter, his eyes abounding in empathy. She knew she should have listened to him when he was explaining the way of current Cambodian society from top to bottom. She saw that he recognized her unease in the face of this unfamiliar corner of the world, her unpreparedness for this challenging new reality of navigating this in-your-face corruption.

"We are in a lion's den, my dear granddaughter. Give him ten dollars, so that we can be on our merry way," he said to her in English.

"Ta! You always taught us about morality and integrity."

"Bend with the wind, *chao srey*."

"I'm sorry, but this just doesn't sit well with me. I'm not exactly at ease with the idea," she retorted, her uncertainty engraved on her face. Then, like a beacon of hope in the midst of her unease, a sign caught her eye. Written in Khmer and somewhat amusingly mangled English, it boldly proclaimed that they don't ask for money, a total opposite of what this man was doing. Maybe she could point to the sign. A glimmer of hope sparked within her, only to be quickly dimmed by her concern—after all, her passport was still in his possession.

Recollections of stories from her relatives and the local Cambodian community flooded her mind, tales of individuals having to grease palms for their positions or jobs. This peculiar situation seemed to fit the bill. Such schemes dominated the Cambodian society, serving to line the pockets not only of the agents themselves, but of those who had got him his position. As she pondered the extent of the illicit gains these customs agents might be reaping from unwitting tourists like herself, a sense of curiosity mingled with her apprehension.

"Oh, for heaven's sake, you're holding up the line. Here's thirty dollars for *her* and for me. I don't have all day. I've got a business to run," a woman's exasperated voice cut through the air from behind her.

Vuthy, with a wide, toothy grin plastered across his face, responded with an air of charm and cunning, "Ah, that's the spirit! A small gesture of goodwill goes a long way, don't you think? Thank you. Bless you, *yi*!"

He continued to beam and engage in lively chatter with the woman in her early fifties. With a dismissive flick of his hand, he handed Etta her passport, hardly acknowledging her, and swiftly turned his attention to the middle-aged woman, practically bowing and prostrating before her, eager to expedite her passage.

"Well, I guess they showed me," Etta remarked to her grandfather as she held onto her passport and sorted through her bag. "I assume she wants me to pay her back," she added, while digging into her tote bag for her envelope of dollar bills to tip the baggage handlers or beggars, as advised by her aunt Thida, who frequently visited Cambodia on her business trips and vacations.

"I don't think so," her grandfather replied, pointing to the charitable woman who was being greeted by cheerful airport workers as they assisted her with large boxes and oversized luggage pulled from the conveyor belt. She walked with her head held high, wearing big sunglasses, as she exited with an air of importance and superiority.

As two men, one young and the other old, approached Etta and her grandfather at the luggage area, the air hummed with the anticipation of reunion and adventure, enough to divert Etta's spirits from the pit of melancholy. Her mood had taken a turn toward something different—a culture shock, one might say—after her run-in with the customs agent.

"Soursdey, che... kong," the young man said and greeted them with that famous Khmer smile. "Welcome to Cambodia." Etta turned to her grandfather, again, seriously pondering whether Cambodia had forsaken its Khmer kinship terminologies in favor of Chinese ones.

"Thank you," Etta replied with a thoughtful gaze. "You don't have to address my grandfather as kong and me as che. We're Khmer."

"Baht," the young man responded, nodding his head as embarrassment colored his expression. Etta had heard from her aunt, and other Khmer of the diaspora, that the Cambodian society had placed Chinese people, customs, and language on a pedestal. Possibly this trend had compelled him to use these foreign terms to address those who appeared affluent, hoping to curry favor and perhaps receive a generous tip. She had begun to see what they were talking about, and she had not even stepped out of the airport yet.

The older gentleman, unfazed by the cultural dissonance Etta felt, inquired, "Where is your luggage? We'll gladly retrieve it and accompany you to your vehicle."

Etta looked around to see lots of East Asian men and women, who seemed to be business people, especially Koreans, coming to take advantage of the easy business opportunities in Cambodia.

As they emerged from the building, a wave of scorching air hit Etta and her grandfather, and they found themselves engulfed by a throng of expectant faces, eagerly awaiting the arrival of friends, guests, and loved ones. Suddenly, a boisterous group surged forward, their smiles radiant and their laughter infectious. "Lok bang," the endearing term for "big brother," resonated from the lips of the elders, while the younger ones joyfully exclaimed, "Lok ta" and "Lok oum," signifying grandfather and uncle in the melodious cadence of Khmer.

Without hesitation, the group swiftly relieved Etta and her grandfather of their duffel bags, their nimble hands deftly retrieving the luggage from the airport employees once they had received confirmation from Etta's grandfather. However, as the realization dawned upon the employees that they might not receive a gratuity from the pair, a look of shock and trepidation settled upon their faces. Sensing their unease, Etta extended a kind gesture, offering five dollars each, which elicited a collective sigh of relief and beams of gratitude from the two men.

"This must be the illustrious and beautiful Davi," one of the group of extended family remarked, singling out Etta. In Khmer culture, individuals often have both an official name and a familiar nickname used by family and close friends. Her grandfather acknowledged the sentiment, and they encircled her, admiring her grace and stature. "American children grow so tall and strong," marveled one of the elders, captivated by her presence.

"Ming," one of the young boys called out to her, using the endearing Khmer term for "aunt" or "auntie"— "you shouldn't have given them any money. They didn't do anything. They were just pushing the cart out."

"That is okay," she responded with a gentle tone, recalling her grandfather's teachings that proper Khmer people speak with a soft and respectful demeanor. "It's a gesture of our gratitude."

"At this rate, you're not going to have any money left because everyone will have their hand out," remarked the young man whom Etta had heard her grandfather refer to as Vey, the grandson of her grandfather's youngest sister. He had believed she was killed by the Khmer Rouge, before reuniting with her during his first trip with his daughter Thida back to Cambodia in the early 1990s.

Etta smiled at him and affectionately ruffled his hair, aware of the playful dynamic she could engage in as the older person. Mindful of the cultural significance that deems it disrespectful for a younger individual to reach for or touch someone's head, considered a sacred area, she freely ruffled his hair as the elder. He smiled at her.

As the sun began its descent, they loaded the luggage into the minivan, settled inside, and drove off. Etta sat by the window, gazing out at the passing scenery with a sense of uneasiness and confusion, while her grandfather conversed with his younger male cousin, younger sister, and her son (his nephew). Vey, his nephew's son, sat beside Etta, smiling and admiring her.

The sky shimmered in a yellow and orange glow as the city of Phnom Penh welcomed her with a traffic jam.

www.ingramcontent.com/pod-product-compliance
Lightning Source LLC
Chambersburg PA
CBHW011138310726

48972CB00009B/2756